CHRISTIANNA BRAND

STARR-BELOW

John Curley & Associates, Inc.
South Yarmouth, Ma.

Library of Congress Cataloging in Publication Data

Brand, Christianna, 1907—
  Starrbelow.

  1. Large type books. I. Title.
[PR6023.E96S7 1984]   823'.912   83–18978
  ISBN 0–89340–673–2 (lg. print)

Published in Large Print by arrangement with the author
and The Mysterious Literary Agency.

Distributed in the U.K. and Commonwealth by Magna
Print Books.

Printed in Great Britain

STARRBELOW

BOOK ONE

One

Through the quiet canals, between the cliffs of their bordering houses, the hired gondola crept on its leisurely way. The bright pole pierced waters as leaden-grey as a sheet of pewter, patched with weed; here and there a gondolier, lounging on water-lapped steps, glanced up with casual curiosity at the fashionable strangers gliding by. Otherwise all was quiet, all was still. "For heaven's sake," said Lady Corby, her vinaigrette to her nose, "what byways are these? Shall we never be there?"

Sir Bertram sat very erect and precise beside her. "We have been many days on the journey from England. What matters an extra half hour?"

"If this girl is not all that my brother has promised. . . ."

"Your brother is a madman, Marcia, I have always said so. For some fancied slight he turned his back upon England, cut himself off from his family, ruined all his prospects; and now expects you, through this paragon of his, to re-establish his name."

"His name is past recall. Who cares now for poor, silly James Devigne and some gaming scandal forgotten years ago? But the girl… If we can but get her home, exhibit her in society, marry her well. …"

The gondola nosed round a corner, its high, black-painted iron prow dipped into the shadows of a bridge and out again into the sunshine. "Very well, my dear; and then – I have told you. We marry her well, as you call it, and what happens? Rich and secure, she gives not another thought to kind Aunt and Uncle Corby – who by no means are rich and secure, and very much the less so for the gamble they have taken in befriending her. For your brother confesses that he hasn't a penny left for the young lady's exploitation."

"He has spent it on her education: singing, dancing deportment – he says she is fit for a palace."

"And I say that once in her palace, she will forget us."

"That is not my idea at all," said Lady Corby grimly.

"Let us hope you are justified. We have come a long way on the chance of it."

4

"You have read his letters: he says she is a very jewel."

"Very well," he said again. "So she may be. It remains for us to be wary in marketing the jewel."

She had been unguarded; she slid back into the role she habitually played before the world, and indeed before herself – a role so grossly false that, if it deceived herself, it deceived no one else. She made a little moue, she shook her little muff at him reproachfully. "Oh, Bertram – you talk as though I would sell the child over the counter!"

He at least was no self-deceiver; or only in glossing over their cold-hearted dishonesties in a sort of ruefully mischievous sense of fun. Nor would he defer to her facade of sweet innocence. "Over the counter – or in the slave market. Marriage – or the other thing. But only the very best conditions, my dear, I'm sure: the most select harems."

She laughed it off, protesting. "Pooh, Bertram, you mock me! This girl is my niece; my poor, foolish brother has begged me to assist her. It will amuse me to place her advantageously in marriage, that's all; and if she's as lovely as he promises – why,

5

so much the better. No one can say," said Lady Corby, glancing complacently at her own reflection swimming sickly in the weed-grown canal, "that I am envious of another woman's beauty, even at thirty-six."

"You are talking to your husband, Marcia, not to your lover," said Sir Bertram. "Forty-two." He added, however: "But at any age, my dear, you'd still have nothing to fear."

For she carried with her an extraordinary air of youth. Her body was tiny and exquisitely trim, her hands and feet miracles of littleness in their perfect shoes and gloves; her face – her face was a mask of youth, not of powders and paints giving a false impression but of the true contours of youth, with smooth-stretched skin, unlined, as a woman's face is lined, about the mouth and eyes; and yet as false as a mask over a face too experienced and worldly-wise to be young. "At any rate," she said, "I shall take the girl back to England and do my best to marry her well." She added, ruminatively: "I think of Lord Weyburn for her." It is strange to consider that in time to come so proud a man should, even unknowingly, have danced to the tune

6

that such a woman played.

James Devigne came forward to meet them when at last they arrived at the lovely shabby old palazzo that was nowadays his home: a tall, thin, peevish, ailing man eaten up with the waste and tragedy of his own life; much older than his sister, and unlike her, looking more than his years. He had married in his late thirties, an Italian girl, whom he had christened Firenze, after her birthplace – a woman of changeless beauty, dark, black-eyed, vital; and at this moment, in her own tongue, voluble. "Very well, James, now I have made your sister and her husband welcome as you said I should. But they are *not* welcome and they may as well finish their wine and depart."

"Be quiet, Firenze, they'll hear you, you will spoil everything."

"They can't understand what I say."

Sir Bertram Corby played with his wineglass to conceal his smile. James Devigne said angrily: "Where is Sophia? Why doesn't she come?"

"Very well, Giacomo, now I will tell you. Sophia is not here."

"Not here?"

7

"She has gone out, she will not see these people and she has gone."

"What nonsense is this? Gone out?" He stared at her unbelievingly. "Of course she must see them: they have come to take her to England."

"And I say they shall not take her to England. She is an Italian girl, she is used to the sunshine of Venice, to laughter and freedom – what would she do in their cold, grey England alone among their cold grey hearts?"

Lady Corby smiled and simpered, sipping with concealed disdain at the sweet Italian wine. "What is your wife saying, James?"

"There has been a mistake. She says that Sophia is out but will soon be coming . . . ."

"I say that she will not be coming at all," said Firenze, in her halting English. She looked at them defiantly. "I apologise, Signora: but it is better to speak the truth." And she cried out again that her child was not fitted for England, she was an Italian girl . . . ."

"She is an English girl," said the father, angrily. "It is right that she should go back into English society and take her proper place there. Every penny I've had has been spent on preparing her for such a future."

"Her proper place! What place have we in English society?"

"I have none, Firenze; the more reason therefore that my daughter should redeem the place I should have had. She shall go back and show them that James Devigne has made something of his life after all, for all they cast him out." The Devignes, he said – not very accurately – had been squires in Cornwall since Cornwall was: they held a proud place in England . . . .

"Very well; but that proud place you forfeited."

"He forfeited nothing," said Lady Corby, interrupting pacifically. "It was all a misunderstanding; my brother is too proud, over-sensitive. But, either way, it's true that his child has a place in society and if she's as lovely as he tells us – what a future, my dear sister, lies before her! With our backing, why, there is no place such a girl might not attain to. Would you not wish to see her splendidly married? – a titled lady, rich, safe, admired, the toast of the town . . . . There is a certain Lord Weyburn, Baron Weyburn of Starrbelow. He is a definite possibility: isn't he, Bertram?"

"Oh, certainly," said Sir Bertram. The

9

gentleman's heart was believed to be elsewhere engaged, but that one need not specify.

"Or a countess. The Earl of Frome is a bachelor, so is Lord Burden . . . ."

Sir Bertram privately thought his lordship, at eighty, a trifle long in the tooth. 'But why stop at earls, my dear? Let Sophia be a duchess and have done."

"Well, and so she might be a duchess. The Duke of Warminster is unmarried . . . ."

"The Duke of Warminster is fifteen years of age."

"Very well, but there's Maidstone, there's Hillington; is Norfolk married?"

"I'm afraid he well may be. Her Grace of Witham, however," suggested Sir Bertram gravely, "may yet predecease the old gentleman." Or – why be too modest? Was not His Majesty himself a widower . . .?

"There you are, Firenze! Our daughter – and nothing to prevent her one day becoming the very Queen of England."

"Only that the King of England is a fat old man of seventy with a dozen fat old mistresses," said Firenze, scornfully; and she cupped her smooth brown hands

10

together in an attitude almost of prayer and asked in her florid Italian way, disdain turning to dismay as she looked into the weak, vain, obstinate face, why they two who knew no other joy should tear from their treasure chest the one jewel they had and fling it away where it would be seen no more....

"You talk nonsense, Firenze: my sister will take her where all the world will see her."

"We are all her world," said the mother. "And we shall not see her."

Outside the narrow window, the narrow canal lay like a ribbon of pewter, splashed with its bright green weeds; across the canal a door opened on to the water with steps leading down to it, and a gondola was tied to a post like a barber's pole, sticking up out of the water – post and gondola painted gaily with the colours of the resident family. The 'poppe' leaned on the gilded poop, his straw hat with its coloured ribbons pushed back on his dark head, and sang a love song that rang out like a coin on a counter, in the evening air. "She shall stay in Venice," said Firenze, "and marry an Italian boy and live here with us for ever."

"That it is certain she shall not do," said her husband.

"And I say if she wishes it she shall. What is England to her, what is it to be a countess, a duchess, the Queen, if you like – in England? She is as Italian as I, born here, bred here . . . ?"

"She has the blood of my Cornish ancestors in her veins . . . ."

"She has the blood of the Florentine princes in her veins . . . ."

And so a great storm blew up in the lovely room, the great bare room that was lovely because of its size and its shape and its old air of faded beauty, rather than by any ornament or furnishing. The Italian woman was cool and taunting, flaming and voluble, by turns, and, in the face of blind obstinacy, touched with despair; the Englishman vain, filled with self-pity and, armoured in this long-anticipated plan of reinstatement, impenetrably strong. Lady Corby, affronted and denied, grew irritable, angry and finally exasperated; Sir Bertram was in favour of shrugging off the whole adventure and wasting no more upon it in money or time. They left at last. "We shall start for England tomorrow," said her ladyship, sweeping out upon the mother's

12

triumph and the father's pleading. "This is the end. We return no more." Nor would they, she said to her husband as their gondola glided back with them towards the Grand Canal. "What use to take the girl if she is to be only grudging and sulky? Who would bother their heads with her, moping after her vulgar Venetians, homesick for these stinking canals. You were right after all: I have been duped and deceived." Besides, she said, consoling her disappointment as best she might with sour grapes, probably the whole thing would have turned out but a figment of her poor silly brother's imagination. "Just a coarse Italian hoyden, I daresay, like her mother, with a skin like a nutmeg and the manners of the sweetmeat women in the Piazza San Marco .... Let us think no more of her. We'll go home tomorrow."

A face peeped over the parapet of the bridge above them, jerked back and disappeared from sight again. Three pairs of bright eyes peered through the tracery of stonework, there was a tinkle of muffled laughter. "Is it they?"

"It must be – who else?"

"Can you see them, Sophia?"

"A leg in a silk stocking: my uncle's, no

doubt – but what use a mere leg in a stocking?"

"The canopy hides them. If they would but look out...! Quick – a pebble into the water! Here, Zaffiro – a pebble...."

Brown hands scrabble in the dust, a white hand takes what the brown hand offers. The unruffled surface of the water splits for a moment, closes; a ring forms and another ring and another ring.... Two faces, startled, peer out from beneath the canopy of the gondola, two pairs of dark eyes look up towards the bridge. Two pairs of brown eyes, one pair of blue look, laughing, down.

The Italian, Guardi, painted Sophia Devigne – in the year 1754 when, after her marriage, she went back to Venice. She had not yet stood her trial then, of course – that celebrated 'trial by society' when, in the Blue Gallery of Witham House, the wife of Baron Weyburn of Starrbelow faced the assembled aristocracy of England on charges of wantonness, fraud and – murder; but already in the portrait she wears her secret smile, the cool, proud, scornful, mocking little smile that she showed to the world throughout all those bitter days. He has painted her in velvet and gold, against

14

a background as dark as the mystery that even in those early years already surrounded her: in a dress of deep green with a cloak of ruby red lined with a lighter green, caught with a great ruby clasp; with pearls and rubies, rubies as large as your thumb and great pear-shaped drop pearls. Her hair is the colour of brass – not the brassy gold of the dyed cocottes but the bright yet heavy gold of unburnished brass; and through its moulded tempest rides, as was the Venetian fashion in those days, a little ship, with a curve of gold for a sail and pearls for its ornaments. It is a picture in reds and greens with pearl and gold; and this is strange for the colour one associated with Sapphire, the colour that gave her her nickname, was brilliantly blue. And yet – he was right, perhaps: for he painted her with eyes downcast as they habitually were – her blue was ever like the kingfisher's blue, glimpsed for a flashing moment and gone again. The rubies and pearls were Weyburn heirlooms, as the emeralds and diamonds were which she later wore; but her sapphires were hidden away beneath white lids, dark-fringed with thick lashes; beneath wide brows, half-lifted always as though in a sort of mocking challenge at the

15

world's curiosity to know what lay behind the secret smile. For a whole long week, in the year 1764, she sat in society's 'courtroom' hearing the world tear her reputation to shreds; cooly, mockingly, secretly, half-indulgently, smiling to herself. There were no words, Red Reddington used to say, lurching, a drunken old profligate to his grave, dying at last with her name on his rotting lips, to tell of the magic and mystery of Sapphire Weyburn's smile.

But in the laughing face looking down at the gondola that day there was no mystery: and indeed no magic, save only the magic of youth and gaiety – and of an absolute beauty, Sir Bertram said sharply in Italian to the gondolier: "Who is that girl?"

The three heads bobbed back. The man said, a little astonished since they had but now come from the Devigne pallazzo, "It is La Zaffiro and her friends, whose names I don't remember. La Signorina Devigne. Here in Venice we call her La Zaffiro – because of her eyes. If you have seen her you will understand." He added, reminiscently smiling: "One doesn't catch a glimpse of them often; but when one does. . . ." He kissed a brown middle-finger and flicked the kiss up to the blue gleam peeping through the tracery of the bridge. 'When one does – who can resist her?"

"He says she is nick-named The Sapphire," translated Sir Bertram. "She appears to be regarded in Venice as – irresistible." He spoke with his accustomed ironical mockery; but his voice held a note of something very much like exultation. "There's your coarse piazza sweetmeat seller," he said.

Lady Corby wasted no time in recriminations. "Tell him to turn the gondola. Back to the pallazzo!"

Back to the pallazzo – where already Sophia, breathless, naughtily triumphant, knelt beside her father's chair and curled a kiss into his palm and besought him now that the invaders had sailed away – to let them be gone: to let all these dreams and schemes be ended for ever. "Keep me here, don't send me away from you, don't send me where you and my mother can't follow, where I shall be all alone . . . ." And she cried out in Italian, Papa mio, papa mio, don't send me out of your heart, don't try

17

to recall them, don't wish your daughter away . . . ."

In vain. There came the rhythmic plop and plash of a gondola poled along the canal towards them, the grating of wood against stone, the chatter of voices: all smiles and serenity again, the aunt and uncle appeared.

A week more and she was gone – packed into the great lumbering hired travelling coach, driving away from all she had known and loved, into a cold new world: a young girl, sorrowful, untutored, apprehensive – innocent. Triumphant, the loving father watched her go.

Two

The entry of Sophia Devigne into English society was more startling than even Lady Corby could have bargained for.

Sir Bertram strolled correct as ever through the clubs and coffee houses, bowing to right and left, hail-fellow here, obsequious there, scrupulous never to offend by ignoring, never to court offense by civilities to those who might in turn ignore him; and in his wake, rumour ran with lighted torches igniting the modest bonfire which was all he required of it. The old Duke of Witham fanned the flames, tottering in and out of fashionable drawing-rooms. "I hear the woman Corby's picked up something quite marvelous in Venice. A niece, she's called – well, that's as may be, natural daughter's more likely; but they say she's a beauty. The Duchess on the strength of it has invited them to her reception; the young woman had better live up to reputation or Her Grace will soon set La Corby to rightabouts . . . ."

And her Grace herself, encountering the Earl of Frome and his friend Lord Weyburn on the very morning of her rout, in Berkeley Square, stopped her carriage and beckoned them over, screeching out at them in her high, hard voice, poking out of the carriage her hard, bright-painted face. "Have you heard the gossip, gentlemen? Something quite amazing out of Italy – Lady Corby produces her at my reception this evening. I trust you will be there?"

Lord Frome bowed his acknowledgements. "Your Grace was so good as to send me a card; I shall be happy."

"And I most happy to hear it. It's not often you leave your Gloucestershire pastures for London." And no loss either, she reflected, wagging her head at them, with its preposterous pile of powdered hair. A dull dog, Lord Frome, not a spark of dash in him and his waistcoat at least four inches out of length to be modish. "And Lord Weyburn?"

No dull dog here! An eye of fire, a proud lift to the head, every gesture elegant with a natural elegance, owing little to the studied poses of the môde – every button,

20

despite a cool indifference to the world of the bucks and macaronis, placed precisely where a button ought to be: tall, handsome, haughty, tempering the mannered drawl of present fashion with a natural quick decisiveness of speech that robbed it of affectation. "I thank your Grace. I am this moment setting out for Starrbelow."

Her Grace protested. She would be disappointed. He must put off his journey, delay it a day, oblige her. "You of all men should remain and meet the fair Italian. The scandal is, you know, that La Corby sees in her the future Lady Weyburn."

"Then I fear that Lady Corby also will be disappointed." He bowed, briefly smiling. "You astonish me, Edward," he said looking after the carriage as she drove away, chagrined. "Do you really go tonight to such a house as Gossip Wit's? And to meet this riff-raff?"

"If you will not squire your cousin there, Charles, then I must."

"Christine? Does Christine go there?" His dark face clouded. "Who takes her?"

"Her mother, I presume. It's no business of mine, my dear Charles, to question Miss Lillane's engagements."

"But it's business of mine. My aunt is

21

a silly old woman, no fit chaperone for her daughter."

"Her daughter does well enough, I think," said the Earl of Frome smiling. "And though I have no love for their several Graces – they are still Duke and Duchess of Witham. Everyone does go there."

"Including the Corby and her performing monkey: really, the Duchess stoops to anything for a sensation."

"I daresay Christine will not be troubled very much," said the Earl, peaceably, "by the poor performing monkey . . . ."

Lady Corby was enchanted by the opportunity held out by her Grace's – elaborately fished-for – invitation. "It is perfect! No such situation for an entrée exists in the whole of London. Everyone of any consequence at all will be there. The Blue Gallery is a hundred yards long: one must come in through a great door at one end and parade the whole length of it to be presented to the Duchess – and it's the custom for the mob to stand back either side of the carpet to watch the new arrivals. Sophia will be seen by everybody in town."

Sir Bertram sat with neat crossed legs on

a brocade-covered couch; on a couch opposite a young man lounged, a rather tall, gangling young man with a forward falling lock of yellow hair; for he had taken off his wig and hooked it negligently over the arm of a chair. He spoke with just enough of an accent – faintly German – to be rather engaging. "How do the women know these things, Sir Bertram? Her ladyship, to my knowledge, has never been once inside Witham House."

"Well – her ladyship goes there tonight at any rate," said Lady Corby, tartly. "And we shall see." She said, sharply: "Turn round, Sophia. Madame Turque cannot reach the side-fastenings."

How can I turn round, thought Sophia, with two men sprawling on couches watching me? Fashions in etiquette seemed lax in Venice to what they were here, but their notions of modesty had been very different. And this dress! Made to some design of Aunt Corby's, boned over the ribs and up to the bosom only: the bosom itself covered by nothing but a gathering of muslin held in place by a few clever stitches. I must speak to her, she thought; I can't go like this into public... And... The custom of having male company present during one's

23

toilette, though apparently accepted, made such discussion impossible. She hesitated. The young man on the sofa looked up at her with a teasing glance of his lazy brown eyes. "Yes, turn, Miss Sophia. Madame Turque can see nothing – and neither can we."

What am I to do? thought Sophia again. The fastening of the bodice felt insecure, it needed attention. "Aunt Corby," she murmured, "this decolleté is too low."

"Nonsense, child, it's the height of the môde. Is it no, Bertram? Reassure her."

Sir Bertram got up with his usual precision and walked round with a critical air. "I doubt, my love, whether 'height' is the word. Are you wise? An unmarried girl."

"She will have the gauze scarf round her bosom and shoulders: you have forgotten the scarf."

"All the bucks will be praying," said the young man from the sofa, "that *she* vill forget the scarf."

"Now, Anton, behave yourself!" She rapped him over the head with her fan, dancing before him, tiny and exquisite in her dark velvet dress, with the young doll-face over the hard face of age and

24

experience. "Come now, Sophia – turn round."

No, thought Sophia: I will not turn round. I must consent to be put on show in the marriage market, because my father has sent me here; but when that is done, if offers come I shall refuse them and then I can go home to Venice. But I shall not put myself on show for these two men to amuse themselves at my expense: they are not in the marriage market. At least, she supposed Prince Anton was not – or surely her aunt would have advised her. Her heart sank a little at her own temerity but she said steadily: "Aunt, I am sorry, but I am not accustomed to being dressed with gentlemen present."

"Nonsense," said Lady Corby again. "I want their opinion." She still stood beside Prince Anton as he lounged, his long legs thrust out before him. He had caught at the folded end of her fan as she tapped him with it and continued unconsciously to hold it, she retaining the other end – an oddly intimate grouping as though, but for the intervening six inches of ivory, they would with an habitual familiarity have been holding hands. He looked over at Sophia appraisingly. "If her ladyship asks my opinion –"

Sophia lost her temper. "Well, sir, but *I* do not ask your opinion; nor require it." She swung round on him in a rush of white rage, so that Madame Turque started back and spilt her box of pins. "I am not used to have gentlemen assist at my toilette, and I wish you to go. Since my aunt won't request you to leave, I request you myself. I shall not go on with my fitting until you withdraw." But she saw her aunt's doll-face grow pinched at the nostrils – an already too familiar danger-flag; and her heart quailed. "I apologise, sir, if I disoblige you."

"Not at all," he said, smiling up at her languidly from the sofa. "On the contrary, you infinitely oblige me – you have turned round."

She stood paralysed with rage and shame, clasping her hands before the half-transparent gathering of muslin at the bosom of her dress; and a slow blush, warm, and russet-red as a berry, mounted in her pale cheeks. He looked up for the first time, lounging still, into her face; and suddenly rose to his feet, letting go of the folded ends of the fan as he did so. "Madame, I beg your pardon. I haf offended you." He took her right hand and held it for a moment in his own and then stooped and kissed it with a foreign click-together of the heels. "I forget that you are not yet altogether of the *ton;* and permit me to add, Madame, may it be long before you are so." He straightened himself. "I will withdraw at once; I embarrass you." As he walked to the door, Lady Corby following like an agitated bird in his wake, he said to her: "If I may advise your ladyship – I vould suggest that the decolleté *is* perhaps a little too low."

Madame Turque continued to pick up her scattered pins. "Now Mademoiselle has made herself an enemy," she said. She added: "I do not refer to His Highness Prince Anton of Brunswick."

Sophia wore white for this first, all important, appearance: a billowing dress of the fine white muslin that had only very lately come into fashion, banded with blue, the deep bright sapphire of her eyes. She wore no rubies in those days and no pearls, for she had none; but round her smooth shoulders above the hurriedly pinned-up bosom of the dress, was caught a translucent blue gauze scarf all spangled

27

with stars of the same bright gold as her hair. So attired, with her uncle and aunt on either side of her – deliberately self-effacing, for this one occasion, in their dark velvet and brocade – she entered at last the glittering portals of the haut monde, and slowly walked forward down the long gallery to where the Duchess of Witham stood, receiving her guests.

In all the fashionable London of the eighteenth century, there was, as Lady Corby had said, no better place to see and to be seen.

Graceful as a white swan in her whispering muslin, down the long, mirrored gallery she came, through the throng of guests; slowly pacing the polished pathway left by long custom in that house, so that each arrival might at leisure be observed, judged, found wanting or, as too seldom happened, approved. At the far end of the gallery, the Duke teetered a little out of line to peer towards her, and the Duchess, flamboyantly young and vital by his side, stepped forward also to stare down the long gallery as she came, gravely advancing upon them under the shimmer and sheen of the chandeliers – the aunt and uncle bowing to right and left, simpering and smiling, a-gloat already at the impression their sacrificial lamb was clearly making upon the expectant throng. Slowly, shyly pacing forward, heart thudding, hands trembling as they clutched the gold-bordered ends of the clouds of gauze – all unaware that beneath the gauze the ill-made bodice had slipped awry, that the lovely breasts lay exposed in the haze of blue transparency for all the world to see. There was a gasp and a titter, hardly stifled, the old Duke tottered a little more forward, licking salacious lips, the Duchess raised painted eyebrows and glanced to where Royalty huffed and puffed in an excess of paraded outrage. Male voices passed the news back, whispering, through the ranks of the whispering crowd: "Naked to the waist, by Gad!" The whispering grew into a murmur, the murmur into open exclamation – "La Corby's brought the girl here naked to the waist . . . !"

The Corbys checked a little in their march but, mystified, continued; and – a girl stepped forward. Against all tradition in that house, right in the path of their progress a girl stepped forward and laid white hands against the creamy shoulders and bent forward and kissed the warm cheek lightly, and stepped back again; with flags of crimson now flying in her own cheeks – but with the disordered muslin now twitched back into place. Sophia, all unaware, beyond amazement however at anything this extraordinary London could do to her, accepted the kiss of a stranger and moved on. The uncle and aunt bowed frigidly to Miss Christine Lillane, and, uneasy, still mystified, moved on too.

And in their wake, the vultures flocked in and the picking-over of the bones began. 'A pretty exhibition, upon my word!' 'At some houses, perhaps – but here! And with Royalty present!' 'They are out to catch a fortune – anything for sensation.' 'At least they have achieved the sensation: all the beaux are dicing already for first try for her favours.' 'The sensation, yes: but will the fortune follow?' 'Not through a wedding ring. A man may look on while his wife exposes her – dowry – to society; but till he has had the handling of it himself, he likes to believe that no one else knew the extent of it ....' And the Duchess, murmuring half-apologies spiced with triumph: 'The Corby woman is a vulgar upstart, Majesty, does not know her manners: we invited her only in the hopes that the girl might prove some entertainment,' and, in response to confidential enquiries in the well-known, gutteral growl: 'Not ready yet, I take it: a month or two will do it but for the moment I truly believe she obeys where she's instructed – and, though your Majesty might not think it by Lady Corby's way of going about it, matrimony is the object: with the accent on "money" ....' (And as far as the house of Hanover was concerned, she reflected, she might as well look for the one as for the other.)

Prince Anton of Brunswick sought out Miss Christine Lillane. He begged an introduction from a common acquaintance, who passed on and left them together. "Madame, permit me to speak a word of – gratitude. So kindly an action infinitely became you."

She flushed a little again, curtseying. "I couldn't see her held up to shame, poor child."

" 'Poor child?" he said, smiling down at her in his own teasing way. "Of the two are you not probably the younger?"

"I am near eighteen," she said, a trifle coldly. "And much, much more in experience of the world." This tiny, shiny world of high fashion, of the *ton*, which all about them was a-sparkle with the gossip, the scandal, the piquant fun of it.

The Duchess bore down upon them. She was a high blonde, rather tall, garish, noisy, impenetrably pleased with herself. "Well, my dears – a pretty trick! But really, at Witham House! – and with Royalty present...."

"Duchess, it was an accident, you cannot think otherwise?"

"Ah, it's you, Miss Lillane? – and it was you that stepped forward? Well, well, it was kindly meant in you, child, but you spoilt a most daring pretty trick, there can be no denying it. 'Twas got from La Woffington, half the world was agog when she did the same thing at the opera: but poor Peg was stripped to the middle to achieve it, and of course wore no scarf; and most dismally failed with it anyway, for none took any note but the ladies. What should the gentlemen care for seeing in public what they all knew by heart in private...?"

Prince Anton bowed, flourished, kissed a much-ringed hand. "An accident. I attended the lady's toilet, I know all about it." He flourished again, looking up into her handsome, ravaged, too-early raddled face. "Your Grace is too good at heart to think so ill of an untaught little girl out of Italy."

"Oh, ah yes – a Venetian, isn't she? I'd forgotten. Well, then, that accounts for it – who knows what fancy tricks these Italians will be up to? And the aunt, of course...." She broke off a mite hastily. A Royal Highness was a Royal Highness still, even only of stuffy little Brunswick; and this particular highness was known to be the aunt's lover. "Lady Corby, of course, would not know what the minx intended."

He caught Christine's eye and she gave him an imploring glance – and a monstrous pretty creature she was too, he thought, so brilliantly fair where Sophia Devigne was creamy and warm of skin: much resembling the haughty cousin (a gentleman of whom Anton, the easy-going scapegrace, was not particularly fond) in quiet beauty of line and moulding, though her smooth brows sloped upward in tapering wings where Lord Weyburn's were dark, with a downward tilt. He gave her a reassuring nod. "Permit me, Duchess. This vos an accident, I know it, I promise you: neither the young lady nor Lady Corby prepared it. And now – Miss Lillane was prompt in covering up the damage. I came to ask her assistance in covering up the truth also as far as the girl herself iss concerned. I find Miss Lillane already in sympathy; and so beg you also, your Grace, to enter into a little conspiracy. To us – this iss a little thing, many ladies habitually expose the full bosom: though not, certainly, in such company, nor on such an occasion –"

"And not in the case of a young unmarried girl," said her ladyship, "making her début."

"Ah, there your Grace has it: she *is* very young – and very modest also, your Grace; through Lady Corby, I know her a little. A young girl, inexperienced, afraid as yet of life. If she knows nothing, and I swear to it! – will you not be kind? Let her not find out. To her it will be – shame: she will not hold up her head again. I know this young girl, Duchess, she is proud and she is modest, and she will be ashamed. Don't let her know! Be merciful!" He kissed her hand once more, pleading. "You alone can do it – command that she shall not be told."

"Not be told?" said the Duchess. "Not be told! Why, child, you must be infatuated with the pretty puss yourself, if you're taken in by that; but you shan't convince *me.*" She passed on with a rap of the fan over his whitening knuckles, a graceful inclination of her head to Miss Lillane. "All planned in advance," she confided happily to the next gossip in her way, "and her ladyship's lover in a taking at our having so easily divined the plot. An Italian, my dear, and up to all the tricks: and so young! Untutored, he calls her; but she knows her way about, I warrant you; and with the aunt behind her. . . ."

The Corbys, not unversed in the art of ignoring snubs, were nevertheless puzzled at the equivocal reception accorded their wonderful discovery. The ladies, not usually slow to advance and look over the newcomer, looked indeed but from behind their fans, raising arched eyebrows at one another: such bucks as gathered round were not those whom one would have chosen nor in view of her air of virtue, youth and good-breeding, expected: it was as though in some point of harmless yet essential etiquette she had somehow blundered. Only Christine Lillane, moving slowly through the room on the Earl of Frome's arm, came forward – he hanging back with an air of disapproval – and took the stranger's shrinking hand on her own. "I have to apologise, Madame, for an earlier intrusion. I mistook you for a friend."

"In this company, Madame," said Sapphire, "I find it comforting even to be mistaken for a friend."

"Then you must permit me to call you a friend indeed," said Christine. She looked about her and made signals with her winged brows. "And in proof of it, let me present – come, my lord, where have you disappeared to? – the Earl of Frome: so that now you have two friends –"

Lady Corby interrupted them, advancing upon them suddenly with those pinched white nostrils of her ill-controlled rages. "Accompany me at once, Sophia, if you please. We are leaving."

"Yes, Aunt," said Sophia thankful to be gone from this strange, uneasy company.

"We shall take no farewells; if on the way out we come upon the Duchess, curtsey and say nothing. You have disgraced us all."

"Disgraced?" said Sophia. "I have disgraced you? How?"

"You have disgraced yourself, and ruined our plans; a girl of your age – well, no man would marry you now, you shall be packed back to Italy tomorrow. As to 'how' – get yourself out of here as quickly as may be, and I'll tell you how, Miss, as we drive home in the coach."

They did, in fact, see the Duchess on their way out; but she did not see them. She was too busy talking, in her high, hooting voice. "An Italian, they say. Oh, aye, say I, well that accounts for it! For who are we to be forewarned of what fancy tricks these Italians will get up to. For all we know, every chit in Venice makes her entrance with her bodice 'accidentally' pulled awry – and a twist of gauze clutched over a stark naked bosom. . . ."

It was from this time that Sophia Devigne acquired a new habit of downcast eyes as though she were ashamed to look the world in the face: of a secret, half defiant, half disdainful smile, as though at the same time utterly to deny that she had cause to be ashamed.

Three

– Sophia Devigne to Miss Christine Lillane: "Madame – I now learn that when last night you 'mistook me for a friend,' it was as a true friend that you acted towards me. It is improbable I shall ever see you again; but if passionate gratitude can make a friend, you have one in me, Madame, to the end of my life. I am now, as ever, your deeply obliged, Sophia Devigne."

And Miss Christine Lillane in reply: "Dear Madame, why should you say I shall not see you again? Pray come to me tomorrow afternoon and we can go driving. As for such small service as I was happy to be able to render you, – why, I saw that your dress was a little disordered and took the opportunity in saluting you, to twitch it into place again. The whole affair was so momentary as to be scarcely observable: give it no more attention, it is not worth being mortified over such a trifle. If, however, you will reward me – come tomorrow. Yours ever most sincerely...."

"The Lily has asked you to go driving?" said Aunt Corby. "Good heavens!" But she was quick to seize on the advantage. " 'Tis quixotic, but if of all women in town she is going to take you up, then everything may not be lost to us after all. A very pattern of virtue, and at the height of the *ton*. If you're seen with her driving –"

"She did me a kindness. If she's all you say," said Sophia with that new smile of hers, half shame, half bitter pride, "I should do *her* no kindness by being seen driving."

"Her reputation is such that it would far outweigh yours. How so young a girl," said Lady Corby with unconscious envy, "could already have established so indestructible a name for purity, I can't imagine. That's why they call her The Lily; and because, of course, one must admit she is dazzlingly fair." Neither name nor complexion, however, she added hopefully, was likely to endure. "But she'll marry Lord Frome, no doubt, before she can lose them. She's been in love with him from her childhood."

"My father will be disappointed," said Sophia. "Did you not promise the Earl of Frome to *us*, in Venice?"

"Then the next best will be to form a

friendship with the future countess. She will be enormously rich: though now she has nothing – lives with her foolish old mother, a widow, in London. But Lord Weyburn.... Why yes," said Lady Corby, radiant, "Lord Weyburn of Starrbelow of course is her cousin. Write at once and tell her that you will go driving."

"It will be of no use, Aunt. I am returning to Venice."

"In view of this letter, that arrangement can be forgotten."

"I don't wish to forget it. I wish to go home to my father."

"Well, you can't," said Lady Corby shortly.

"I shall not remain here to be stared at and cackled over."

"Pooh, nonsense: hardly anyone noticed, as Miss Lillane tells you. It was of no consequence, none at all."

"That is not what you said in the coach," said Sophia.

"I was angry, but after all, it is nothing. Mistress Woffington appeared stripped to the ribs in a box at the opera; Lady Lammingham's bosom, being her only beauty, she scarcely covers at all: 'twas only its being there, at the Withams', and royalty present – the court is so frowsty: and you of course, young and unmarried. . . . Besides, it wasn't your fault; I recollect now you said the bodice was ill-fastened, and then it was hurriedly pinned up because you thought the muslin too low. . . . Madame Turque," declared Lady Corby, in a fine indignation, "will find herself dismissed from my favour, from this hour."

"That at any rate will be convenient," said Sophia, dryly, "since she has not yet been paid."

She had learnt to make that sort of remark from Sir Bertram. "However that may be, Miss, you will accept Miss Lillane's invitation. You remain in London," Lady Corby melted into sweetness. "Reflect, my love, that your uncle and I have paid out a great deal of money in your behalf which your father is entirely unable to repay. So that what I request you to do –"

"So that what you request me to do, Aunt," said Sophia, "I must do. No need to continue – the 'reflection' is unanswerable." And she curtseyed briefly to her aunt: and smiled.

Christine Lillane – and Sophia Devigne: whom the wits, in an age of nicknames, dancing obediently to the little piped tunes of Sir Bertram, duly came to christen Sapphire 'because of her eyes' . . . . (How long ago – what a world of weeks ago! – that far away day when a voice had said lightly, 'Here in Venice we call her La Zaffiro – because of her eyes'; when a flick of brown finger and thumb had diverted her destiny on the wings of a kiss. . . .)

Sapphire Devigne: and the Lily of Lillane.

The Earl of Frome drove down to Gloucestershire with his friend and neighbour, Lord Weyburn. "How think you, Charles, of the intimacy of your cousin with this Italian girl?"

"Very ill," said Lord Weyburn briefly, sitting upright on the box of his coach, well wrapped against the nipping November air; the smooth reins lying controlled yet easy across his gloved palm.

"I too. The uncle and aunt are received it seems – the more so since they contrived an entrée with the Duchess. But the woman is said to be an adventuress – their house is no place for your cousin."

42

"And is moreover haunted by that mountebank from Hanover."

"Lady Corby will keep her safe from *him,*" said Lord Frome. "He goes in fear of her; so the gossip says – I know nothing about it. But so should I, I confess," he added, smiling, "were I in his shoes."

"I can think of no man less likely," said Lord Weyburn, "to be in them."

The Earl of Frome, magnificent in title and possessions, was in himself by no means magnificent. It spoke much for the universal respect which, despite her youth, Christine Lillane had magic to command, that no suggestion was ever entertained that her regard for him had its origin in his property rather than himself. He was a smallish, plump, almost chubby man: kind of heart, generous and true, but very rigid in his respect for the conventions, properly proud of the greatness of his position and conscious of its responsibilities: for all his somewhat cherubic appearance capable of unremitting dignity, a trifle humourless, often stern: a man whom lesser men might not like but whom all must respect. Christine, visiting her kindred at Starrbelow over the years, had known him from her childhood and in her quiet

43

fashion, reserved and cool, had loved him near as long. Unmarried at well over thirty, it was widely believed as Lady Corby had said, that he was waiting only for her eighteenth birthday to propose; though others prophesied as freely that he would remain a bachelor to the end. The earldom would be safely taken care of by his brother's splendid line of boys.

Christine's birthday would fall upon the coming Christmas Eve. "I shall give a ball for my cousin at Starrbelow," said Charles Weyburn. "That among other things will serve to bring her away from London and these disreputable friends. I only wish it were sooner."

"Are they in fact disreputable? I know nothing of them, but by hearsay: I'm a stranger to your London life – Frome's good enough for me."

"Disreputable enough, I take it. As to the girl, I know nothing – save that she exposes her bosom in public and that that same bosom is lovely: though I have not seen it, nor the rest of the lady, for myself. But the relatives are certainly such as to make it desirable that this infatuation should come to an end."

"I can't quite imagine Christine

44

'infatuated,' " said the Earl, smiling.

"Can't you?" Charles Weyburn lifted his whip and flicked its long lash with unnecessary asperity over quivering chestnut flanks. He said only, however: 'You know that I feel my cousin a special charge upon me. Her mother's quite useless, a nervous, silly woman and since my uncle died I've regarded myself, in some sort at least, Christine's guardian. Moreover, should I die childless, she would be my heir – she and her children after her."

"At your age," said the Earl, smiling, "it's early, isn't it? – to be talking of dying childless."

The coach rocked, dipping and swaying along the deep-rutted country road; all about them was silence, but for the rattle of the wheels, the creak and jingle of harness, the hollow clop-clop of the horses' hooves. Charles Weyburn also was silent – staring ahead of him over the chestnut backs along the road that wound through the winter meadows to Starrbelow and home. 'At your age, it is early to talk of dying childless.' Ah, but I shall not die childless, he thought, if the mother of my children is not to be Christine?

45

Christine! His cousin, Christine – fair as a lily, spotless as a lily, remote and untouchable on her pedestal above him, pervading all his dreams. Strong with the inward strength of the solitary, high in courage, bold, independent, a little ruthless – in this lay his only weakness: that a girl's white hand held all his heart. He said at last, slowly: "This leads me to say . . . I should forewarn you, Edward, as a friend, that – that I intend to propose to my cousin on her birthday night. It is, to some extent at least, my object in giving her the ball."

Lord Frome looked down quietly at the gloved hands resting in his lap. "Do you? Then 'as a friend,' Charles, I wish you all good fortune." He raised his head. He said: "You of all men, I have long thought, are the one to make Christine happy. You have wealth and position to offer her – well, so have others; but you have other advantages, you're the right age for her, and a gay fellow with a place in this same fashionable world we were speaking of, such as a beautiful woman must naturally wish for. You're a month in London, I know, for every day *I* spend away from Frome." He had lowered his face again; but now he looked up and repeated, smiling his steady smile:

"I wish you all joy, if you succeed with her."

"Thank you." But in the added intimacy of their close companionship, perched up alone on the box in the brisk chill of a sunlit winter's day, he put out a delicate feeler. "May I presume to ask – and if I may not, of course you won't answer – whether my good fortune would be your ill? I have sometimes thought. . . ." He broke off. He said with unwonted hesitancy: "I would not wish to enter upon ground that you had a right to consider your own."

"Only the lady could confer such a right," said Lord Frome, "and without her permission, it would hardly become me to confirm or deny that I aspire to it." Lord Weyburn lifted the whip again but he put out a quick hand. "Come, Charles – spare the beasts: they at least have not offended. Let your cousin have her ball and let who will propose to her that night – the more conquests for her to remember one day, the better." He added, shrugging, as though to turn the conversation: "But that you will by this or any means separate her from her lovely Venetian – I take leave to doubt. She has sworn to bring the girl into society after the débacle of her first appearance – and

47

Christine has a faithful heart."

"Yes," said Lord Weyburn. "Christine has a faithful heart." Is it faithful to *you?* he thought. Can it be true that, as they say, she has always loved you? This man, this short, stubby, stolid man with his set ways and his pedantic speeches...? And yet... And yet, he thought, I in my own way also love him, knowing him as the man he is. And he looked into the smiling face of his friend and saw behind the smile a strength as steady as his own, a courage as high as his own, a greater gentleness, a loftier integrity: a man who could win and hold the love of a woman fit to recognise him for what he was. If she knows him, he thought, if she sees him as I see him, as he really is – then she is lost to me. "Yes," he repeated, bitterly, not thinking of Sophia Devigne, "Christine has a faithful heart."

And so it was that Sapphire at last came down to Starrbelow, in the week before Christmas, 1753: came down with a coachload of gay revellers, bright as parakeets in their velvets and furs, loud as parakeets in their chatter and laughter, flocking out of the coach and into the hostelries, crowding round the great blazing log fires, sipping their hot possets, warming their frozen toes, greeting with parakeet cries other coachloads of parakeets all, all converging upon Starrbelow. Every house of consequence in the neighbourhood was thrown open to accommodate guests, making up parties for the ball. Christine, meeting with an unequivocal refusal from her cousin to do more than entertain her friends – and these must include the Corby's, and, it appeared, Prince Anton too – for the actual duration of the ball itself, had perforce found them rooms at an inn. "Never mind, my dear; no doubt Lord Weyburn would have arranged matters better if he could," said Lord Corby. This was her great chance to bring about her coup, and she would have slept in the stables to settle the matter. "We shall stay over Christmas, Miss Christine, and make a holiday of it. No doubt we shall see you during the rest of the time?"

"Oh, yes, Lady Corby, of course I shall come over to you."

"And Sophia will come over to you," said Lady Corby, sweetly. "Never mind us, we are used to it; but Sophia will be so happy to see a great English house."

"Yes, of course, Lady Corby, if Sophia

would like to see over Starrbelow; and Frome Castle also, I could ask permission of the Earl. . . ."

Lady Corby cared not two straws for Frome Castle – that Sophia should be accepted at Starrbelow was the height of her scheming. She said, however, with a wink, that no doubt Miss Lillane would have a *special interest* in showing her friend over the Castle.

"As to that, Madame, I must simply ask the Earl's permission," repeated Christine coldly; but her heart leapt, nevertheless, at the thought that what this ill-bred woman hinted must come true.

"I should like to see Frome," said Prince Anton. "Our Hanoverian castles are not at all like yours."

"For the moment, however, my dear, they will have to content you," said his mistress, sharply. "We must not intrude upon the confidences of young ladies." She withdrew to a small inner room where Sir Bertram was sitting, circumspect as a mole in his handsome black coat, silk ankles crossed, buckled shoes perched neatly on the fender. He looked up at her. "Come in, my dear, and sit down. An excellent claret

50

– it will refresh you and you look in need of refreshment."

"If Anton is to be off chasing Sophia wherever she goes, he will spoil everything."

"I told you," said Sir Bertram, equably pouring wine, "not to bring him down."

"I did not 'bring him down'; I don't carry him round with me like a lap dog –"

"Don't you, my dear?" said Sir Bertram, handing the glass.

"– he was invited and accepted of his own accord."

"After much angling on his part through Miss Lillane – I heard him and warned you accordingly, but you are perhaps a little over-confident, my dear, in the inferiority of Sophia's charms to your own: doubtless justifiably so." He settled himself more comfortably in his chair. "Is he paying his own board here, by the way, or leaving it owing with ours?"

"I know nothing about Prince Anton's financial arrangements."

"I am sorry to hear it; for the past eighteen months, they have been indistinguishable from our own."

"You can hardly call ours 'financial arrangements,'" she said, grimly; sitting down at the table, however, with the glass in her hand.

"Well, I don't know. What other term would you apply to a growing burden of debts? His debts and ours?"

"You appear to forget that when he first came to England –" began Lady Corby.

"Ah, when he first came to England! – an amiable prince, apparently closely attached to the court; and with money to burn. But, my dear, the attachment has proved insecure; and the money has all been burned."

"With our ready assistance," said Lady Corby.

"Well, yes. But it made, you recollect, but a very small conflagration; he appears to be in dread of the wrath at home when his application to frivolous concerns becomes known to the illustrious relatives; and since he cannot apply to them, all the money he needs must be supplied by us. If 'supplied' is quite appropriate: perhaps I should say rather 'has had to be owed by us.' Indeed," said Sir Bertram, reproachfully refilling his glass and holding the wine to the light, "if we ever paid bills, I should really have a right to complain that your lover is an extravagant luxury."

"He is not my lover," said Lady Corby, automatically; but she added with real meaning that he would be more likely to be Miss Sophia's lover if she didn't take care.

"But you will take care, my dear, I'm sure," said Sir Bertram, comfortably.

Sapphire came very late to the Starrbelow ball. It would be her first 'entrée' since the night at the Duchess of Witham's, her appearances in society in the intervening time having been on small occasions and always in the company of Christine. Now she must go alone again, with her uncle and aunt, must hear her name called again, must walk again into a great room filled with people – with every eye fixed on the bosom of her dress and a sneer and a whisper behind every fluttering fan. At the very thought, she was filled with a dread so powerful as to be physically prostrating, and half the evening had passed before, sick with terror and shame, she allowed herself to be dragged by her aunt into the carriage that was to carry them the distance between the inn and the house. By this time, she knew, it would be vain to hope that her friend would be waiting to conduct her in: Christine must long ago have been forced to leave the great hall and join in the dancing with her guests. Indeed, they could see her through the bright-lit windows as they drove up the long drive, whirling on the edge of the waltzing throng with Lord Weyburn himself: could see them stop as the music ended and step out on to the frosty, starlit terrace. Is she happy now? thought Sophia, sparing out of the absorption of her own dread a moment for her friend. Has her belovéd spoken? Is it all settled, is she betrothed?

But Lord Frome had not spoken. He had danced with Christine in his turn, had walked with her, alone, along the Starrbelow gallery beneath the old portraits of her ancestors; holding her hand on his arm and wishing her happiness on this wonderful night of her birthday ball and for all the years to come. But he, who held her happiness in his keeping, spoke of it and in the very act of speaking spoke it away – for he spoke of nothing else. Now if ever, the time to tell her what she longed to hear, was come; and he said nothing. He smiled into her eyes with his own kind, loving, belovéd – too long belovéd – smile; and kissed her hand and tucked it into his arm again. "The fiddles are starting up, I must take you back to the ballroom; your next partner will be waiting."

Sick with the last flickering of all her high flame of hope, she temporised. "I need not hurry. Unless, of course, you're engaged to dance?"

"No, no," he said. "I am no dancer, as you know. I dance with you, but that is for other reasons: for – for the happiness of it. ..." She dipped him a little curtsey, clutching eagerly at the compliment implied, but he broke off, he lightened his voice and said, smiling: "One may dance like a bear oneself, but it can't but be a pleasure to lead out on to the floor so lovely a lady, in so lovely a dress – and on her birthday night!" In the ballroom below the music began in earnest but he had halted his steps and stood facing her; and now only said unhurriedly: "You're sure I don't detain you? You need not go yet?"

"No, I have a – a little while yet. There's no occasion for formality with my next partner. It's only my cousin."

"You dance next with Lord Weyburn?" His whole attitude altered immediately, he took her arm again and led her towards the stairhead. "Perhaps after all I had better return you to the ballroom. In the pleasure

55

of your company, I'm forgetting my manners; and to my host of all people." Down the broad stair he led her, almost urgently, and across the hall with its attendant footmen and through the crimson curtains that hung in their velvet folds at the doorway to the ballroom. Lord Weyburn was standing there, looking a little anxious. "I deliver Miss Lillane up to you, my lord; with apologies for my part in keeping you waiting. We were detained by your great grandfathers – we have been quizzing them up in the Long Gallery." Lord Weyburn looked at him sharply but in the smiling face could see nothing but the casual pleasure of an evening's entertainment. Here was no accepted suitor: that was certain. Either he had proposed and been rejected, in which case, of course, true to ettiquette and to his own consideration of the lady, he would show no sign; or he had not proposed at all. And if he had ever intended to propose – surely no time would have been so propitious as now? With a heart all of a sudden as light as air, Lord Weyburn offered his arm to his cousin Christine.

Dazed with disappointment and grief she danced like a ghost of happiness in her white birthday dress, through the lovely room; sick with the return of numbed senses to the sharpness of her sorrow, allowed him to lead her out on to the deserted terrace. Vaguely she saw through the undraped window the surge and sway as the guests regrouped themselves, to listen inattentively to the music of the spinet in the intervals of the dancing; and Lord Frome standing alone in the embrasure of an opposite window. A coach had just driven away from the portico; and she could see Prince Anton of Brunswick come through the ballroom doorway and stand uncertainly just inside it, looking about him. Clearly her friend was at last arriving. Sophia's need recalled her a little to life, she revived her attention and now gave recognition for the first time to what her cousin was saying – that he loved her, had loved her always, would love her for ever, that something like a terror of joy gripped his heart because she did not at once repudiate his love, because he dared to hope that her silence might mean consent.... Stupified by her own grief, conscious only that at any moment Lord Frome might turn and see her outside the uncurtained window, she could only stare back into Charles Weyburn's eyes, could find no words to speak. "Christine, say something – say something!" But as she gazed speechlessly up at him – she, the remote, cool, controlled Christine who, had she not loved him would surely by now have kindly and quietly denied him? – hope grew in him, and grew. "Can it be possible...? All these doubts, all these fears... Christine, don't hold me in torment here, say just one word." But her tongue was paralysed. "Then, dearest, say nothing; but if you say nothing – am I to take it that this nothing means everything to me?" He stood apart from her, not touching her; and still she uttered not a word. "Oh, Christine!" he said. "You are mine!" After all this world of uncertainty, never daring to hope – can it be possible that you are mine?" And he put out his hand to her, slowly, almost as though he were frightened, and like a man in a dream drew her to him; and at last with a swift movement caught her close in his arms and kissed her undenying lips.

She wrenched herself free of him; and in that instant saw Lord Frome turn his head and look directly across the ballroom towards the window. One thought only flashed through her mind. He will see me here in my cousin's arms – I have lost him for ever.

And she raised her hand and with all her force struck Lord Weyburn across the face.

He stood motionless for a moment, gazing down at her, utterly incredulous. At the sharp sound of the slap, heads turned, a silence fell. Lord Frome started, stared: and suddenly turned on his heel and pushed his way through the throng towards the ballroom door, the footmen lifting the velvet curtain to let him pass through. Lord Weyburn moved at last. He stepped back, his hands fell to his sides. He said, "Your pardon, Madam!" and made her a bow and a flourish – very pale, with only a slowly mounting flush on his face where her hand had struck; and turned and went back into the ballroom leaving her standing there.

All about her the gardens lay dark and silent, lit only by the stars, as, weeping, she fled past the glittering windows, out into the night alone.

He went back into the ballroom, slowly, not putting up his hand to his face: moving slowly forward into the brilliant ballroom where some imported maestro tinkled unattended his little silver notes from the rosewood spinet – the crowd parting to make way for him, falling gradually silent as though from some creeping contagion of muted tongues – moving slowly forward in the sombre magnificence of his jewels and brocade, not deigning to put up his hand to cover the mounting flush where her hand had struck. A voice said at last, to break the uneasy silence: "What, Charles – has The Lily turned you down?" and there was laughter, a little high-pitched and nervous; Charles Weyburn was never a man to trifle with. A voice said: "She'll come round, Charles, never fear." A woman standing near him said: "She'll have you in the end."

"No," he said. "That is all over." And this time he did put his hand to his cheek, and touched the red mark; and the rest of his face was white with a white, cold, frozen anger that stripped away the artificial indifference of society manners, bared the outraged pride for all the world to see. He had made her an honourable proposal and for answer – this!

The Duchess of Witham, avid as ever to be at the storm centre, had squeezed her way towards him. Such an excitement! –

and when they had all believed that only the dull Earl of Frome was involved. Rather, a thousand times, Weyburn. "For shame, my lord! Our poor Lily – such a pother over nothing! But I vow you shall have her." He did not answer, looking with chill disgust into her gloating eyes. "Or if you will not, why then we must find you another." She rapped him with her fan, looking delightedly about her. "Come, don't look so glum my lord, put a bold face on it: here's not the only pretty girl in England. Come to my next rout and I'll show you half a dozen I warrant you, good wives enough and fit for any man's arms."

He bowed to her icily. "I thank your Grace; but I want no other wife in my arms." And he raised his voice suddenly and swore it aloud. "As long as I live – I'll hold no other wife in my arms."

She threw up her hands with their glitter of rings. "Why then there's nothing for it after all. You must marry Miss Lillane."

"That is over," he said again, and he bowed once more and made to pass her. "Now, if your Grace will pardon me...." But she cried out, high and hooting: "Not so fast, sir! Not till you promise me."

He looked at her stupidly. "Promise you?"

"To marry Christine Lillane."

To marry Christine Lillane: who had replied to his honourable proposals with a – public – slap across the face. "As soon, Madame," he said, "would I promise to marry the next woman who walks through that door."

A few shrugs, a few titters, an exchange of indulgent smiles. But a voice said: "A thousand guineas on it, my lord?"

He checked; he was brought up short. He said, over intervening heads. "A wager? On what?"

"On what you've just said, my lord. That you'll marry the first woman to walk through the ballroom door."

Ah, now indeed the languor deserted them! Lord Weyburn of Starrbelow – who was known never to refuse a wager; and the challenger (did any then observe that covert glance towards the door) the Princeling, Anton of Brunswick, whom his lordship was known to regard with little-concealed contempt. Excitement rose in them, rose like champagne bubbles all about the packed ballroom till the very candle-flames in their crystal chandeliers seemed to quiver with anticipation. Painted fans made screens for exchange of shocked comment, white hands were struck motionless, holding the open snuffbox: all heads turned at the sound of murmuring in the hall outside. Belated arrivals were being questioned by the footmen, were giving their names. The voice repeated, insistently, on a note of odd urgency: "A thousand guineas, my lord?"

The moment lasted an hour: but as the footman's white-gloved hand lifted aside the red velvet curtain, Charles Weyburn cried out: "Done!"

And the curtains parted: and Sapphire Devigne came in.

Four

They are all staring at me, thought Sapphire. They are all remembering. It is an eternity since I came through the doorway and stood here and felt their eyes on me; and this chill immobility and this silence will never end.

But it ended. A figure advanced, handsome, magnificent, in dark velvet and brocade, and bowed, and took her small hand in a long white hand. A voice said: "Lady Corby... Miss Devigne... I am happy to welcome you to Starrbelow." His voice rang out very cold and clear in the great room where the only other sound was the tiny, far-away tinkle of the spinet; she could hear the rustle and whisper of her aunt's dress as Lady Corby curtseyed, the creak of Sir Bertram's corseting as he bowed. She dropped into a curtsey, and could not see herself, as he saw her, poised there for a moment like a porcelain figurine, cool white dress, warm white skin, bright gold of hair, eyes cast down: red lips smiling the little smile. He raised her, still holding her hand, and led her forward into the room; and as on that other evening – nobody spoke. Now, even the spinet had ceased its tinkling; and into the silence, like Hans Anderson's mermaid whose every step was to cause her the agony of sharp knives cutting into the flesh, Sapphire Devigne entered upon her destiny.

Lord Weyburn was apologising for the absence of her hostess. "No doubt she will be here in a moment. I believe her friend, Lord Frome, has gone in search of her."

She was a little surprised – she had seen the Earl of Frome a moment ago, standing in the hall with his carriage cloak on. But she could not give her full mind to it. All about her, conversation was resuming, the fiddles were tuning up for the dancing, the whole frozen room coming to life again; all eyes, she knew, were upon her – and into her quailing heart had been thrust a new, sharp stab of presentiment, a new threat born in that single moment when she had looked up from her curtsey and into his eyes… I must speak. I must say something…. She stammered out that this was a happy, a very happy evening for Miss Lillane….

"Happy? Why? Because Lord Frome has gone in search of her?"

She opened her eyes and looked directly at him and for the first time Lord Weyburn saw the blue blaze of sapphire. "I meant only because it's her birthday and you're giving her this ball."

"Oh, aye," he said. "The ball. That is your notion of happiness, Madame, is it? A birthday ball?"

She might have retorted that the ball to her was away from it. She replied however, indifferently, falling back upon the new manner, the new, cool front of ironic disdain with which, before all the world but Christine, she covered her vulnerability, that she had been merely making polite conversation. "If every exchange of civilities is to be so critically analysed, I had better keep silent."

"Even silence may be open to analysis."

"Do you keep silence also then, my lord! and we may analyse one another without giving offence."

A spark of anger, yet not without a grudging admiration, kindled his eye. He bowed. "I trust that so early in our acquaintance, I have not offended?"

"If you have, sir, it need not signify,"

said Sapphire. "Our acquaintance is likely to be so short that there will not be time for you to do so again."

It was his turn to look startled. Rumour had reached him that Lady Corby had destined him as a match for her niece, nor had he been slow to divine that the lady's lover had tricked him into his present pass – that Prince Anton had been well aware, having just arrived at Starrbelow in her company, that Sophia Devigne would be the next woman to pass through the fateful door. This at least did not look like complicity on the young lady's part. "Why do you predict that our acquaintance shall be short?"

"Because, sir, my 'notion of happiness' is so far removed from balls and routs and the rest of your English joys, that I purpose to return to Italy as soon as I may."

He bowed. "Our English joys will be the less for your going."

"No doubt," she said, coolly. "But the hounds will soon find some other poor creature to bay." And she also bowed, withdrawing. "The music is beginning, my lord, your place is with the dancers. I will return to my aunt."

But he caught her hand and pulled her

back to him and once more she looked up at him, startled, and once more he caught the flash of blue. "To your aunt! And then – to Italy? Why, Madame, you do nothing but threaten to run away." And he put his hand behind her waist and pressed her forward into the dance with him, and she went, neither resisting nor going willingly. "You shall not return to your aunt – nor to Italy either if I can prevent it," said Lord Weyburn of Starrbelow.

Lady Corby paraded the ballroom on her husband's arm, bowing this way and that effusively, despite the cool reception her greetings received. "Keep your eye on her, Bertram; I can't afford to be seen watching...." She fluttered her fan and dipped a curtsey to a nervous looking little woman huddled in a corner with a couple of cronies, watching the dancing. "Bow, Bertram, quickly; it is Lady Lillane, Christine's mother. Do keep your wits about you," she hissed sharply, under cover of the smile. "She could be useful."

Sir Bertram bowed vaguely in the general direction indicated. "I can't watch Sophia and be on the look out for useful old ladies as well: I am not cross-eyed."

"It would not help you if you were," she

said, with, what was rare in her, a genuine ring of laughter.

"Yes, it would; for I could watch Sophia, and by keeping a permanent grin on my face, convince the old pussies that I was smiling at them."

"How does she seem to be doing? Does he look impressed?"

"I think one might say," said Sir Bertram carefully, "that he looks impressed; yes. Whether he looks very pleased, is another matter."

"Is she not smiling?"

"Oh, yes, she is smiling," said Sir Bertram; they both knew by now what that could mean.

"Oh, Lord! That girl will undo herself and all of us. . . ."

"She has done that once already, my dear," said Sir Bertram, laughing in his turn.

"Pouf – that is long forgotten: it is she alone who makes much of it. And yet – what a hush when she made her entrance just now! I thought she'd refuse at the last minute, after all our trouble. If Lord Weyburn had not come forward, she would have. How goes it now? Are they speaking?"

"She is speaking; by the look on her face – and his – I should say she was speaking her mind."

"You don't mean – he seems angry?" In her anxiety she stole a glance herself, from behind her fan. "How strange he looks; so pale, and there is a flush all down one side of his face... But as to the expression, wouldn't you say that he looked not so much angry as – well, as intrigued? And, look! – positively, he is leading her into the dance. Come, Bertram, we had better dance, too; we can watch best that way."

"Not I," he said. "What do you keep your tame monkey for? Dance with him."

But Prince Anton was not in the ballroom; and when, later, they looked for him in the drawing-rooms and about the long buffet-tables laid out in the dining hall, he was not there, either. For Prince Anton of Brunswick, having sold his soul to the devil, and realising too late that it was so, had gone out into the wilderness: where his master waited.

A message came for Miss Devigne. Miss Lillane was unwell, she was lying down in her room with a headache. Would Miss Devigne come up and see her there?

70

It was a lovely room, the room Christine always had when she came to Starrbelow, kept especially for her: a small room with tall windows looking out over the wooded park where the deer grazed beneath the great, spreading beech and chestnut trees; with a high ceiling, painted with a design if naked cupids, playing among the clouds, all tangled up with pink and blue ribbon bows. Christine lay in her white ball-dress on the white fourposter bed: looking indeed, Sapphire thought, like a lily that had been flung down, broken, there. "Christine, are you ill?"

"No, no, though my head aches dreadfully...."

"And you have been crying?"

"I have many things to cry about," said Christine, turning her head away on the lacy pillow.

"Has Lord Frome...?"

"Lord Frome has said nothing. I danced with him, I walked with him alone in the gallery – oh, Sapphire, you may almost say that I threw myself at his head; and he has said nothing, I have been mistaken all along...."

She could be tender with only this one friend – she who had been so gay and tender

71

with all the loving, belovéd friends, but a few brief weeks ago; but now she sat down on the edge of the bed beside her, all blue and white and gold, and took the pale hands in hers and smoothed back the disordered hair. "Oh, dearest – what can I say? I am so sorry; and yet – surely it must be all a mistake, it must come right in the end . . . ?"

"How can it 'come right'? If he is ever to speak – surely then was the time? And now . . . Oh, Sapphire, dear Charles, who has always been so good to me . . . !" She put up her hand to a throat that ached with tears. "Are they all gossiping about me, down there among the dancers?"

"About you? Why no – why should they?"

Christine lifted her head from the pillow to stare at her. "You mean – you have not heard?"

"Heard? No – heard what?"

Christine did not answer. She said: "Is Lord Frome below?"

"He crossed with us in the hall, going out, just as we arrived. I'm afraid . . . Well, it is true, Christine, that I have not seen him since."

"How long have you been here, Sapphire?"   "An hour – an hour and a half? You came out on to the terrace with Lord Weyburn as we drove up the approach." She said: "You have not been weeping all this time, dearest, up here alone in your room?"

"I have been weeping: what does it matter where one weeps? I was in the garden; and then, when you were all dancing, I crept up here." She thought it all over, miserably. "So Lord Frome has gone home, you see, Sapphire, and will not come back tonight. He – does not like scenes; and he does not like women who make scenes – and if he did not like me before, what chance is there now that he will change his mind? My cousin, Charles, out on the terrace, spoke to me honourably and asked me to be his wife; and when, taking my silence for consent, he put out his arms to me, I – I hit out at him, hardly knowing what I did, because my heart was breaking for Edward – for Lord Frome. And Charles said nothing but walked away from me and into the ballroom; and you tell me now that Edward has gone home?"

"Oh, darling, no: we don't really know that – I tell you only that I have not seen him in the ballroom. As for Lord Weyburn," said Sapphire, with a flash of her own wry pride, "he has lost no time in consoling himself with another."

"With another?" said Christine, astonished out of her self-absorption. "Charles? With whom?"

"Ah, my pet, you are not so lost in love, as to be devoid of a touch of chagrin?" said Sapphire, laughing. She shrugged. "Have no fear, however, you are in no danger of losing your admirer through his attentions to this particular lady: nor, though he would not care as to that, is she in danger of being hurt by them." And she got up off the bed and made an ironical curtsey.

Christine sat upright, lovely as a wild-flower in the tumbled disarray of her dress and hair. "Lord Weyburn – has been making love to you?"

Sophia smiled her little smile. "You are so surprised?"

"Only that he so lately had made love to me," said Christine, hurriedly.

"Ah, no." She said, sadly: "That he should flirt with another woman to assuage his wounded pride, that would not much astonish you, Christine. But that he should choose Sapphire Devigne, that by-word among your London outcasts, just clinging with one poor hand, and that only through your loving kindness, to the mud-scattered skirts of the *ton* – that does amaze you." She shrugged again, the gentleness in her face hardened to that look of scornful pride that was coming to be habitual there. "I don't know why it should. He chose me the more to affront you by the very contrast; and at the same time to make sure, lest at any time you showed signs of softening, that you would never suspect him of *serious* attentions elsewhere. This is a comedy only too often played."

"Yes," said Christine, very thoughtfully. "Yes."

"So ready in agreement," said Sapphire with a mock bow, "is not flattering. But you pay me the compliment of sincerity: which must take its place."

"Oh, Sapphire!" Christine jumped off the bed and ran to her friend, putting her arms about her. "Forgive me, I was far away, I was not thinking of you at all; or of what I was saying." And she held her at arms' length, looking into the lovely face that but a few weeks ago had been so frank and sweetly smiling and so young. "You make too much of it all, this foolish incident at Witham House – it is spoiling you, Sapphire, you are building it into a tragedy

75

that will ruin your life. It is forgotten already by everyone but yourself."

"I am remembered, Christine, as that Italian adventuress who, to attract attention in the marriage market, went to the Duchess's rout with her bosom exposed."

"Oh, Sapphire!" she said, half-despairingly. "You have been brought up according to other lights, you do not understand our English ways, you make far too much of it all. Besides, you are not unchaperoned. The blame, if any, must attach to your guardians."

"I am no tender admirer of my aunt Corby, Christine. But she was not guilty of any intention there."

"Probably nobody really believes she was. But she is – not popular – in society, and if something goes a trifle wrong with her plans, why there is gossip and a little malicious pleasure no doubt: but at her expense, not yours."

"I am believed to be an accessory to her 'plans.'"

"By very few. At worst you are thought to be the innocent victim of a silly little ill-contrived plot; whose worst fault, after all, was that it was a lapse of taste." She looked anxiously at her friend. "I have told you all this so many times, Sophia, I thought I had convinced you."

"So you almost had," said Sophia, "until this evening. Otherwise, I should never have come at all; as it was I was ill with dread. . . ."

"But needlessly; what little breeze of gossip there was, has long ago blown itself out, the whole trivial incident is forgotten, nobody thinks of it."

"Oh, certainly. I could almost hear them not thinking of it, so profound was the silence as I entered the ballroom tonight. . . ."

Entering the ballroom: standing in the doorway in her snowy white dress against the looped, curving background of the red velvet curtain, all unconscious of that voice that had cried out a challenge, all ignorant still of the voice that had answered: 'Done!'

"Not a soul spoke, Christine, every head turned as I came through the door; every eye, I daresay, to the bosom of my dress. . . ."

"If they were silent, it was not upon your account. You forget," insisted Christine, "that a new scandal had raised its head. Tonight, in public, I slapped Lord Weyburn's face. If they were silent, it was

77

the silence before a real storm – your little breeze, Sapphire, was as nothing to a scandal involving Lord Weyburn, of all people, and the Lily of Lillane; and all the world knows, but himself, of my love for the Earl of Frome. Three untouchables, found vulnerable at last. . . ."

"Well, we will not fall out over our claims to be objects of scandal, Christine." But her heart was sore for her friend. "Rather a thousand times it should be I than you. . . ."

There was a knock at the door. Christine's maid entered carrying a folded paper. "From his lordship, Madame."

"From Lord Frome. . . ?"

"From Lord Weyburn," said the servant quickly, sorrowfully watching the disappointed face.

Christine handed the note to Sophia. 'My dear cousin – I scribble this hurriedly, as you will understand. You must return to your guests, your absence is causing comment and it will be far worse for you if you are not seen again – and holding up your head. I regret that tonight I should have proposed a question which merited such an answer. The question was put, however, and the answer given. Let us therefore agree to cry quits: let the matter never again be referred to between us – be assured, at least, that the question will never be repeated. But you must come down now to your guests....' There had come a pause here, the ink on the quill had dried, the quill been dipped again. The note continued: 'Pray ask your friend, Miss Devigne, if you will, to join our Christmas gathering and remain a few days.' Another pause. 'If there is gossip or if you fear gossip, she will stand your friend and with her wit and courage which I truly believe to be great, will help you through. I suppose her aunt will wish to come also; better invite the whole party. But come down now: it is necessary. Hurriedly... I remain your cousin, and from now forward merely your cousin, Weyburn.'

"What – Sapphire Devigne to stay at Starrbelow – *and* Sir Bertram and Lady Corby," said Sophia, folding the note and handing it back. "The very rooks would take flight and the elms be deserted."

"Sapphire! – you must stay."

"Not I," said Sapphire. "To be sneered at by my fellow-guests, to be further insulted by Lord Weyburn's counter-flirtations: thank you, no."

"Oh, dearest, you are so bitter. What

nonsense is this? Why should my cousin not sincerely admire you?"

"With his cheek still tingling from another woman's rejection? I'll warrant him," said Sapphire, overwhelmed suddenly by the bitterness of what she took to be merely his cynical choice of her defencelessness for attentions in fact directed towards her friend, "I'll make his cheek tingle and not with the flat of my hand." And she struck her own hand against her forehead and cried out, like a child in the dark, to think that she, Sophia Devigne, who such a little while ago had been far away at home in the sunshine of Italy, surrounded with only love and tenderness, greeted with smiles and simple friendship as she walked lightheartedly through her happy days, and been reduced in so short a time to this: a young girl still, and yet, it seemed to her, long schooled in wary appraisal of hidden, unlovely motive, hard of head, chill of heart, using her natural wit as a weapon instead of a charm, using her gift of beauty as a mask to hide a mortified and resentful heart. "Go down, Christine: call back your maid and let her re-dress your hair, and go down to your guests. I will walk down with you and stay with you a little while but no power on earth shall keep me at Starrbelow beyond this night."

"Oh, Sapphire, I beg! I hardly know Lord Weyburn's other guests, how can I keep up appearances a week with no close friend here of my own?"

"You have your mother here."

"You know my mother, Sapphire. She ... Well, I mean no disrespect, but my mother is too nervous, too – too undetermined, she is no friend for me, no support to me, at a time like this."

"I will not stay, Christine. I have some pride left, poor tattered flag that it may be, and I will not stay."

Christine did not answer; but after a moment she opened her little travelling-desk and from a drawer took a letter. "Madame – I now learn that when last night you 'mistook me for a friend,' it was as a true friend that you acted towards me." And: "If passionate gratitude can make a friend, you have one in me to the end of my life...."

"Very well," said Sapphire, handing the letter back to her. "I will stay." And she said, as she had said to her Aunt Corby not very long ago: "Whatever you ask me to do,

Christine, I must do." But this time the blue eyes genuinely smiled.

It was not so late when they returned to the inn, but that Lady Corby whispered a command, and Prince Anton met her accordingly in the private sitting room set aside for their party, when the rest had retired to bed. But he said uneasily, the gutteral intonation unusually pronounced, "In a public inn, Marcia – iss not this indiscreet?"

She had been waiting for him, standing in the shadows of the great brick chimney-piece, and now she did not move but just raised her little hand, like a doll's hand, and beckoned him over to her, smiling up into his eyes. "Indiscreet or not – come here and claim your reward!" But as she reached up to put her soft arms about his neck she added, murmuring: "Or at any rate an earnest of rewards to come."

He almost shuddered under her kiss but, fatally weak, allowed her to hold him, stooping over her from his considerable height; and something of the magic of her power over him returned with the kiss. But when at last she released him, he moved away and stood unhappily, one hand against the brick chimney piece, head bent, the straight fair hair falling forward over his forehead as it often did – for it was his habit to wear a wig as seldom as possible and he grew his hair longer than men who habitually wore one; and repeated only: "Iss this not very indiscreet?"

"Bertram knew I was coming. After this evening, I had to talk to you."

"And I to you, Marcia. The moment this vos done, I haf regretted it. I think it must be undone."

"Undone?" she said, staring up at him in amazement. "You must be mad."

"I vos mad when I did it. I had gone in ahead of you, as you said I should since we arrived so late. . . . As I came into the room, he spoke, he said he should marry the first that came through the door. I knew the chance was great that the next to come in would be you with Sir Bertram and Sophia. I saw the chance suddenly, I knew you desired this marriage for her, I had not time to reflect – almost before I knew it, my voice cried out."

"An inspiration, Toni!"

"But no. It vos wrong. I can't let it rest like this, I can't let her go in ignorance, condemn her to such a fate."

Her face hardened under the china doll look. "Oh, if your objection is only that it harms Sophia...!" But she sweetened her voice, she forced herself to smile. "Why, dearest, you're being foolish. 'Condemn her to such a fate!' – when you've just said yourself, it's the fate we've 'condemned' her to all along. That she should become Lady Weyburn – it has seemed to me the highest pinnacle of happiness the child could attain to; and her happiness," said Lady Corby, shrugging as though such a truth must be self-evident, "is all I ask. What does it matter how the work is begun? He will pay her attentions now because of the wager; fall in love with her, marry her, and – there we are! Did you see his face all evening? He's already enchanted."

"Sophia will soon disenchant him," said Anton, grimly.

"Sophia is difficult. *We* know, Toni," she said, confidentially deprecatory, "what Sophia can be. But to him, you see, it's provocative, he's intrigued by the difference between her cool manner and the flattering of the rest of these chits that pursue him."

"Very well, then; if all goes so well, let

me call off the bet, let the affair simply take its natural course."

"But my foolish one, what harm is there in it, why not let it remain as it is?"

"It vos not a fair bet," said Prince Anton. "I knew she would come."

If it were truly only this, she thought! If it were not that in his heart he cares more about what happens to *her* . . . . Her own heart – honest in only one thing, her passion for this handsome boy, so many years her junior – sank at the thought that even this wager might prove the rock on which the affair between them might founder. She went off into peals of her pretty, tinkling laughter, however, coming up to him, putting her little hands up on his shoulders, resting her dark head against his heart. "Not fair! Oh, Toni, you are so sweet and so comical! You are like a child playing tag."

"It is an affair of honour," he said stiffly, enduring rather than accepting her embrace.

It was an agony to her to feel, to sense that drawing-back; but she forced herself to ignore it. "An affair of honour? Why, then, I suppose it is – and in that case, Toni, it *is* serious. For, to unmake the bet, you must confess that when you made it you knew it to be, as you call it, 'unfair': and that will not look pretty."

"Everyone must know thiss already," he said wretchedly.

"A few may suspect it; but you must keep quiet and if it is ever mentioned, then will be the time to start, to stare, to declare upon our honour it never occurred to you till now ... to rush off to Lord Weyburn, conscience-stricken, if it comes to the last, and say that this matter has been brought to your attention, that of course now you see it in this light, you must cancel the bet. But be warned by me, I implore you – to 'confess' will be to give yourself away. And besides," she insisted, "we hoped for the marriage for her anyway; without this, it could still have taken place."

"If it does so now, this will cost me a thousand guineas," he said gloomily. "And I have not got it."

"I will pay it; Sir Bertram and I will pay it."

"You have not a thousand guineas either, Marcia."

"Precisely! – and does that trouble *us?* When Sophia is well married," said Lady Corby, "money will be flush. He is

86

enormously rich, she will have but to reach out her hand into the coffers. . . ."

"Do you suggest I shall borrow from *her* – to pay off her husband?"

"Pouf, nonsense: I say only that her wealth and position will all be owing to us; and she is not a girl to forget her friends." She smiled up at him. "Nor am I, when I am rich, one to forget my friends."

"I will not haf your money, Marcia," he said stiffly. "Nor hers."

"You will have to have somebody's money, my love, to pay off even half your debts, a tenth of them; or you'll find yourself on the wrong side of Papa, excluded from Hanover and your ultimate destiny, the fair Princess Gertrud."

"She iss not fair," he said sulkily. "She iss like a young carthorse."

"Good," said Lady Corby, with satisfaction.

"You are pleased for me to marry a carthorse?" he said, half-laughing. "This iss not very kind."

"It is not kind of you to marry at all, when your Marcia needs all your heart."

"But I must marry at the last," he said.

"Yes." She closed her eyes for a moment against the reality of it; but, go warily! her instinct told her, you hold him because you are worldly and cynical and it is all a charming game; if he ever suspected what it really means to you, he would take fright and be off. He 'must marry at the last' – it was a fact, she had known it always, she must face it now; and make use of it. "Yes, you must marry. And Marcia is unavailable – and penniless. But the Princess Gertrud is rich, my poor Anton; is it not so?"

"That she is rich is not important; I inherit my own estates."

"But she is a suitable match for a nephew of the Elector; and a nephew, moreover, not so very far removed from the throne itself."

"To you thiss iss unimportant," he said, resentfully. "To you, Hanover is a dull tuppenny kingdom which turns out dull, elderly misstresses for your king – who, however, I remind you, Marcia, vos not too good to come from Hanover himself. . . ."

"And look at him!" said Marcia.

"I, at any rate, have respect for my country; and I do not think it a small thing that – though God forbid! – I might possibly be called upon one day to rule it."

"And therefore must provide yourself with a suitable Electress. Of course, my dear; you are right, it's a serious matter. But

I, meanwhile – why you cannot be astonished that I should not be sorry the young lady is like a carthorse! And you have a year or two yet to sow your charming wild oats."

"I should have discretion, however, in the sowing. And, Marcia, it has not been discreet to come over and waste this time when I should be studying your history, your constitutions, etcetera; to spend my whole competency in so short a while –"

"And spend it in the company of Marcia Corby!"

"An affair of gallantry –" he began uneasily.

"An affair of gallantry – ah, yes, in England! But in Hanover, my pet, will papa take the same view?"

"Your own king –" he began again.

"Ah, yes, our own king – who by the way, as you have reminded me, is rather more *your* own king – has had his affairs no doubt: and finds his mistresses in Hanover, what's more. But I cannot suppose Gertrud's stuffy little royalties will be quite so complacent as our poor Queen Caroline. . . . Or as they say she was," she added, rather hurriedly, "for I'm sure I was too young to know about such things when the Queen was still alive."

"And Gertrud is too young now."

"But her parents are not."

"Nor mine. If my father should find how I haf spent this time...." He looked suddenly very young, his face was troubled, he met her eyes with a sort of pleading. "Sometimes I ask myself, Marcia, whether I should not – If we should not –" He left the fireplace and moved right away from her, stood in the window, one hand holding back the heavy curtain, looking out at the first grey streaks of the dawn. "Has the time come, perhaps, to end it all?"

Life had dealt unkindly with Marcia Corby. Married off at an early age (yet well knowing what she did) to a man, much her senior, whom her parents had deceived about her fortune, she found too late that he, in turn, had been deceiving them. Thus mutually betrayed, they had settled down to a jog-trot partnership, loveless yet by necessity loyal; united only in a common cold-heartedness, a common determination to fight without quarter for such material benefits as they demanded from life: since life had robbed them of purer means to happiness. For twenty years they had

90

struggled side by side; and, 'Sometimes I feel,' she would think, peering at her old-young face in the looking-glass, 'that behind this mask lies all the age and evil knowledge of the serpent of old Nile. . . .' And now . . . . Into her life had come, a year ago, this young man – who was not like the other young men she knew, the old-young men to match her old-young face, the cynical, raffish, middle-aging men playing with rather desperate abandon as the years hurried on, their games of gallantry that were not at all gallant, their games of love which were utterly without love. Anton, genuinely young, fresh to the ways of the world and the *ton*, handsome, charming, in those days rich, in those days debonair, had been too inexperienced to recognise the serpent that stared out at Lady Corby from her own glass – had fallen genuinely, gayly, richly and happily in love. To her it had meant – at first, another conquest, only; but as time went on and his guileless sincerity flattered and reassured her, something far more – something to lift her heart above the dreary round of petty deception and roguery, the cheating, the dodging, the debts, the thieving – call it by what other name one would; the lies.

Something to raise her own value in her own long-disillusioned eyes, something to give back for a little while at least, a real look of youth to the mask of youth she habitually wore: something to treasure, something to cling to, something, as far as her cold heart could know such an emotion, to love. A vindication, coming late but not too late to be precious to her, of the right she had once had, innocent, lovely and young, to a decent man's love. And now.... A short while later, schooled all too quickly in the manners and modes of her world, he tugged at his silken tether and longed to be free; and had not even the courage to say so, must pretend he would stay if he could, but did not dare. He is poltroon, she thought, looking at his handsome, white, unhappy young face; a great, whey-faced, faltering, innocent baby, weak as water and not knowing what he wants – unless it may be that sly-smiling witch of a girl. But she shall not have him. Such as he is, he is mine and I need him and will keep him: I won't let him go. "Anton," she said, "are you telling me you wish to leave me?"

"Not *wish* to," he said, weakly protesting.

"The truth is, you fancy yourself in love with this girl."

"I – in love . . . ?" he stammered, startled, colouring.

"And that is why you want to break off this bet. Well, I tell you, fairly, Anton, it shall not be. Sophia Devigne is not for you. . . ."

"Sophia?" he said. "I . . . I don't . . . ." He stuttered and stammered "I swear to you, Marcia, there's nothing between us, nothing. . . ."

"Then keep it so. She is not for you, Anton; you must marry your German girl in the end and it would be fatal to get tangled up over here with an unmarried woman. With me you are safe." But she added: "As long as you do what you're told."

He raised his eyebrows, shadowed by the falling lock of fair hair. He was, after all, a prince. "As long ass I do what I'm told? What iss this – a threat?"

She came across to him and stood facing him, very small, very lovely in her bright dress; very strong. "Yes, Anton – if you like to call it that – a threat. Sophia is destined to marry Lord Weyburn; our fortunes depend upon it, mine and Sir Bertram's,

93

and, if you will be wise, yours too."

"I tell you, Marcia, I do not vish for her money...."

"And I shall not allow you to upset my arrangements," she concluded, disregarding him.

He said, with a touch of scorn, "How vill you prevent me?"

"Ah, you don't quite believe me, Toni: but it's simple enough. For, rather than let you spoil my plans – and this is the 'threat,' my dear – I shall acquaint your parents, and dear Gertrud's with the manner in which you have spent your time and your patrimony over here. You understand?"

He looked at her with something like fear; but he said, rallying a smile and a shrug: "A pretty scheme! Lady Corby presenting herself at my father's door with a story of having a liaison with his son and helped to dissipate his fortune. I don't quite see you," he said, looking down at her with something of the teasing smile Sophia had come to know, "in so very unpromising a role."

She considered it ruefully. "Nor I. It would not become me at all." She paused just a moment for his little gust of triumph. "No, I couldn't go myself; I should have

94

to send Sir Bertram. The husband, enraged, breathing fire and thunder, demanding redress, would cause quite a stir, I flatter myself, Toni, at the court of Hanover?"

His face changed. He said sullenly: "Sir Bertram would not go."

She laughed. "No, I don't think he would; and if he did he would manage it badly – can you see him playing such a part?" And she came up close to him again, and again put her little hands up on his shoulders and smiled like an angel into his face. "Come – I am teasing you, darling, of course I shall not send Bertie, or go myself. But you must be a good boy, my love, and do what your Marcia tells you – and forget all this nonsense; and when the time comes, you shall go back safe and solvent, to the little carthorse." And to be on the safe side, she added, for he was as weak as water, naughty boy! where a pretty face was concerned, he had perhaps better not see Sophia for a little while.

"This is impossible; tomorrow we all go to Starrbelow."

"In the circumstances, will it not be wiser for you to return to town? We shall follow at the end of the week."

"Oh, but no," he said. "I am invited to Starrbelow."

"We will make our excuses. . . ."

He was a young man, weak, perhaps rather vicious, easily led, caught up in an affair 'of gallantry' which had become too complicated for his limited experience; but he was also a nobleman, reared in the formal atmosphere of a court. When in this trivial affair of behaviour, she brooked him, he knew where he stood. "Lord Weyburn invited me, Marcia. I haf accepted. Tomorrow I shall go to Starrbelow ass I said I would." And he looked out at the dawn and corrected himself: "Today."

Five

Starrbelow, whose name in former days was Starrbelow-Edge, lies at the foot of the easternmost ridge of the Cotswold hills; its land on the western side marching with the far wider estates of the Earl of Frome. Frome Castle stands higher than Starrbelow, crowning a rounded hill from which it dominates, four-square in its Tudor magnificence, the country below – the 'slender landscape and austere,' lying serenely, silver grey and green in the thin, clear Cotswold air. But Starrbelow looks out over level land; its lovely yellow Cotswold stone is set in a green park, only a little undulant, beyond which stretch the flower-bright meadows and the rich farm lands; only behind it the ridge rises up, heavily wooded, sharp and high as a cliff. So Sapphire saw it, driving up the long approach in the thin sunlight of a winter's day, with drifts of melting snow where flowers and leaves would come again; and could not dream that one day, rich in everything but love and happiness, this would be her own.

There were, in all, thirty guests at Starrbelow for that Christmas house party; but there had been a reshuffle, she found herself assigned a room that might have been set apart for one of more consequence, surely? than Sophia Devigne: a room looking out over sunken gardens, centering on a lily pool, of stunted plants forming loveknots and intitials entwined, trimmed with tiny clipped hedges of box – a room hung with parchment all round its high walls, with painted scenes: a meeting, a love scene, a presentation scene – young lover, young love, and welcoming parents; the formal betrothal scene. Every servant at Starrbelow knew, and paid her deference accordingly, that this was, traditionally, the room where a prospective Starrbelow bride first slept; everyone at Starrbelow knew – but not Sophia.

The Duchess of Witham was among the guests. "You'll put up Gossip Wit for me?" Charles Weyburn had said to his friend, discussing the plans for Christine's party; and, "Not I," said Lord Frome. "That hooting macaw? I wouldn't have her in my stables, let alone my house."

"My sentiments, exactly. But my aunt Lillane insists. The Wit could be a dangerous enemy to Christine."

"Christine has nothing to fear from the Wit, nor from any other woman either."

"All young girls in society, Edward, are at the mercy of gossip. Look at this unfortunate whom Christine has befriended. . . ."

"Your cousin is no poor little wretch from heaven knows where – and with an aunt like La Corby. Slander can't touch Christine."

"Even direct rudeness; a rebuff, a passing sarcasm in that high, carrying voice. . . . The Duchess is part-master."

"Christine would look at her with her blue eyes unclouded, and raise those winged eyebrows of hers a fraction and pass on her way; as though she and everyone present must wonder that any lady could so betray herself into unloveliness. And what is more, the rest would take their cue from Christine."

Lord Weyburn laughed. "You have a great confidence in my cousin."

"I have confidence that she need not pander to such women as her Grace of Witham; at any rate, I will not entertain the

99

lady, even for you, or even for your aunt, or even for Christine. Tell off thirty or forty of the others and I'll house them for you in my great barracks, with pleasure. But even Frome is not large enough for me and Gossip Wit."

So the Duchess of Witham was entertained at Starrbelow, because everyone disliked her; and the Countess of Lammingham because everybody liked her, and Lady Thawne because everybody laughed at her, and Lady Pamela Newton because everybody laughed with her: and Lady This for some other reason, and Lady That for yet another.... And in their train came the gentlemen, dawdling or mincing behind them according to their various ways, poor old Witham very doddery, Lord Lammingham very correct, Lord Thawne very much depressed, Lord Newton in the seventh heaven of devotion to his Pamela; and among the This's and That's, three men whose names, for Sapphire' sake, were, within less than a year to become household words: 'Red' Reddington, hard-riding squire of the small but lovely manor of Harley-sub-Edge, near by, – Sir Francis Erick, as blonde and china-blue-eyed as Christine herself, – and Lord Greenewode, his familiar and friend, as tall and dark and melancholy as Sir Francis was bright and blonde and gay. And all these people knew, of course, that Lord Weyburn has wagered a thousand guineas with Prince Anton; but even those who had room for pity in their hearts, could do nothing to warn their victim – a wager was a wager and one could not conceivably depart from the accepted code.

Lord Weyburn met them as the carriage stopped at the great front door steps, with Christine at his side. She had regained her poise; and to see the two cousins there, he tall, slight, dark, handsome, coolly aloof, she tall also and slender, dazzlingly blonde and blue eyed so that she seemed all pale gold and azure, and wearing that same cool aura of reserve he wore – you would not dream what passions in the past few hours had stirred them both. There was a general plan for a ride that afternoon, to the hills above Frome Castle (Lady Corby smirked at Miss Lillane, but The Lily coldly turned away her head). He feared, however, said Lord Weyburn, bowing, that Miss Devigne would not ride?

"Thank you, no, my lord," said Sapphire, and would not be at the trouble of asking him why he should suppose it in advance.

"If we could command sea-horses, perhaps...."

"Sea-horses? Oh – you imagine that because I come from a city of water-ways, I can't sit on a horse. But – similarly – we have no roadways in Venice, yet your lordship perceives that I have the use of my legs."

"And employ them to perfection, Madame – as I know from your dancing last night."

She inclined her head in indifferent acceptance of the compliment, sweeping before him in her bouffant, trailing skirt, through the doorway to the hall. A servant motioned them all up the wide stairs to their rooms. Lord Weyburn held her back, standing looking up at her, one hand on the newell post. "Will you not change your mind then and come with us today?"

"I thank you – no."

"You are piqued because I fancied you couldn't ride? But where, in Venice...?"

"I have not been hobbled like a goat all my life in Venice," she said; and burst out, flashing blue: "There are horses in Italy as good as any nag in England, I suppose; and riders to leave your trit-trotters in the park a thousand miles behind."

"You are vehement in defence of Italy...."

"She needs no defence," said Sapphire, dropping back immediately into indifference.

"Some day, I hope, you will think as loyally of England."

"That is not very likely. Loyalty implies some familiarity with the object, and my only wish regarding England is to leave it as soon as I possibly may."

He bowed his regrets. "The more reason why you and I should ride while we yet have the opportunity."

"For the third time, I thank you – no." And she went up the stairs after the rest to her room. "I understood," she said to Christine, flinging her hooded cloak upon the great four-poster bed, "that I was coming here for your protection. But it seems I shall soon be as much in need of yours, it is I who am to be persecuted. Your cousin is no gentleman."

"Because he asks you to ride?"

"Because he persists. What does he care whether I ride or no?"

Christine stood looking out across the

sunken garden beneath the high window. "You are so angry: and so suspicious, Sophia. May it not be that my cousin simply wished you to ride? – for truly, dearest, I believe he likes you."

"Your cousin has been successful then, already. Last night he thought only of *you*. Today you believe he likes me. Tomorrow, may you not be a little jealous?"

"You don't believe that, Sapphire?"

"Of course not: but Lord Weyburn does – it is his only object." And she burst out again that it was heartless, heartless. . . .

"Oh, dearest – heartless? What can you mean by that?"

"I mean nothing," said Sapphire, quickly. "Your cousin believes that it will pique you if he makes love to your friend. When I say it is heartless, I mean that were I an innocent, as I was a few brief months ago, I might be credulous, I might suffer; and so it would be heartless. But I am not innocent: your beau monde has cured me of all that and in a wonderful short space of time indeed. I am credulous no longer, I cannot be made to suffer: for 'heartless' read 'cynical,' therefore, read 'insolent.' Your cousin insults me with his attentions: I find him insolent."

But Christine was hardly attending. Beyond, the sunken gardens; beyond their walls, the park; beyond that park was Frome. "Sapphire, you must ride with me this afternoon. We are to go up behind the castle; my cousin will suggest that we call there. Edward last night was angry, I know it: he cannot bear women to make scenes. He left the ball because of what I did – and, oh, Sophia! I know he won't come back. So I must go to him."

"You go to him! Christine, you have no pride."

She flushed. "I think I have; and yet – when one is in love, it is true that pride seems a small thing, insignificant. . . ."

"Not to me," said Sapphire.

"But you are not yet in love."

"Ah, no," said Sapphire. "I had forgotten that. Well, so we are to run after this paragon of yours who, I must say it, Christine, seems to me a monstrous prig and that is all."

"He is not. . . . You don't understand. . . . Well, at any rate, Sophia, I want to go to Frome. If my cousin takes us all there, no one can suspect me of – of pursuing . . ."

"If your cousin takes you, there's no need for me to ride."

105

"But supposing he does not think of it; then you could say – could express a wish to see the castle. . . ."

"The simple answer is, Christine – I have no habit."

But Christine had a habit, had spare habits, half a dozen habits left hanging in various closets from a lifetime of cousinly visiting at Starrbelow. And so Sophia must ride and did ride, sitting like a proud, disdainful young queen on the pretty mare Lord Weyburn, triumphantly smiling, chose for her. There were a dozen riders; close, divided, strung out, close again, they cantered jingling through the park, clattered across a road newly cut through the valley, climbed, the ponies pecking gamely with their gentle heads, up the steep hill that brought them out at last to the ridge above Frome. A lone rider met them there and stared with frankly appraising eye at Sapphire. "Who is the pretty puss on Weyburn's new mare?"

"A puss indeed," said Lord Greenwode, reining in beside him. "And with claws to scratch. Beware of her."

Red Reddington looked closer. "Is she not the girl . . . ?"

"Yes. Last night at the ball. His
106

Lordship wastes no time."

"Neither would I," said Sir Francis Erick, laughing, "had I made the bet."

"But will she have him?" They sat their horses casually, long easy in the saddle, the reins held slackly, looking out across the lovely hills and valleys, down on to Frome Castle. Squire Reddington was square and thickset, reddy-brown as to complexion from exposure to all weathers, hard-riding, hard-drinking, hard-living, some said dissolute; and yet he looked at Sapphire with a sort of gentleness about his bright brown eye. "She looks – a cut above these scheming city wenches."

Lord Greenewode shrugged. "She plays it like a veteran however. She's cat-and-mousing with poor Charles already: tosses her head and flirts her fan and does not mince her language; and will not dance, or won't converse, or deigns not to take his arm – but in the end is seen to dance and talk and hang on him. I wagered today she would not ride with him – yet here she is!"

"And yet I'll swear, knows nothing of that other bet."

"No, no: there I agree. The aunt's been

long set on poor Charles – she's told the girl what game to play, that's all."

"Somehow," said Reddington, "one grieves to see her quite so apt a pupil." He gethered up his reins and clattered off. Sir Francis, smiling blue-and-blonde, said to his friend, "I'll say Amen to that."

"Alas for dreams," said Lord Greenewode. "I'm a cynic."

Prince Anton sat slouched loosely in the saddle, his feet slipped out of the stirrups, his long legs dangling. He had ridden all the while beside Christine Lillane and all the while had struggled with the longing to tell her of the danger he had brought to her friend. Fear held him back; fear of his mistress's reprisals, fear of the blackmail she had hinted, fear that she would indeed inform his father of what would bring an end to all his future hopes. Life at home in Hanover was very simple: what passed here for competence, there was wealth, what here was tedium inexpressible at home was ease, position, comfort, self-respect; and he knew that there could be, ultimately, no other life for him; nor, when he returned there, could he support any other. At home it was all or nothing – for those who were of the royal circle and yet not in it, literally nothing: no gay fringe of society as there was in England, where a man might be a gentleman and rich and respected, though he be hardly tolerated, if at all, at court. And if all this came out.... Impossible to explain: impossible to explain to those to whom the Court was the very crown and centre of social attainment and joy, that here in the circles in which he had moved, it was all as nothing, not important enough to be even a laughing stock: where one must put in an appearance now and again for loyalty or expediency's sake (stifling one's yawns through the long, dull, homely evenings with the widowed old king and his family of squat, ugly mistresses, all of them advanced in age before he had ever aspired to them); dressed in clothes specially kept for such occasions, of a fashion ten or fifteen years outmoded, so that one might not outshine the sartorial ambitions of His Majesty.... When he went home, he knew, easy-going and mercurial, he would sink back happily enough into the ways of home: would accept with simple happiness the rich, dull, well-born wife, the annual baby, the succession of openly acknowledged mistresses; nothing else – when he went back home – was thinkable. But if Marcia carried out her threat, it was lost to him for ever – and he had nothing else. And if he confided in Christine, Marcia would carry out her threat.

Christine, innocent of his musings, rode silently beside him, preoccupied with troubles of her own. Would Charles suggest riding down to the castle? The Earl would be alone there, he had accommodated only such guests as had come for the ball alone and were returning home the following day. Those that were staying for Christmas, formed the party at Starrbelow. She looked imploringly at Sapphire, sitting in her green velvet habit, silent, among a group of gentlemen: all having laid wagers, had she known it, as to who would be first of their number to induce a flash of those blue eyes of hers. Sapphire met the glance, shrugged, turned to Lord Weyburn. "May we not ride down nearer, and look closer at this wonderful house?"

He was faintly astonished; it was the first time she had so much as expressed a preference – unless it be a not very flattering negative one. "Why, of course. We'll all call upon Edward." But the slope was steep immediately below them and the going difficult. "We had better cut across through the field here and take that path by the wood...." He pointed it out to them, gesturing with his crop.

Mrs. Forgard was with them, a noted horsewoman. "For my part, I'll take the slope and go down and across the big meadow; we can really let out our horses here."

"I'll go with you," said Squire Reddington; one or two more said, "And I."

"Perhaps it will be best," said Lord Weyburn, "if we divide then, and I'll take the less experienced while you ride on."

Everyone looked briefly at Sapphire. She glanced at Christine. Christine had ridden this country from her childhood; she said, not sufficiently masking her charitable intention, "I'll ride with Sophia."

Sapphire sat very taut on her little, dancing mare. She said, after only an infinitesimal pause: "Very well – come with me," and just touched her beast's flank with her heel and plunged straight down the slope.

Red Reddington caught up with her, three fields beyond the foot of the hill, galloping beside her on his great chestnut, outstripping her, riding a little across her horse's nose, to shout back at her. "Rein her in! Pull her up! You're putting her at it too fast!"

Sapphire sat truly in the saddle but her hands in their leather gloves were white with strain. She shook her head dumbly. The little mare flew on.

He understood. He shouted: "Can't you slow her?"

She shook her head back; two tears of something like terror welled up in her eyes, rolled down her white cheeks, were dried in an instant by the rush through the keen wind. If I fall, if I injure the mare, if I disgrace myself before them all, once more...!"

They took a small ditch, hedged on one side: she sat her mare like an angel but her heart was in her mouth. They were in the big meadow now, a great, humped, close-cropped, hard-surfaced field: there was room to manoeuvre and, before the further hedge was reached, he had edged his horse again across the mare's nose, slowed her down, steadier her; would not stop her but cantered his chestnut comfortably beside her. And he looked into Sapphire's white face and gave her a wink and said, "Bless you! – I won't tell!"

He was not of the world she had learned so soon to distrust. She found herself saying, simply, "That would be kind."

"You ride her like an angel; but she's difficult." He jerked his head towards the little mare. "Weyburn shouldn't have put you up on her."

"He hoped I would come down off her," said Sapphire, wearily.

"Hoped you would fall! My dear Madame...."

"Oh, not so as to hurt myself: just to look a fool. Baiting Sapphire Devigne is the current amusement – where have you been that you haven't yet found that out?"

He wondered if she knew the full truth of what she said: whether she knew of Lord Weyburn's bet. A monstrous business, he thought, if she did not; yet, strict in the code of his times, he must himself keep silence. He led the conversation into safer channels. "You come from Italy, Signorina, I believe?"

She swung round upon him in the saddle, all her face suddenly lit to happiness. "Oh, to hear you say that word – 'Signorina!' It is such a long time-since I was 'Signorina' to anyone. Only to hear

113

you say it is like. . . . She broke off. She said, "Forgive me – I am being foolish."

"It doesn't seem very foolish to me," he said.

"Does it not – such an outburst?" She said wistfully: "I am so sick with longing for my home. Just a word and – it was like – like a candle flame, suddenly lit in one of our dim, old churches. . . ."

He looked round at the broad rolling meadows, lying grey-green about them in the thin winter sunshine; at the bare grey branches of the trees, at the great, grey castle, brooding grimly over all. He said, smiling at her: "Do you find our England like a dim old church?"

"Why, no," she said, laughing outright. "Indeed it was a bad comparison; for though our churches are cold and grey when they are empty, in Italy they are very seldom empty; and when they are not, why, then they are filled with light and colour, the music rolls forth, the air is delicious with incense, and all the people come with their families and talk and chatter and say their prayers and talk and chatter again; and the children run about amongst them and it is all warm and familiar and – kind; their churches are their homes to them, their

114

second homes, they are in their Father's house."

"That is not the way with us in England."

"Neither in nor out of your churches."

"You are severe on us, Miss Devigne."

"Not upon you, I hope," she said quickly. "You have been nothing but kind." And she smiled at him, the old warm, gay, confiding smile of her girlhood in Venice, a thousand shames ago. Lord help me! he thought, if she turns those blue eyes on me one instant more with a look of such sweetness, I'm a lost man. . . . But the drum of hooves in the meadow was heard coming up behind them, and the look was gone. "Here comes the horses," he said. "And the hounds," said Sapphire.

The party of riders overtook them, all lost in frankly surprised admiration of Miss Devigne's prowess on horseback: none among them would have dared put his mount at such a pace down that steep and across that meadow. Lord Weyburn came last; seeing her safe, with Reddington always close behind her, he had held back to assist another guest, Prince Anton, who had perforce ridden with the rest but whose experience was hardly sufficient for such

115

hazardous going. He left him now to laugh over his discomforts with Christine, and cantered up after Sapphire. "You were magnificent!"

Gone was the gay and simple smile. She lifted an eyebrow, faint astonishment tipped with scorn. "Because I could cover a couple of fields and yet keep myself in the saddle?"

He had been unaffectedly delighted. In face of her stony unreceptiveness, however, he resumed immediately his accustomed manner: that manner that was but a carefully studied, pale reflection of the exaggerated fashion of the day – the hint of a drawl imposed upon his own quick, decisive way of speech, the set periods which became second nature, the studied compliments which were the môde – the gesture of a well-kept hand half buried in snowy-white cambric frills. "Keep your saddle! Why, you ride like a goddess, you were Artemis, Diana the Huntress...."

"That would be a reversal of roles for me," said Sapphire, bitterly.

He missed her meaning. He said, laughing, "Why, in fact it would; for Diana, I believe, hunted afoot and rode no horse." He looked appraisingly at the mare now trotting gently beside him. "She is new and as yet unchristened for our stables. Have I your permission to name her Sapphire?"

"You will name her what you like, my lord. I give and withhold no permission."

Squire Reddington, his knight errantry accomplished, had fallen back with the other riders; a wager had been laid and it was commonly accepted that each side must be afforded fair opportunity of winning. Lord Weyburn said: "You are unkind, Madame."

"I am indifferent," said Sapphire.

"You are at least not gracious. I intended a compliment."

"A sapphire is a gem, sir; you may call your horse that without consulting *me*."

"So is a ruby a gem, or a diamond or emerald. But I wish to call my horse Sapphire. Come," he said, laughing a little, pleading, "it is not a great favour to ask."

"I have not refused it: you may call your horse what you will."

He considered. "Well then – a wager! What shall we wager?" A gate to Frome Castle gleamed, gilded wrought iron, ahead of them – not the great main gates that opened out on to the village, but smaller gates, at the end of an oak avenue, leading

117

to a path through the woods. "A race – I will race you to the gates. And if I win, you shall give me permission to call my mare after you; and if you win – why, if you win," said Lord Weyburn, "I'll give you the mare herself. Come! – what do you say?"

The going here was easy enough. "I'll ride to the gates and get there first," said Sapphire. "But I'll wager nothing upon it."

"What, not wager? – my beautiful mare to the use of your name!"

"It is not my name; and I would not accept your mare."

"Very well then: if not your name...." He shouted a word back to her but she did not catch it, already his horse with the little bay mare after him, was galloping wildly up the long avenue that led to the gate; leaving the rest behind, trotting idly, weary from the long, downhill, difficult ride, gossiping among themselves as to what this sudden dash might portend. The ground was spongy, soft yet resilient, with its bed of damp, dead leaves, the horses' hooves made only a heavy chuff-chuff as they thundered between the double line of oaks with a scatter of rotting acorns and dankly-snapping twigs; the air was full of a scent that was new to Sapphire, the scent of the woods in winter, it was cold and keen on her tingling cheeks and suddenly the greys and browns of the chill countryside seemed drear to her no longer, but alive with colour of their own, with silver and gold; and here and there the dark green of mistletoe, sucking the oak's blood to feed its pearly white berries, clinging to the bare old branches with little, green, elbowed arms. Her velvet hat tumbled back as she thrust-on the mare after the thundering big black horse ahead; she pulled it off with one hand and flung it away from her, and the startled mare tossed up her wild head and rolled her wild eye and this time fairly took the bit in her teeth and bolted, uncontrolled, up the straight avenue and veered and jumped the shallow ditch and fled off across the tree-scattered, hilly parkland, was wrenched round, found the avenue again and, exhausted after two such escapades in the space of an hour, came to a shuddering standstill at the gilt gates, where Lord Weyburn, sitting the big black horse, calmly awaited them. "For a moment," he said, easily, catching at the mare's bridle close to the bit and holding her still, "I thought she was too much for you; but just as I would have come after you, you had her in control again." And he edged his horse round until they sat close, knees touching, half facing one another and said, laughing, "At any rate – I win!" and put up a hand and caught her by the tumbled bright gold hair and lightly pulled back her head and, leaning forward, as lightly kissed her lips.

She had steeled herself against that grey glance of his, half admiration, half scorn; against the too-rare flash of his smile, the ring of his voice, the cool, formal touch of his fingers when they met or parted. But this – there had been no preparation for this. She felt his hand hard against the swift, backward, evading jerk of her head, she felt his firm mouth, dry-lipped, brush against her own – felt herself caught suddenly and held, her breasts crushed hard against his breast, felt her lips open under his lips: open, relax, respond; seek and receive.... Her blue eyes flashed up into his, drowned in an all unlooked-for longing, a new-purely physical, deep, sweet agony of only half-understood desire; weak with the will to succumb, to resist no longer, to answer the call of his own swift flame of demanding passion, as unlooked-for as her own. For a long, long moment she lay against his breast, held close in his arms; and dragged her mouth at last from his, only for the sweetness of offering it to his kiss again, and, with all heaven in her great blue eyes, looked up into his face. . . .

And saw there – the sudden withdrawal, the return of chill doubt, suspicion, distrust, disdain. With the parting of their lips, the old, cold sword of their common mistrust thrust its way between them, severing in one bleak moment two hearts and two bodies that in as brief a moment had come to their destiny, had come together as one. The blue eyes clouded, stared with blank horror into grey eyes grown hard and contemptuous with the flooding-back of remembered griefs, with the recollection of what he believed he knew to be her perfidy; and ignorant of that secret reason for his mistrust, saw there only a mocking triumph in so easy a conquest. One small gloved hand gathered up, automatically, the reins on her horse's neck, she raised the other as though to strike the smile from his face and saw that in truth no smile was there. Her hand dropped to the gathered reins, she bowed her head to conceal the starting tears. Why should I strike him? He offered me an insult and I in return have exposed my surrender like the slut he believes I am. Love him? – oh, God, yes! – what should he know or care for my love, who pursues me only because I am cheap and easy and unprotected, because the pursuit may serve to tantalize Christine whom he really loves....

He made no move to stop her as, white and weeping, she turned her horse and fled from him down the long avenue of the winter-sleeping trees.

Back at Starrbelow she went straight to her room and sent a maid to ask Lady Corby to attend her there. Aunt Corby said sharply, "Why did you not stay with the others?"

"I did not wish to. They went on to the castle; two gentlemen rode back with me...."

"If you'd gone to Frome Castle...."

"Well, I did not go to Frome Castle, Aunt. I had something better to do." She had gone to the closet and was tossing her clothes out onto the bed. I had to pack. I am leaving here. If you come with me, send for your woman and begin packing too."

"Leave here...? Pack...? You must be insane, Sophia."

"Very well, I'm insane. At any rate, I'm leaving this house."

"But Christine...."

"Christine must do without me. She has managed her first entrée into society after last night's debacle – the rest will be not so difficult; I know, I know it all. And by now she will have met Lord Frome at the Castle, she has no more real need of me...."

"Sophia, I am telling you – if you had gone to the Castle...."

"Aunt Marcia, before the party returns from Frome I shall have left this house. If you are not ready by then, I shall go without you: as far as the inn, perhaps, I can go nowhere else – but here I won't stay. Are you coming or are you not?"

"No," said Lady Corby. "And neither are you going. You are staying with Christine." And she held up a hand that silenced Sophia until she had finished her sentence. "If you had gone to Frome Castle you would have known already that Lord Frome has left England. The moment the rest of his guests had gone, he started for the continent – leaving no address."

"Well, all I can say of your lover," said Sophia again, "is that he must be a prig."

Christine leaned her white forehead against the cool pane and stared out over the park with sorrowful blue eyes. "You must understand Edward, Sophia. He hates – unreserve."

"But to fling off abroad because a young woman loses her head a little and strikes in the face a man who affronts her. . . ."

"You have just been affronted, you say; and by the same man. But you did not strike him."

"I intended to do the next best thing – to quit Starrbelow. Now, once more, through your troubles, Christine, I am tied here." She bit on her lip with the shame of it, the humiliation. "What can he think? – once again I alter my mind. . . ."

"What do you care for what my cousin thinks? You do not like him, he annoys you by his flirtations, that is all." She begged: "Sophia, don't leave me. Stay my friend."

"Oh, I am your friend – more your friend, Christine, than you will ever know." But she melted from her mood of resentful irony. "Don't mind me, dearest, your cousin challenges me with his attentions

124

and it irks me not to end them once and for all: it is no more. For the rest...." For the rest, she said, surely Christine should take heart of grace. "Lord Frome would hardly journey to the continent for every young woman whose conduct failed to rise to his standards. Does this not show he loves you?"

"Then the worse for me, Sophia, if I have failed him."

"He will come back, my pet; be patient. And," she said smiling, "I, I promise you, will be patient too...."

Lord Greenewode rode across the park with Sir Francis Erick. "Alas for your sentimentalisms, my dear Frank! Your dove is attacked by the eagle, we all saw it happen, and though Weyburn smiles grimly and returns no answer when he's quizzed with it, I'll swear by the set of her back, the arch of her throat, nay, by the look on her face as she rode back through the park with Red, that she gave back the kiss. And a most accomplished performance, moreover, or I know nothing of women! Whether or not, however, she flies off home, with fleathers ruffled to a fine show of indignation – and flies no further! That's ten guineas Reddington owes me: he wagered she wouldn't endure it." He added: "If you ask me, Frank, Squire Reddington fancies the dove for his own côte."

"She'd better beware of *that* het," said Sir Francis, uneasily.

Lord Greenewode laughed. "What – you too? You are all bewitched by this little Italian schemer."

"I think it is the aunt who pipes the tune; the poor little girl just dances."

"I have small faith," said Lord Greenewode, looking with his sad, dark eyes at the merry blue eyes of his friend, "in your poor little girls who dance to such tunes as that...."

And there was dancing indeed at Starrbelow in those days, a sort of fever of revelry that gathered momentum as the week went by and all the world watched the progress of the eagle in pursuit of the dove. From London came news of mounting excitement, of side-bets far exceeding the value of the original, of gossip and scandal eagerly devouring the latest tidings of what went forward at Starrbelow; of green-eyed envy of those who were here to judge for themselves moment by moment the swing of events. The scandal sheets flourished

126

with lies and distortions and ugly, ill-composed sets of verse, every booth in the pleasure gardens had its version, sentimental or obscene, of the Lord Weyburn's wooing; Lady Corby's maid grew insolent-rich on bribes. At the storm centre, conscious of mounting, inexplicable excitement, conscious of being – but well used by now to being – the focal point of gossip, Sapphire walked and rode and danced; speaking little, wearing the secret smile, lowering her white lids ever over the anguish of the proud blue eyes. 'Only give me strength to endure it with patience, and one day Christine must release me from the debts of my gratitude: one day she will be happy again and I dismissed.' And God grant, she prayed, that Christine might never know, what no one must ever know – the true cost to her, the true pain behind the superficial pain of enduring the insult of addresses which she believed to be paid to her only by way of revenge upon her friend. Meanwhile, she had long ago written to her father imploring him to pay off at all costs, to mortgage her whole future if he must, to pay off such debts as they had incurred with Aunt Corby. One day this will be over for ever, one day I shall return to Venice. . . .

She held the answering letter in her hand, on the day that Lord Weyburn proposed.

She held the letter in her hand, tucked into the little velvet muff; but she knew its contents by heart already, a letter from her mother, not her father, written in Italian, in the sloping Italian hand she wrote herself: belovéd daughter, figlia mea – imagine my distress – your father unwell – opened the letter – have not dared to show it to him yet. . . . And money, money, money . . . . No money even for the journey home, let alone to repay all that had been poured out on her by the Corbys during her sojourn in England. All, all had long ago gone on training her for this part which it had ever been her father's incomprehensible longing that she should one day play: in the dancing lessons and the singing lessons, in the lessons in deportment and the arts a young lady of the English *ton* must practice: in suitable housing, in suitable furnishing, in suitable dress so that when the time came, as he had known it must, she should be at home in the world which had once been his own. No money left: no money to repay all that had been spent since. And yet – 'And yet if you are unhappy, my dearest, my darling, cara, carissima, then of course you must come home. He must be made to understand and accept, your aunt can be paid off at last, she is rich, she will not mind the waiting; we can work, you and I will work and save and over the years, somehow we will repay. Think seriously of it, for it will break his heart; but if you are unhappy, of course you must come home. . . ."

It had been handed to her late in the evening, she had read it by the light of one of the great, glowing braziers that ringed the moonlit silver of the frozen lake where small boys roasted chestnuts and handed them round to the quality, gaping at the fine ladies in their velvet cloaks and furs. 'If you are unhappy, then of course you must come home. . . ."

Lord Weyburn walked across the ice to her as she wandered solitary by the margin of the lake, her thoughts a thousand miles away. "You are alone, Miss Devigne?"

"By preference, my lord."

He put up his hand to steady himself against an over-hanging bough. They were at the far end of the lake, away from the clustered groups closer to the house. He

129

looked into her face and saw that it was softened, not the face he knew, habitually smiling that little scornful smile. If she would but look at *me* like this, he thought.... And he remembered the response of her kiss by the gilded gate and thought that if she were but true, no woman in the world could be more fit for a man to call his wife. For under the scorn, he thought, she is warm and kind; and tender and passionate and, God knows! – beautiful; and clever and wise and witty and gay – if she were but true. But could she be true? A trick had been played and all she had done since had shown her – surely? – to be cognisant of that trick; she had played a game that had never seemed other than false – withdrawing, withholding, repudiating, threatening: always in the end to give way. And yet – this look of softness, of gentle sorrow.... His hand touched the little velvet muff. "It's the turn of the year. You are thinking perhaps of home?"

"Yes," she said. "Of Venice."

"Venice must be beautiful in the winter?"

"Venice is always beautiful," she said, sick with nostalgia.

"I have seen Canaletto's pictures; and Signor Guardi's."

"Oh, yes," she said. "Francesco's – the Guardis are friends of ours at home. And their pictures are lovely; and yet – who can paint Venice? – when she is all grey and silver in the winter time, with the sunshine thin on the islands beyond the still water, as I have seen it so often; and the fishing boats making black patterns across it with their high, curving prows...." and she opened her dark blue eyes full upon him and looked for the first time steadily and directly into his face: and looked through and beyond him, out of her sorrow into forgetfulness and so back to joy again; and did not see him at all.

He stood looking down at her, very near to her; and knew again the longing to take her into his arms, to hold her close, to catch her to him with violence and hold her close and in a passion of violence, make her his own. I am sick, he thought; I am sick of a fever – and he swore to himself that this was not love but only a sickness, a fever, of physical desire that tormented his waking hours and all his dreams. But in the moonlight, he saw how the tears glittered on the thick lashes fringing her heavy white eyelids, and all in a moment his mood changed to one of tenderness and a sort of peace. "You are crying," he said, and bent his head and kissed her gently, brushing her eyelids with his lips, tasting the salty sweetness of her tears; and put his arm about her and held her lightly, as though she were a much-loved child. And she, half unaware, lost in her dreams, relaxed against his shoulder, luxuriated in the old forgotten joy of simple kindliness and tenderness, the old, safe, uncomplicated happiness of home. I am going home, she thought. No need any more to scratch and fight, no need any more to defend with the new-forged weapons of her bitterness and scorn, the citadel of wounded pride: no need any more for the heartache and the pain. When hope is dead, love will die too and I shall forget. Once away from this place, seeing him no more, suffering no more this mockery of courtship for Christine's benefit – I shall forget. 'If you are unhappy, of course you must come home. . . .'

He stood for a long time, leaning back against the great tree with the overhanging bough, holding her lightly, almost impersonally, in the circle of his arm; and after a while slipped down his hand and took her hand from its little muff and held it in his own; and after a while again, raised it to his lips and kissed her fingers and laid his cheek against it and at last, she unresisting, let his mouth wander over it, softly and sensuously, tasting the scented sweetness of it for a moment with the tip of his tongue; all the time holding her gently, relaxed against his breast. "You are delicious," he said to her. "You are like the salted apricots we preserve here in the summer months at Starrbelow – your tears are salt and your hand is honey-sweet when I touch it with my tongue." And he brushed back a stray curl that had fallen, heavily gold, against her cheek and said: "You belong to Starrbelow. You must never go back to Venice."

"If you are truly unhappy, of course you must come home...." "I am going back there," she said dreamily, only half hearing him. "I am going home to Venice."

As though some delicate piece of glass had been dropped and broken, the mood changed, shivered into a thousand fragments, the look of sweetness and tenderness that had come to his face, was gone. He said abruptly: "Why do you persist in this wearisome game of evasion,

133

why these ever-lasting fabrications about your going home? We both know very well that you are remaining here."

"I?" she said, startled. "Remaining here? In England?"

"At Starrbelow." He said roughly: "Let there be no pretence at least between you and me. You are remaining at Starrbelow – as my wife."

Now indeed he got the full blaze of her eyes. She stared at him in utter astonishment. "I? As your wife? I don't understand you, my lord."

What an actress, he thought; or – could it be possible...? Well, he could soon discover: he had but to put her to the test, he had but to ask and if she refused, if she persisted in refusal, then he would know that she at least had been no party to the conspiracy. A fine position for a prospective lover, he thought to himself, ruefully: if I am accepted, I shall know her for a cheat and adventuress; only if she is true and – and therefore infinitely lovely and desirable, shall I have lost her! Meanwhile, she gazed rapt in astonishment up into his face. "I do not understand you."

"Then you are more – innocent – Madame, than I took you for." And I a fool, he thought, to lose my head and bruise my heart again, to be taken in by this play-acting little coquette. He smiled down at her mockingly. "Do you not know as well as I –?" He broke off, he began again. "I must be one of the very few men existing, must I not, Madame ? – who can literally say that at the first instant he saw her, he knew that a woman was destined to be his wife?"

And I? she thought; what did I not know in that first moment, walking forward into the silence, meeting your eyes . . . ? But she could not believe, she could not trust, she stammered out faintly again: "I do not understand you, my lord. Is this some new insult?"

He moved impatiently. "It appears to be my fate that any woman I offer my hand to regards it as an insult. You at least, however, have not slapped my face."

"It is but a week, sir, since – that other offer."

"That book is closed," he said. "A new one is opened."

She looked at him doubtfully: "In the course of one week?"

"In the course of one hour: in the course of one moment. I left my cousin, I walked through to the ballroom, a door opened and you came in; in that moment, the book of Christine was closed, was sealed up forever – and a new book opened." And he thrust his hand into a pocket and brought out something that glittered in his palm, a rainbow of ice and fire. "Come, Madame – here is the Weyburn betrothal ring. I have carried it since the night of my cousin's ball: since the night she refused it." He did not say, 'since the night I made a wager which I now must win'; but he looked a challenge and she, all ignorant of the test inherent in the challenge, was too stunned to do more than gaze back at him, trembling and bewildered. "Then give me your hand." And he took it roughly, almost violently, forcing it apart from its fellow, and thrust the great ring on her finger and let go of her to execute a bow and a flourish, ugly with the mockery of her duplicity and of his own sharp pain at finding her false after all. "Forgive me if I leave you now and go back to the house and prepare them for the news. I will summon an escort; the future Lady Weyburn must not wander the garden alone like some unknown – adventuress." Without a further word he was gone, walking away swiftly towards a group of servants beside one of the braziers. He returned with a couple of men. "Attend Miss Devigne at her leisure back to the house." To Sophia he said: "You will need a moment, doubtless, to prepare yourself for your – reception," and he bowed once more and caught and kissed the nerveless hand weighed down with the great diamond ring; and was gone again.

Very pale, dazed, trembling, speechless, she stumbled after the lackeys and back to the house.

Six

In January, letters came from Venice. Her father, ambition satisfied, now realised too late that his treasure was cut off from him for ever and, aging and delicate, was fretting himself into a fever of remorse and anxiety. It was impossible, of course, the mother wrote, that he should come to England, nor could she herself leave him. It was a great deal to ask: but could not Sophia return to Venice for even a little while before her marriage. . . ?

Lord Weyburn had left Starrbelow almost directly after the betrothal and gone abroad, declaring his intention of seeking Lord Frome who appeared to have cut himself off altogether from England. Sophia took the letter to her aunt. "I must go to Italy."

"Nonsense! Go to Italy! Your wedding is planned for next month."

"Then it must be postponed; I must go to my father."

"You are mad, Sophia: you have a

138

trousseau in the making, a thousand matters to deal with."

"What does that matter, Aunt Marcia; my father is ill and my mother needs me."

"A ruse, you foolish child; a ruse on her part to get you back to Venice – and to keep you there."

"Then it partly succeeds, for I shall go; and partly fails, poor mother! – for I shall not stay."

"If you go," said Lady Corby grimly, "you may as *well* stay."

"What does that mean, Aunt?"

"It means that your lover seems not so hot, Sophia, but that your absence may cool him off altogether. How much have you seen of this man you are to marry? Almost the very day after your betrothal, he rushes off abroad leaving his guests to the mercy of his Aunt Lillane, a week later he returns – without Lord Frome – and crosses with you coming back from Starrbelow. Now he is heard of in Bath – and is content to have you, it appears, lounging with Christine about London with Anton at your heels...."

"At your behest," said Sapphire, "as my watchdog."

"I put a good face on it, Sophia, lest

Weyburn hear of it. And now," said Lady Corby, angrily, "when surely he would be coming soon to town to assist with the wedding arrangements, you, forsooth, must go flying off to Venice."

"I will come back," said Sophia.

"But will your lover come back? Have a care, Sophia, lest he elude you altogether. Though that, I suppose," she added, thoughtfully, "he can hardly do, after all."

"Why do you say so?" said Sapphire, sharply.

"Why, because – only because he has given you his promise."

"As to his promise, from that I can release him." She shrugged; she said with affected nonchalance: "Why should you suppose him likely to wish it? Is this not the usual conduct of an affianced gentleman of the *ton?* I had assumed more assiduous attention to be not the fashion."

"Of course, of course: Weyburn is not a man for outward demonstration, he loathes all appearance of weakness.... It will be different, I warrant you," said Lady Corby, confidentially winking, "in the privacy of marriage." Heaven forbid, she thought, that the filly take fright now and rush off out of the contract! And as to Italy

– she supposed the girl would go, and if so she must go too, or heaven knew when she would return; and one must, for the sake of the future, keep in her (increasingly capricious) good books. "Of course, dearest, you must go to your parents if they need you; and I could not let you travel alone, Bertram and I will come with you. . . . We shall be back, I daresay, before the month is over."

But before the month was over the father, for whose poor, unworthy ambition the lamb had been sacrificed on so bitter an altar, had died, still unsatisfied; and it was March before Sophia could leave her mother and come back with her aunt from Venice. Of Lord Weyburn, there was still nothing to be seen; but Prince Anton of Brunswick met the coach at the Rochester stage.

March, April, May. May at Starrbelow: with a thousand candles shimmering like fireflies in the silver gloom of the tiny chapel in the park, and a thousand, thousand bright flowers starring the fields and gardens in the bright sunshine outside. . . . And Lady Corby, brilliant in velvets and furs, and Sir Bertram discreetly

141

splendid in black and silver brocade; and Prince Anton hang-dog in sober brown, and Christine, muted yet radiant, in sky-blue to match her eyes – for the Earl of Frome, returned at last from abroad to stand friend at his friend's wedding, was calm, friendly, solid, as though they had all met here but yesterday.... And Lord Weyburn, standing before the altar, awaiting his bride, tall and straight in his dark flowered waistcoat and dark, magnificently embroidered, yet sombre coat – too sombre altogether, whispered the household servants clustered round the chapel door, peering in at the great folk – disappointingly few – assembled for the wedding; but the bride's father was recently dead and the bride herself not long returned from abroad so perhaps there had not been time for a more elaborate show.... And now....

And now, standing in the shadows of the arched doorway, a mist of white, a blaze of blue: poised there for a moment, moving softly forward, materialising out of the gloom into the candlelit brightness before the altar.... A few words spoken, a gold ring given, a strange name written – the new Lady Weyburn comes down the short aisle, white lids lowered, on her husband's arm.

Outside the door of the chapel stood a coach and six horses, the coachman on his box, a man at the leaders' heads. Lord Weyburn paused in the tiny porchway, Sophia's hand still on his arm, and called a name. A steward stepped forward, astonished. "My lord?"

"Coram, I leave Starrbelow in your charge. My lawyers in London will communicate with you; otherwise, take orders from Lady Weyburn." He took from his sleeve a folded paper and handed it to Sapphire. "Here, Madame: this empowers you to collect on my behalf, a thousand guineas owing from your accomplice. You may have the spending of it together with all my heart." He bowed to her briefly, bowed to the company, standing, open-mouthed with amazement, grouped about her; and before anyone could collect himself to speak, had leapt up to the box, taken the reins from the coachman's hands and was driving furiously down the long curve of the drive to the wrought-iron, gilded gates. The mud struck up by thundering hooves, was spattered across the bright faces of the flowers.

143

Seven

It was a very lovely spring at Starrbelow, that year – that year of Sophia's marriage, 1754: a lovely spring, lying over the gray-and-green Cotswolds like a golden blessing, soft skies, soft sunshine and soft, warm rain to bring out the sticky chestnut buds to their furled green leaf, to bring a clear sheen to the fresh young meadow grass – to wash away the mud from the bright faces of flowers, bespattered by churning wheels....

She remained there, very quietly, the new Lady Weyburn: saw no one, went nowhere, did nothing: waited, perhaps – but no sign came. People said, later, that she gave him a week – two weeks; that she wrote to him, but received no reply. That she heard from his lawyers in that time, it is certain: his financial arrangements long-planned with this knowledge in his mind, were made clear to her, she found herself free (under certain restrictions) of his homes in country and town, free of a large income placed unreservedly at her command, free to come and go – as long as she kept out of his way; free, a girl barely eighteen, to live as she would – as long as she left him alone. So she gave him a week – it was said – and then another week; and at the end of that time, she sent for her friend, Christine, or Christine came unbidden – came down from London carrying with her, no doubt, a journal with a gossip paragraph (which certainly appeared there on June the eighth or ninth of that year): L–d W–n reported very snugly established at Bath, dicing nightly for high stakes at intimate parties, presided over, in the regrettable absence of her newly wedded ladyship, by Miss L--y P---e, with her accustomed charm. . . .

What *is* known is that on a late afternoon, three days after her friend's arrival with these tidings, Lady Weyburn ordered a horse saddled for herself and dismissed the groom (over his respectful protest) and alone rode forth – past the gilded gate where so short a time ago she had raced with Lord Weyburn and he had claimed his reward, along the silver path through the woods, now bright with young green; across the broad meadow where Red Reddington had halted her bolting mare and had promised her, 'I won't tell!'; up the steep incline, the mare's head pecking gallantly as she picked her elegant way through the lush young grass, up and up to the ridge above Frome Castle.... Red Reddington spotted her there, a rider sitting motionless as though awaiting something, as he rode up to the ridgeway crossroads with Sir Pardo Ryan, both on mischief bent. They had had some idea in their heads of calling in at the hostelry at Camden where there were two pretty wenches for the tumbling, if it suited their fancy; but the rider had seen them, had spurred the horse into action – and out of the sunset, cantering towards them on Weyburn's little bay mare 'he had christened her, in the end, The Kiss', had come, of all people, her ladyship herself; who had not been seen since her marriage and desertion, now nearly three weeks ago. "By all the saints, Red! – the bewitching grass-widow in person!"

"She'll not want to meet us," said Reddington. "We'd better turn back."

But she waved her crop and called out gaily to them and came bucketing up on the pretty little bay, and reined her in. She looked very little like a widow, moreover,

146

in green velvet and a gaily feathered hat. "Sir Pardo! Mr. Reddington! – good evening. How charming to encounter you here!"

Two such rakes and a pretty woman alone with them on a summer's evening! – even the gentlemen themselves were shocked. "Have you no attendant, my lady, no groom with you?"

"No, I'm a rebel, Sir Pardo, against attendant grooms – and unattendant bridegrooms to boot. I have mouldered long enough in my decent obscurity, done penance enough for the crime of being wronged and deserted. All of a sudden the devil was in me and I banished my attendants and have ridden forth in search of –"

"Another devil?" prompted Red Reddington, laughing.

"And have ridden this hour; but until this moment – as Sir Pardo would say, divvle a devil have seen!"

"But now see two of us to make up for it," said Sir Pardo in his soft Irish brogue.

She laughed at them, the blue eyes flashing, looking up at them from beneath the smooth eyebrows, under the curving rim of her riding hat. "Which makes three."

"Two ugly devils and – Lady Lucifer, Daughter of Light."

"What shall we do, brother devils, in this brief respite from the ardours of Paradise?"

They concealed their astonishment, somewhat taken aback: was this the silent, disdainful beauty they had striven to make some headway with during Christmas week while Charles Weyburn made good his wager? "Is it not true, Mr. Reddington, that you have a famous peach brandy up at the Manor House?"

"For gentlemen, Madame. Rede Manor for a lady, unchaperoned? ... What, Pardo, is not Lady Ryan at home?"

"Why, sure, and would be happy to entertain her ladyship."

"That would be most kind; and yet ... I have heard Lady Ryan, Sir Pardo, described as an angel...."

"Which she is to put up with me, sure," agreed Pardo, readily.

"'An angel from heaven' – so I have heard it said. But gentlemen, are we not for the moment refugees from heaven? So, Mr. Reddington – peach brandy?"

"So ho!" said Sir Pardo to Squire

148

Reddington, as they swung their horses heads and trotted after her. "It seems that the gossips were right – and we need not ride to Camden for wenches after all."

"It seems so," said Reddington; but he remembered her simple gratitude when he had stopped her horse in its nervy flight across the great meadow – and for the first time in his life could find it in his heart to be sorry that a pretty woman should turn out to be easy game. . . .

She rode with them next day; and the next day and the next – and once again all the county was agog with gossip. Miss Lillane was reported (via the Starrbelow housekeeper) disapproving, in dudgeon, declaring herself ill and keeping to her room – though whether her malaise was not true and rather the cause than the effect of her ladyship's bid for freedom, became a debatable point. Lady Lillane was distraught, wringing her hands outside her daughter's locked bedroom door and imploring her not to involve herself in any more of Sophia's scandals, now that Lord Frome was at home again and everything so promising. "Running backwards and forwards between us and the Castle," gabbled the outraged housekeeper into eager ears, "beseeching the Earl not to credit that Miss Christine would lend herself to her ladyship's goings on: as if she would, our young lady that's been in and out of Starrbelow since the day she was born and knows how to conduct herself, I hope, if others don't.... But the Earl knows our Lily better than that. 'Compose yourself, Madame,' he says – I had it from Thomas Footman there, he heard it with his own ears: 'compose yourself, Madame. I'll believe no ill of anyone till I see it for myself; and never any ill of Christine.' And it's my belief, and Thomas Footman's too, we'll have her Countess of Frome before the year is out. But as for this other.... Caught my lord, we all know that, with her witching ways and pretending to want none of him: and him tied fast by the wager.... And now! quiet enough, I'll grant you, the first days, sitting moping like a bird, staring out all day over the drive where he drove off, as though he might at any moment come riding back up it and take her in his arms like a prince in a fairy-tale. But then suddenly – up and off she goes, riding out by herself; and that evening she's drinking like a man at the Manor with the Squire and that no-good Sir Pardo; and it's my belief she rode deliberately to intercept them, for the stable boys say she asked a couple of times if it were not true that the Squire would ride over of an evening to Camden; and which way lay Camden from the crossways upon the ridge. . . ?"

And now it was whispered that Old Nick himself, in the person of Lord Franks, had joined the new partnership; and if that were so, Lady Weyburn's frail reputation indeed was gone. Moreover, it was true. She had met him while she sat at her ease with her new friends on a bench in the sunny garden of the Camden tavern – Lady Weyburn of Starrbelow, in such company, in such a place! He had strolled up and said a casual word to Red and Pardo, and leaned from his great height and looked into her eyes with his own glittering, black eyes and – chucked her under the chin. And she had raised her hand that held the half-finished tiny glass of cherry brandy, and coolly, unhurriedly, you might say almost without animosity, thrown the contents of the glass in his face. "Mind your manners, sir," she had said; and put the glass back quietly on the wooden table between them.

He had started back, half losing his

balance, recovered himself, wiped the sweet red liquor from his blanched cheek; never taking his glittering eyes – grown cold – from hers. "Your pardon, Madame: I took you – naturally – for a village wench."

Sir Pardo and Squire Reddington had leapt up, of course, enraged for her, and alarmed; but she waved them negligently back to their places. "Put up your cudgels, gentlemen: my lord has learned his lesson and will be more civil, for the future – to the village wenches." And she had motioned him to a seat beside her, laughing in his face; and called out in the new, gay, arrogant voice she used, for more brandy; and drawn him, the incident apparently forgotten, into the conspiracy that had been the subject of their interrupted murmurings. Aunt Corby was coming to Starrbelow – she had that morning had a letter – with all her train. And the very thought of it filled her with ennui; but how to get rid of her now?

"Why, by writing, Madame, and telling her not to come."

"But she comes already, and at my request; and with her band of friends. I wrote several days ago, inviting her, telling her to bring a party with her. I detest my aunt, but I thought I must bear with her company for the sake of the company she'd bring: for what other friends has my lord and master left me?"

"He has left you a fine choice of neighbours, at least," said Sir Pardo.

"Alas, I had written before I met with my two devils – my three devils," she amended, bowing an invitation to Lord Franks, somewhat to Reddington and Sir Pardo's dismay. And the worst of it was, she said ruefully, that the advent of this unwanted guest had lost her the best friend in the world she had. "For Miss Lillane, my dear Christine, disapproves, my devils and gentleman! She disapproves of you and of my rides with you, she thinks Lord Weyburn would not welcome Lady Corby's friends in his house, and therefore *I* should not. For Lady Corby will bring down Miss Eustis, of whom, specifically, our Lily disapproves, and Mrs. Mettle, a gossip of hers, and such rakes, I daresay, as Miss Eustis and Mrs. Mettle can persuade. And Prince Anton, whom, I confess, in the past I have found – not inattentive, comes with her ladyship of course; and of this, above all, my dear Christine disapproves. And she will not stay by and see the wife of her Cousin Charles so indiscreetly conduct herself, she cannot give such goings-on at Starrbelow the countenance of her presence there. Wherefore, she and her mama have withdrawn themselves, have left me: Christine and I have quarrelled." And she laughed a little wildly and waved the empty glass in the small white hand with its meaningless wedding-ring and confessed that one must not whisper it but her dear Christine was something of a little prude – nor, perhaps, would they be astonished to learn that the affronted ladies had betaken themselves no further than Frome Castle. The Earl had opened his gates and taken in the refugees from scandal – and who dare swear they'd have run so fast, had no such tempting asylum offered sanctuary ...?

But meanwhile she had found her – three – devils, and she owed no duty to anyone, and life was gay; and now she was to be plagued by Aunt Corby. Was there not a man among so many, cried Sapphire, who would save her from this turbulent aunt ...?

So began, on a sunny evening outside a village alehouse, the first adventure of the

Treasure Seekers' Circle – which in the few brief weeks of its existence bade fair to outrival in notoriety all the hell-fire clubs put together, not excluding Medmenham itself: so began the first of Sapphire Weyburn's deplorable 'escapades.'

Lady Corby, needless to relate, was delighted with the present condition of her niece's affairs. True, upon the first shock of her desertion at the church door, Sophia had turned away all company, her aunt's included – even her belovéd Christine, white and weeping, had been packed back ruthlessly to town; and had insisted with unexpected strength and purpose upon being left alone at Starrbelow. But so young a girl, rich, beautiful and now entirely unconstrained, would hardly remain for long buried in the country with only the company of a pack of grudging servants, feeling their master tricked into marriage and now banished by it, and resenting her presence there. Friends, company, she must soon have; and where should she turn for them but to Aunt Corby, the fountain of all the place, wealth and splendour which she now enjoyed? There was an anxious moment when Miss Lillane appeared to have got in first: what if Sophia threw in her lot completely with the Frome Castle set and after all failed in her duty to closer kin? But Christine, ever moping after her dreary earl, proved, evidently, an unstimulating companion: hard upon her departure for Starrbelow, the much desired letter arrived. Sophia found herself very dull in the country, Christine had arrived but had brought her mother with her and the old lady was grating on already raw nerves. Would not Aunt Marcia, of her mercy, collect a few friends and come down to Gloucestershire, losing as little time as possible ...?

Aunt Marcia lost no time at all. It proved a trifle difficult to persuade friends who had been warm enough in the interval before the marriage, but now seemed to shrink from a bride whose own husband apparently thought her not fit company; but, tant mieux – she had tried to compose a house-party of the highest respectability and might now without scruple invite those whose company she herself really preferred. So into the coach with herself and Sir Bertram, bundled Dolly Mettle and a new friend, Betty Eustis; and to offset them she had captured Sir Henry Kidd –

already much alarmed at the company he found himself committed to and planning to escape from Starrbelow as soon as it proved possible; and the Honourable John Fair – dear 'Honjohn' of whom, so many years later, Lady Weyburn was to declare, standing at bay before her persecutors, that, in the words of Sir John Marvel, he, at least, 'nothing common did, or mean – in all those memorable scenes!' He had been very young in those days, and very green; and dangling a little after Miss Eustis who, despite her appearance to the contrary, was neither young nor green. . . .

That in bringing her aunt down to Starrbelow, Sophia was in any way influenced by the fact that where Aunt Marcia went Prince Anton of Brunswick went too, never, for some reason entered Lady Corby's innocent head; and when, too late, some such vague suspicion occurred to her, it was easy enough to keep him pinned out of harm's way, at her side. She could not, after all, know of the Treasure Seekers' Circle, and its plans to dispose of her.

So Christine, retired to Frome, and though she would not, it seemed, entirely cut off her friend from her love and counsels and continued to ride and drive with her now and again, refused to enter her cousin's house at Starrbelow or to meet the riffraff assembled there; nor did the Earl offer entertainment at the Castle. Lord Franks, however, was not so particular – and, indeed, had no cause to be – and a rout was declared in honor of the boon companion and her new boon companions and friends: they must all drive over in a couple of coaches for the ball and stay overnight.... So 'the county' was horrified by a new scandal: Lady Weyburn of Starrbelow – queening it in the splendid decaying house where for twenty years no decent woman had set foot, sleeping in a bed where no woman had slept but for one purpose, since old Lady Franks had died.... And the next day dallying and delaying until dusk set in and not until then chivvying her party into their coaches and setting off home, all a little the worse for drink, along the lonely, darkling, hilly Cotswold roads.... Sir Bertram and Lady Corby rode ahead with Mrs. Mettle, Miss Eustis, Prince Anton of Brunswick and Sir Henry Kidd – Prince Anton very sulky as seemed nowadays his habit, as he skulked about, chained like a large, gangling dog to his mistress's side; Sir Henry morose and unresponsive, bitterly regretting his mistake in accepting for the visit, and longing to be out of it all. Sapphire, in the second coach, was with her three devils – to the scandal and secret jealousy of the other ladies – and had co-opted a fourth in the person of Honjohn, to the particular disgust of Miss Eustis; except that, already though but a boy a famous whip, he had insisted on driving and so was out of Sapphire's immediate way. And on the high, moonlit ridge above Frome where the long road rides the sharp back of the Cotswolds, three horsemen rode out from behind a clump of trees and took up their positions, quietly, strung out across the path of the leading coach.

Your money – or your lives!

The coach drew up with a clatter of horses' hooves, Sir Bertram poked out his head at one side and Prince Anton at the other, the coachman called out on a high note of fear: "Highwaymen across the road." Behind them, the second coach lumbered up and stopped. Of the three supposed occupants, only one head poked out of that, and that a woman's – nor was there anyone to observe at the moment, that she was laughing.

In a straight line, slowly, the three riders moved forward, masked, cloaked, pistols at the ready. Nobody spoke. As they neared the first coach, one man slipped down from the saddle and went to the leader's head, his pistol pointing steadily up at the driver's heart; a second rode on to the following coach; and out of the shadows a fourth man slipped and gathered the three horses and stood quietly holding them. The third, a man of great height, called out sharply: "Remain within! Nobody to leave his place!" His eyes glittered behind his black mask like diamonds. He dismounted and walked round to the window of the leading coach, pistol cocked, "Ladies – your jewels!"

The ladies, terrified, clung to the three men within, hampering any attempt at rebellion, imploring conciliation. The ornaments they had worn at the party had been collected – by Lady Weyburn's (somewhat insistent) advice – for easier care and carriage in a single box, Lady Corby's jewel case. Mrs. Mettle and Miss Eustis were clamorous for their personal safety. "For God's sake, my lady, never mind the trinkets, hand over the box and be done!"

Prince Anton struggled violently to be free. "Unhand me, Marcia, let me deal vit dis ruffian...." Sir Henry, also, beat off restraining hands. The two glittering eyes behind the mask looked on in amused contempt at the struggling mass penned in the coach; the single eye of the pistol swung a little, this way and that. "Come, Madame, take your friends' advice – hand over and be done."

Within the coach – confusion: outside, a rattle of commands, voices raised in argument, a sudden silence – a shout of alarm from the highwaymen at the horses' heads. The tall leader swung about a little but did not relax his grip on the pistol. At the opposite side of the coach, the door was pulled sharply open. "Aunt Marcia, the box – give me the box."

"Sophia!"

"Hush, he'll hear you. Quick – give me the jewel box.... Give me the box, I say, I have a plan...." She seized the box from under their feet and turning, flung it away from her, to lie hidden in the long grass beneath the stone wall that closely bordered the road. "Now – where is your dressing-case?"

"My dressing-case?"

"Hush, quiet – the dressing-case, hand over the dressing-case, he'll think it's the jewel box, how should he know differently...?"

Over their frantic whispering, the voice of the third man calling from the hinder coach. "A woman... Crept out by the far side.... Can't leave the horses' heads, the coachman has a firearm...." You could picture him standing with his back to his leader, his eyes fixed upon the firearm, calling over his shoulder. "She's gone round to the other side of your coach."

The tall leader spoke a word to the second man, wheeled his horses and rode round the great black bulk of the coach. Sapphire stood, panting, at the open door, the leather dressing-box in her arms. "Ah, Madame – I thank you, you do my searching for me!" He spoke to his fellow in charge of the first coach, and the man left the horses, but warily, keeping his weapon fixed upon the coachman, and sidled round to the door of the coach and took the box from her; the third man, also still covering John Fair, perched up on the driving seat of the rear coach, backed away and joined them. They stood, the four, grouped in the moonlight: two cloaked and masked figures, backs to one another, firearms levelled up at the coachmen, a third between them, very tall, very dark and bright of eye, looking down at the girl in a green velvet cloak, crouched, suddenly uncertain, staring up at him, backed against the carriage door. "We leave you then: but before we go – permit me to thank you, Madame." He added, sotto voce: "And to repay an old score," made a low bow and a flourish, swooped suddenly – and catching her in his arms, bent her head violently backward and, so holding her, pressed his half open mouth upon hers. She struggled, beating violently at his breast with clenched hands. His fellows, startled, turned upon him. The coachmen, released from the threat of their firearms, gathered up the reins and got their uneasy teams under control. Prince Anton flung open the door and, over her arched body tried to force the man off her; and, his friends also seizing him by the shoulders and pulling him violently away, Sapphire wrenched herself free, found herself dragged back into the leading coach and the door slammed. Prince Anton had succeeded, the man being held powerless in the grip of his own friends, in tearing the pistol from his grasp and, now covering all three with it, backed away from them and around the coach and hurled himself in at the opposite door. The horses, released at last, took to their heels and urged on by the terrified coachmen, fled wildly off, the coach rolling and jolting behind them, down the moonlit road; and Sapphire, half in, half out of the window, snatched the gun from Prince Anton, leaned out yet further and, steadying her arm as deliberately as possible on the sill of the lurching vehicle, fired it point blank at the highwayman's heart.

The fourth man, meanwhile, had stood by quietly, holding the highwaymen's horses, taking no part. John Fair leapt down from the following coach... "Here, fellow, bring your horses over here and hang on to my leaders...." The groom obeyed, running crabwise up the road, trailing his string, trit-trotting with nervously tossing heads behind him. John Fair ran over to the little group crouched in the ditch by the side of the road. "For God's sake – is he dead? Has she killed him?"

Sir Pardo and Red Reddington knelt in the long grass beside the wounded man.

"She's winged him: only winged him... Here, Franks, pull yourself together, you're not dead yet...." They heaved him into a sitting position, packed precious handkerchiefs, linen and lace, around the spurting wound. "Can we get him to the coach?"

The groom dragged the leaders forward, struggling to control the three loose horses besides. "Is he bad, sir?"

"Only the shoulder... Can you steady them, Bates, while we try to get him in...?"

"Thank God she's not killed him," said John Fair.

"He asked for what he got – setting about her like that, and she not able to cry out for fear of giving the game away... Look, he's coming to," said Sir Pardo. He leaned into the coach for a flask of brandy and poured some down the injured man's throat. "Come, my lord, wake up! – you're not dead yet, I say."

They got him into the coach at last and he lay back in a corner, his lean, lined face very grey. "Better bring him back to the Manor," said Squire Reddington, "and send for a doctor from there. You can come along with us, John, and continue to

165

Starrbelow later, and bring her the news. Pardo, you'll stay overnight with us at the Manor?"

"I'll do that," said Sir Pardo. He bent and picked up the two boxes lying in the grass by the wall, one where Sapphire had thrown it, the other where he himself had dropped it when Lord Franks fell. "You can take back the jewels with you, John – 'saved by Lady Weyburn's resource and courage!' As for La Corby's cosmetic box – alas, the bold highwaymen, holding us still at pistol point, have made off with that, thinking it contained the jewels – dragging their wounded comrade with them!" He could not help laughing, even then, at the success of their plot. " 'Twas a famous notion, sure, and'll keep her ladyship out of the way most conveniently: for she'll not appear without her rouge-pot, that's certain...."

"Come on into the coach," said Red Reddington, "and don't gabble so much." He jerked his head warningly in the direction of the groom. "Up on the box, John, and drive on slowly to the Manor House. Hey, Bates, can you manage those three back to the stables?"

"I managed them here to meet you, sir,"

said Bates a little sulkily, having intercepted the warning nod.

"Do the same home, then; and – not a word, Bates, of this evening's doings: that's understood?"

John Fair sat up on the box, quietly and steadily driving the team so that the joltings of the coach should not jerk open the wound – which, however, appeared now to be bleeding less. From within, voices reached him, raised in anger. " 'Twas your own fault, my lord, setting about her like that. . . ."

The answer was inaudible. "A joke?" said Red Reddington. "To force yourself on her when she was helpless to resist?"

"Do you call this 'helpless to resist'?" said Lord Franks' voice, feebly, but raised to defend himself.

"She had no gun when you fell upon her; and couldn't cry out for fear of giving us away. A mean advantage, *I* say, to take of a woman – and a friend."

"And so say I," said Sir Pardo.

"She threw her wine in my face and I meant but to even the score with her: 'twas by way of a joke. But I confess I a little bit lost my head . . . She looked so devilish alluring," he said, ruefully laughing, "looking up at the 'highwayman,' pretending terror, with those great blue eyes. It isn't often she used her eyes: but when she does . . ." He used an ugly term.

"For that," said Reddington, "if you were not helpless, I'd knock your teeth in. . . ."

Lord Franks laughed his rasping laugh, gritting his teeth on the stab of pain as his shoulder moved. "By heaven, you're very solicitous of the lady's name – more so by a long way than ever she is herself. Why this fuss about a kiss in public? – she's ready enough with them in private, as you doubtless all know. . . ."

"I know nothing of the sort," said Red, heatedly.

"Do you not?" said Sir Pardo. "That's not what you've said to me; nor what I've found myself."

"Very well, then, I unsay it; nor will I hear it spoken of in my presence. . . ."

"Well, well," said Lord Franks, more comfortably, having drawn the argument away from his own misdemeanour, "let us not bicker over our conquests or we shall never have done. In this case I set out, lightheartedly enough, to settle a score, and now the lady has resettled it and I wish her

168

no ill for it: I shouldn't have let those eyes get the better of me and I'll send her my apologies – with a pair of ruby buckles for her shoes to match the red devil in her blood: our Lady Lucifer, Daughter of Light!" He pushed aside some protest from Reddington, declaring he'd believe the Wicked Squire was in love at last and would break the heart of every doxy in Gloucestershire, and lighten their purses for the future by adhering to but one. "Offer her buckles yourself, and see if she'll not take them! For my part, she threw out a hint as we danced last night; and if her stick of a husband isn't here to give her gew-gaws, who's he to complain if others do it in his place...?" But what a termagent, he added, laughing ruefully again; what a spitfire! "I'll swear she shot to kill...."

If Sapphire, the first fury of her outraged feelings abated, felt secret alarm as to the outcome of her action, she showed no sign of it. The man had assaulted her: she had shot him in self-defence. She hustled the ladies to their bedrooms, sent for food and wine and sat down with the two remaining gentlemen in the candlelit gallery whose windows over-looked the drive down

169

which, twenty-one interminable days ago, Charles Weyburn had ridden away for ever out of her life. "But Sapphire – but my lady – if you haf killed this man. . . ."

She leaned back against the tall, white marble mantlepiece, a glass in her hand: in the flicker of firelight, the tones in her red velvet dress shifted and shone like the tones of the wine in her glass. "It's no crime for a woman to defend her honour. If a man assaults her, it's no crime for a woman to shoot him."

Sir Henry Kidd lifted his head, startled, and looked directly at her. She said: "Why do you stare at me, Sir?"

"I am waiting," he said.

"Waiting? For what?"

"For you to say something, my lady, something more."

"I say it's no crime to shoot a man who assails one's honour. You are waiting for me to – add something to that?"

"Something very much to the point," he said. "Something that can hardly have escaped the attention of anyone so – if I may be permitted to say it – so intelligent, as your ladyship; something one would have expected to be the first thing that would leap to the mind. But you have not said it, my lady; you have not said that it is no crime to shoot – a highwayman."

She stood very still for a moment, the glass glowing like a ruby in her white hand. Then she laughed a little ruefully. "So – that is the worst of dealing with these keen-eyed lawyers! – you have found us out?"

"Do you mean to say, Sapphire," cried Prince Anton, forgetting in his agitation to change it to 'my lady,' "that all this thing hass been a deception – a –," he fumbled for the English word, "a Betrug, a fraud...?" "A fraud?" she said, laughing. "Pish, nonsense! Let us call it – an escapade."

"To what purpose?" said Henry Kidd, steadily.

"To what purpose? Our escapade? Why – for amusement, sir."

"I see. But as you have reminded me, I am a lawyer. Is your amusement to cost the ladies upstairs their jewels – and the dressing-box?"

"The jewels lie hidden by the roadside and will be returned."

"I see," he said again. He thought it over for a moment. "Yes, I see. But the dressing-box?"

"The dressing-box – why, sir, the dressing-box is now most unfortunately in the possession of the highwaymen."

"Who, however, were not highwaymen?"

She looked suddenly a little alarmed. She said, and now he could have sworn she improvised, glancing uneasily at Prince Anton: "But who are – are members of a club, you see: a club of – of treasure-seekers, Sir Henry, bound by their rules to obtain certain objects, certain not easily obtainable objects. . . ."

"Such as – Lady Corby's dressing-box?"

"A lady's dressing-box; why, yes, you see, one of them, Lord Franks I think it was, was set this object for his attainment – or lose his election to the club. Other members of the club," said Sapphire, bravely struggling with extempore. "to pledge their best assistance." She laughed, eyeing him warily over the rim of the wine-filled glass.

"The other members of the club being – yourself, Squire Reddington, Sir Pardo Ryan and the Honourable John Fair?"

"Do you mean to say, Sapphire, you haf robbed Marcia off her precious box?"

172

"Don't tell on us?" implored Sapphire, on a note of alarm again.

"But Marcia cannot – That is to say, Lady Corby must haf this box, she does not travel without it, it is her first object of care always. You will return it to her, off course?"

"Why, as to that you see – it is Lord Franks who now has the box: it is his 'treasure,' possession of it constitutes him a member of the – the Treasure Seekers' Circle. . . ."

"And meanwhile," said Sir Henry, relentlessly pursuing the course of his thoughts, "Lady Corby, of course, without her box, will be unable to appear – er – properly dressed; that is to say, will be unable to appear at all." And he looked at the Prince and thought: 'He at least is not a party to this.'

"I shall do my utmost to persuade his lordship to part with his treasure, Sir Henry."

"His lordship – or his heirs," suggested Sir Henry.

"Or his heirs," she agreed, shrugging. But she had little hope, she added, that Lord Franks, if he lived, would prove easy to deal with in the matter; he was not now, after all, very likely to be anxious to oblige her in anything, however much she might wish it. . . .

"Oh, I am sure you wish it most devoutly, my lady," said Sir Henry; and he could not forbear from asking her curiously: "Are you not at least a little alarmed, Lady Weyburn – lest the man may be dead?"

"Why no, said Sapphire, gazing back at him limpidly, not in the least alarmed: for had not Sir Henry pointed out to her that it was no crime, in self-defence to kill – a highwayman.

Ten years later she was to stand before him, a woman accused – was to face him before all the assembled aristocracy of England, accused by him and by them all of the wantonness springing from those first wild summer days at Starrbelow. But she could not know that, and meanwhile pursued her own wayward way; and late in June announced imperilously that Aunt Corby was in need of medical attention – the poor denuded lady still keeping her room – and they must all move up to town. . . .

She spent a night with Sir Bertram and

Lady Corby at Albemarle Street; but one night only. Lord Weyburn had left instructions that when in doubt she should apply to his lawyers, and next day she drove to their office – in a hired carriage; the last she ever used in London – and sat with Mr. Boone in his quiet room looking out over the grey old cobbled street where a lady's equippage had seldom been seen before. "You should have let me called upon *you*, my lady."

"I have no address at present," said Sapphire, shrugging.

"You have Lord Weyburn's house in Berkeley Square."

"Have I?" said Sapphire. "I did not know, or I was not sure."

His lordship's instructions are that you are to be treated exactly as though – as though...."

"As though I were his lordship's wife by preference," suggested Sapphire, "instead of through a vulgar wager."

Mr. Boone coughed and bowed and looked awkwardly down his long, legal nose. "His lordship has been most generous in his arrangements."

"Oh, certainly. Let me see if I understand them correctly. I am to have

175

the use of either of the two houses – when he himself does not happen to wish to use them. What is to be done, may I ask, if I am in Berkeley Square when his lordship arrives? I take it he does not propose to remain with Miss L---- P------ for ever?"

"Miss –?"

"In Bath," said Sapphire.

"His lordship will give due notice of his coming."

"And her ladyship will strike her tents and scuttle out of his way? If Lord Weyburn feels restless at any time, it seems hardly an idyllic outlook for *me*, Mr. Boone – driving back and forth between Starrbelow and London, bowing to my husband out of the window as our coaches cross." She shrugged. She examined minutely the seaming of a glove. "Supposing, Mr. Boone, that I were to return to Italy?"

Mr. Boone looked startled. That eventuality, apparently, had not been considered. "I shall have to discuss the question with Lord Weyburn."

"Please do," said Sapphire. "As soon as possible." She gave her entire attention to the glove. "Will he be soon again in town?"

"I understand," said Mr. Boone

miserably, "that his lordship proposes passing through town about the end of July."

"I see. Meanwhile, I have the use of the family house?"

"Oh, certainly, my lady. And the carriages – I am horrified to see your ladyship so equipped, with no attendance but a maid and a hired coachman. Your ladyship must remember," said Mr. Boone, proudly, "that you are the wife of Baron Weyburn, of Starrbelow."

"That is a tragedy," said the wife of Baron Weyburn of Starrbelow, "that I am very unlikely to forget." And she swept him a curtsey and gave him one blue blaze which Mr. Boone, also, thought he was unlikely to forget.

So Sapphire installed herself in the lovely house with the high pillared portico and the long lines of tall windows exquisitely balanced in their regular pattern across the glowing pinky-red new brickwork; and within a week had made it the most notorious house in town.

Lady Corby, terrified, summoned her niece to Albemarle Street. It said something for Sapphire's reputation, indeed when after but a few days of her occupation, such a woman as Aunt Corby dare not be seen entering the portals of Berkeley Square. "Sophia, are you mad? What are these rumours I hear of you and your behaviour?"

No hired coaches, no simple white and blue dresses for Lady Weyburn now. She sat in the little back drawing room that would have been but a cupboard in her own great house, arrogantly beautiful in a dress of light green satin with a splendid crimson velvet cloak, rubies in her ears and on her fingers, ruby buckles in her shoes; and now at the door, the fine matched Weyburn greys fidgeted in their trappings as the family carriage waited, coachman, footman and page in attendance (her ladyship had told the coachman she would *not* be long). "Rumours, Aunt? Did you bring me all this way to ask me a question to which you already know the answer?"

"I know the answer; but is it – can it be – the truth? That your husband's house is frequented by all the rakehellies of this town. Lord Warne, Lord Greenewode, Francis Erick, Ross, Toms Jeans...."

"Prince Anton of Brunswick," said Sapphire, continuing the catalogue.

"I am happy to have Anton keeping

some check on your doings," said Aunt Corby stiffly.

Sophia laughed outright, fluttering her fan, the naughty side outward. "Ha, ha, ha! Poor Anton my watchdog – well, well!"

"Do you know, Sophia, that it is said that half these men are your lovers?"

"Good gracious," said Sapphire. "I must be kept very busy."

"Are there so many of them?" said Lady Corby, nearly fainting.

"There are twelve – if you count the two or three country members."

"I do not understand you, Sophia. What I wish to know is – are you taking lovers?"

"I have as many lovers as – as your ladyship has," said Sapphire.

Lady Corby closed her own fan sharply and rapped with it on the table; just so – how very long ago, and yet but a few brief months ago! – had she rapped Prince Anton over the head because he agreed that Miss Devigne's dress was too low. "A married lady of some years standing, Sophia, may – discreetly take a lover. That is something different from a woman in your position playing ducks and drakes with her husband's good name, with his home, his possessions, his money.... In God's name,

179

what will Weyburn say when he hears of this?"

"As long as he does not say it to me," said Sapphire, "I care not two pins what he says. So why should you?"

Lady Corby cared because through her niece she had hoped to dig deep into the Weyburn resources. "He will cut you off with a pittance, forbid you his house...."

"He will be very foolish to do so," said Sapphire, shrugging. "He has given me a taste of wealth and I might find myself unable to live without it. He may drive me to – earn – it, in a way even less creditable to his precious family name." And she drew back her pale satin skirt and showed the ruby buckles blazing on her insteps and lowered the hem again without a word; but she smiled. Lord Franks was known to boast that any woman in London could be bought with a pair of jewelled buckles: they were at present the rage.

Lady Corby looked at her niece in utter terror. "To think, Sophia, that you are the innocent girl I brought over from Italy less than a year ago!"

"Indeed, yes: I have a great deal to thank you for, Aunt Corby," said Lady Weyburn;

and rose and swept out to the waiting carriage.

The Treasure Seekers' Circle meanwhile, improvised for the staunching of Sir Henry Kidd's inconvenient curiosity, had become established fact and within a brief week was the talk of the *ton*. Red Reddington and Pardo had come roaring up to town in her train, Lord Greenewode and Francis Erick, his familiar, had joined immediately and brought in a group of friends, Prince Anton, now openly ever at Sapphire's heels, was an ardent member – on the score, no doubt, of 'keeping an eye on her ladyship' for the benefit of her ladyship's aunt. And Sir Cecil Prout was a member. An object had been suggested for Prince Anton's acquiring – a hoop from the Duchess of Witham's petticoat. Sapphire had proposed it – conducting the first full meeting of the Club, sitting wickedly elegant upon a curved and gilded couch in the drawing-room at Berkeley Square – one woman among a dozen men, half of whom, at least, no decent women would know. "A hoop, I say, from Gossip Wit's petticoat."

The Honourable John went off into gales of his boyish laughter: the cleanest wind

181

that blew through the lovely rooms in these days of Lady Weyburn's early occupation. "That iss too easy," said Prince Anton, laughing too. "I must but creep up the backstairs and kiss the maid."

"I amend: a hoop from the petticoat her Grace is *wearing*," said Sapphire, sparkling. Her hands held, as ever nowadays, a wine-glass; she looked at him over the rim, across the red wine. "Come, Prince – you accept?"

"Sir Cecil Prout should be the one to send after petticoats," said Anton. "Since she publicly declared he should never have left them off."

"I have not the pleasure of Sir Cecil Prout's acquaintance."

"He is a foolish fop," said Tom Jeans, who was among them, "but he would amuse your ladyship."

"Let us make him a member, then, and the hoop his challenge. We must keep up our membership: Lord Franks in his venture was supported by four lieutenants – it's agreed we may call for as many volunteers as we require. Very well then – now for Prince Anton. He has wriggled out of the – hoop; what else can we devise for this member, brother devils?"

"His Majesty's snuff-box," suggested Francis Erick.

She clapped her hand over her mouth. "Anton! You dare not?"

Prince Anton leaned forward in his chair, looking back at her, unsmiling. His face had aged of late, there were fine lines about his eyes that gave him a haggard look, the broad planes of his handsome face were pale, and the long-knuckley hands clasped together between his knees in a familiar gesture, were tensely clasped these days. He said, slowly: "Why no – her ladyship is right: I would not dare. Thiss iss – for others; for me – I am too near the court, thiss iss not fair to my father and I must not." He bowed to Sapphire, bending his head down, not looking up at her. "I may forget that I am a chentleman; I must not forget, however, that I am a Prince."

Sapphire also bowed, a little mockingly; and she smiled at him – but it was the new smile, the smile that had been born at the Duchess of Witham's ball. "I will not contradict you, sir: in either respect." She shrugged. "Well – you are absolved your royal cousin's snuff-box. You shall have instead – come, gentlemen, what shall he have? – the Prince is difficult to

183

accommodate. A page from the visitor's book at Witham House?"

"We have already used Gossip Wit," said Prince Anton.

"A page then from – from the record book of some Fleet-wedding parson?"

"They are abolished," said Honjohn, "since last quarter-day."

"Not abolished: made illegal. Many still exist, however, who may legally perform marriages – he must get one of those." (Did she glance over at Anton then, as was afterwards suggested, with a look that said: Splendid! – we have delicately steered them in the direction we meant them to take at last: an excuse for extracting that page. . .?) " 'Tis a hard task to set him, gentlemen; but he has had other choices." She laughed. "I will come with you, Anton; disguised as a bride . . . !"

And so the club casually born, went forward and – disgracefully – flourished. Lord Warne had been set, that very day, to try for a wine-cup from the nunnery of the Daughters of St. Paul on Blackheath, and at supper arrived, triumphantly bearing with him not only one of the nuns' wine-cups but one of the nuns as well – who first affected terror and tears and then went

184

off into giggles and then was quizzed by half the gentlemen present and proved to be only some doxy of an actress pressed into his lordship's service for the occasion. It was generally felt by the company that his lordship had gone a little far in introducing so unequivocally undesirable a young person to her ladyship's house; but Lady Weyburn took it with the utmost complacency and only saw to it with tact and charm that she was complimented, paid off and dismissed, without the necessity of inviting her to join familiarly in with herself. But in future, she said, she thought the rule should be: no ladies. "I will play all parts when it comes to feminine assistance and I assure you, Brother Devils, shall not be found wanting. Sir Cecil Prout must let me have a share in the matter of her Grace's petticoat; and – you will not forget, Prince Anton, your blushing Fleet bride . . . ?"

Eight

On August the first – and we must keep
these dates before us, for they were to
become important later – on August the
first, then, 1754, Lord Weyburn returned
to London from the pleasures of Bath. The
marriage had taken place at the end of May;
and of the intervening nine weeks Lady
Weyburn had spent the first two in solitude
at Starrbelow, the next two also at
Starrbelow but in anything but solitude;
the remaining five in a mounting crescendo
of wildness and folly – there were many to
give it a far worse name – in town. If she
remembered the lawyer's warning that his
lordship would be passing through London
at the end of July, she paid no heed to it.
She was conducting a meeting of the
Treasure Seekers' Circle when, late in the
evening, his coach drew up at the door of
the house in Berkeley Square.

He stood in the great hall, tall, slender,
handsome, swinging the light travelling
cloak from his shoulders, handing his hat

and his gloves to the manservant. This was an old man, long in the service of the family. He ventured, wretchedly, that her ladyship was in – in the drawing-room, my lord. . . .

"Her ladyship?" said Lord Weyburn, astounded.

"Her ladyship is – entertaining, my lord."

"Do you mean – Lady Weyburn? Lady Weyburn is in the house?" On the man's unhappy, half-apologetic nod, he added, still incredulous: "Did she not know I was coming?"

"I conveyed your intentions to her ladyship, my lord, as you instructed me; I had heard from you with orders to prepare for your arrival this evening."

"But, then – what did she say?"

"Why, merely that I doubtless knew my duties, my lord, and should make all arrangements accordingly." He hesitated. "Her ladyship is occupying the yellow suite; I have prepared your lordship's own room as usual. . . ."

A woman came down the great, broad curve of the stair: not Sapphire but some painted doxy with Sapphire's ivory skin and brass-gold hair, dressed in a gown of white that looked like a wedding-dress,

187

dragged down half off her shoulders: with some tawdry finery of white feathers and veiling in her hair and an over-loading of diamonds – which, however, were real diamonds. He stood in the shadows of the hall staring up; behind him the man made a sign of dismissal to attendant footmen and himself slipped away. In a moment Charles Weyburn was alone with her. Three steps from the bottom of the stairs, one hand on the marble rail, she stopped and lifted her heavy eyelids and looked full at him. He closed his own eyes for a moment against the – terror of it; the sick disillusion, the mounting disgust and rage, the astonishment, the fear. Red as a rose against the white dress, a glass of claret glowed in her hand. He said: "Dear God in heaven! – is this you?" She looked back at him unsmiling, over the shifting rose-red light in the glass. "Do you not recognise me, my lord? I am much as you saw me last."

"That at least," he said, "is not true."

She put on a look of doubt. "This was the very dress."

"But not the woman," he said swiftly; and looked away from her, away from the wreck of the woman who a few brief weeks ago had worn the dress – the wreck of the

188

young girl in the white dress whose eyes had suddenly stared up at him with a look of startled innocence, of bewildered pain that had haunted him ever since. He blurted out: "And anyway – why do you wear this dress?"

"Oh, the dress?" She laughed, pecking at it with her free hand, looking down disparagingly at its snowy white muslin, dropping a fold of it from fastidious fingers, brushing it into place again with a backhand flick as though this old rag of a wedding-dress were something hardly worth consideration at all. "A masquerade. We have all been down to the Fleet."

"To the Fleet?"

"You have heard of our Circle of Treasure Seekers, sure?"

"I have heard some rumour. . . ."

"The Circle has been down to the Fleet, today: the object, a page from a registry book – I acting the part of the bride."

"In the wedding-dress in which you were married to *me?*"

"The wedding-dress? Why, as to that, my lord, I thought as little of the dress, I fear, as *you* did when I wore it last. The prize is the thing: and we have attained the prize."

He bowed stiffly. "I felicitate you, Madame. An admirable object and an admirable way, I am sure, for Lady Weyburn to be spending an evening. Do I understand that your 'circle' is assembled here, in my house?"

"Which, I understand was to be also *my* house, my lord."

"While I was absent. Did you not understand from my lawyers, that we were not to be here together?"

"But it is your coming," said Sapphire, coolly, "that has brought us here together." And she gave him a little, impudent bow and turned away and began to remount the stairs. "Well – will you join us; or not?"

"I thank you, no," he said.

She paused again, looking down at him now from a greater height, with a look of mock regret. "I am sorry. There are friends of yours among us: Mr. Reddington is here, and Sir Pardo, and Lord Franks. . . ."

"Lord Franks! Here? You admit that man to your acquaintance?"

"Why, yes: we had a little difference, a while ago; but he apologised and – made amends; and we have remained good friends. You heard of that affair in Gloucestershire?"

"I heard nothing of a particular affair. Lord Franks is not a man for any decent woman to recognise."

"Oh, dear." She shrugged. "Well, it is too late now. But it is difficult, you see, to choose one's friends discreetly – I was till a year ago, a stranger in England and have had, of course, no hand to guide me; moreover, the choice has not been great – the respectable fight shy of a wife whom not even her husband will condescend to know. At any rate, sir – you will not meet Lord Franks?"

"I will neither meet him nor permit him to remain here in this house; whether it be yours or mine. I must ask you, please, to request your friends to leave."

"Oh, certainly. It will not be the first time, I daresay," said Sapphire, laughing, "that some at least of them have been asked to remove from a gentleman's house." She added: "Am I also 'requested to leave'?"

"As you are here, you had better remain. I, myself, will go elsewhere tomorrow."

"You are all consideration," said Sapphire; and she bowed to him, still laughing, looking down at him from the curving balustrade above his head, holding the glass in her hand: a white wraith in the

191

shadows, now, only the diamonds glittering like ice in the rays of the great, hanging, central chandelier – a white wraith, a radiance of cold white ice and snow: with only a blot of red wine like a bloodstain, where the human heart should have been. . . .

He washed himself, changed his travelling clothes, toyed with some food and wine. He heard the unmuted chatter and clatter of the departing guests; and a voice he recognised. Napkin in hand, he started up from his chair. "Ask her ladyship to come to me immediately – no, take a message: ask her ladyship if she will receive me as soon as is convenient." He waved his hand at the table. "Have all this cleared away. After that, let the servants retire."

"I will wait up for you, my lord."

"No, no, go to bed, you have been travelling all day. I need no attention." And I need no listening ears, he thought to himself, and no gossiping tongues – she and I must speak now, once for all. "Ask her ladyship to dismiss her maid: I have matters to discuss with her."

The servant departed, winking to himself. Lady Weyburn returned with him immediately. "You sent for me, my lord?"

"I asked you to receive me, Madame."

"Well, well – I'm not particular about the minor courtesies." As the servants retired, closing the door behind them, she came up and stood before him boldly on the hearth-rug, looking up questioningly into his face. He said: "Your guests have gone?"

"At last." She shrugged. "They were a little hard to persuade."

"None more so, no doubt," he said, smoothly, "than Prince Anton of Brunswick?"

She looked somewhat startled. "You yourself have entertained the Prince, at Starrbelow."

"Not, however, as your professed admirer, Madame."

"Nor is he that now. Why, pooh! – he's my Aunt Corby's lover," said Sapphire, recovering her spirit a little. "All the world knows that."

"All the world knows also that he has grown less assiduous of late."

"Not upon my account, sir." She looked at him boldly again from beneath painted eyelids. "Do not wish poor, mistress-ridden Anton on me – I have other fish to fry." And she thrust out her foot in its white slipper with the great ruby buckle and looked down at it, as though reminiscently; and laughed again.

He followed her glance. He said sharply: "What is this?"

"A foot, my lord. In a white shoe – which foot and even which shoe you have seen before."

"But not with such a buckle. These were not among the Weyburn jewels."

"Were not; are now, however." She looked down at them complacently. "I have several pairs."

"Such things are of considerable value. Where did you get them?"

"From a jeweller's."

"Who paid for them?" She hesitated, almost imperceptibly and he insisted: "Who paid?"

She put on a pained expression. "Why, my lord – I did."

"Let me see the bills for them."

"I never keep bills, I've destroyed them. You do not suggest, sir, that I did not pay for the buckles? For that," said Sapphire, "would suggest in its turn that *I* was paid – with them."

He turned away his face from the bold,

194

painted stare; his own handsome face, sick with offended pride and feeling, hid itself in the shadows of the bent head. He said at last, quietly: "The time has come for us to arrive at an understanding. Will you tell me with simplicity – what is your purpose in all this?"

"In what, my lord?"

"In this determination – for that is what it is – to disgrace my name: which is now the name you, also, bear."

She shrugged. "It is not a great encouragement to uphold one's name, if one bears nothing else but the name."

He shook his head impatiently. "Don't fence with me in this matter. I ask you again – what is your purpose?"

"May it not be simply that I enjoy it?"

"No," he said. "I knew you, a little at least, in former days; and I do you the honour to believe that this is not truly your idea of happiness."

"Oh – happiness," she said bitterly. "I spoke of 'enjoyment'; let us not mention between us such a word as happiness."

"Then what is your purpose?"

"May it not be – revenge?"

"Revenge?" he said, astonished. "For what? Because, having been tricked into

195

marriage, I did not remain, the devoted husband, to be tricked again?"

She stood very quiet, her hands folded on her fan, and only the glitter of her rings in the candlelight, gave away the secret of their trembling. "As to that," she said, "I say now and never will again – and if you do not believe it now, you never will, and for my part never need – that I knew nothing of the wager nor lent myself to any trick." She waited. He said nothing. She said: "This you won't believe?"

"This I – can't believe." He burst out: "All of your conduct... You coquetted with me: would not dance with me, but danced, would not ride with me, but rode; returned my kiss that day we raced to the gate in the woods, and then were 'insulted' and rode off home and would stay at Starrbelow no more: and yet stayed. Why did you marry me, if you knew nothing of the wager...?"

She broke in on him. "Very well, my lord, very well: you don't believe me, let that be enough. Now, as to the rest – you object to my conduct, I 'disgrace your name.' What do you say to my – returning home?"

"To Starrbelow?"

"No," she said. "Starrbelow is no home to me." She looked him in the face. "I want to go home, my lord – to Italy."

He caught his breath. "To Italy!"

"I will go away, out of your life, home to Venice. I will go back to my mother; and that will be the end."

He did not reply; he walked across the room and stood with one hand on the rose brocade curtain, looking down, unseeing, into the quiet street, where only the flaring torch of a passing link-boy illumined the midnight dark. He said at last, "When do you wish to go?"

"At once," she said quickly.

"And never return?"

"What should I return for? No, I will not return."

"So this is it?" he said at last, slowly. "This is the reason? You foul my name so that I shall be glad to be rid of you – to send you back to Venice where your heart has always been. This has been your purpose?"

She looked up sharply. "No. No. You did not want me, you'd be glad to get rid of me on any terms – why should I have gone to the trouble of . . . ?" But she broke off. She said with a deliberate shrug: "But

197

why do I protest? Perhaps this was the reason after all."

Sir Henry Kidd might have said that once again she extemporised; but if Charles Weyburn noted it then – and later he was to use it against her – he pushed the flicker of recognition from his mind. "For this! You married me for wealth and position in England; and when you found that you had wealth, indeed, but no position here, you decided upon wealth alone, in Italy. And for this, to gain your ends in this, you have smeared my name with the filth that smears your own, half the profligates in town defile my house, you have debauched yourself with men no decent man, let alone any woman, will know – even Starrbelow, even Starrbelow itself has been made unclean by your need to disgrace yourself so that I may be glad to get rid of you; even there you have taken your dissolute lovers and made the place hateful to me. . . ." He flung back from the window, he confronted her, still standing with bent head by the empty fireplace, and raised his hand as though he would strike her down. But he lowered his hand. "Yes, go," he said. "You are right – you could have gone without this."

"I will go," she said. "But – in one thing

you are wrong. I have had no lovers at Starrbelow."

"What do I care, Madame, where you have had your lovers?"

"You care that I may have made Starrbelow unlovely in your sight. In this, therefore, believe me – I have not disgraced Starrbelow."

"Do you think I have not heard of your conduct there . . . ?"

"Not at Starrbelow," she said quickly. "My friends came there, it is true: my aunt brought two ladies whom you would not have liked – and neither did I. But no one else came to the house, to whom you could object."

"Prince Anton of Brunswick came."

"Prince Anton of Brunswick is nothing to me, my lord."

"Is he not your lover, Madame?"

"No," she said. "No."

"From the moment you came to London, this man has been openly your admirer. . . ."

"I was ignorant and frightened: he was kind."

"He followed you to Gloucestershire, hung about you during Christmas week at Starrbelow – was your partner, deny it

199

though you may, in the matter of the wager. From the time of your betrothal to me until our marriage, he was with you constantly."

She did not reply that for much of that time she had been in Italy; she said, instead: "And where were *you* then, my lord?"

"Not hanging round the skirts, to be sure, of the woman who had tricked me into marriage. But he was there – is it not true?"

"I was with my aunt; where my aunt is, Prince Anton is." Now she did say: "Besides, I was abroad."

"In January you were not abroad; in March, April, May, you were not abroad – you were in London and so was Prince Anton of Brunswick – is this not true? Is it not true that he came to our wedding wearing a look as of a man about to be hanged, is it not true that within two weeks he was down with you again at Starrbelow, is it not true that you rode with him secretly in the woods? – that you were seen there, were intercepted there . . . ?"

She closed her eyes, swaying a little, putting out one hand to the mantelshelf to steady herself. She said, however, with a light laugh: "Dear me! – Christine has been – indiscreet – in her letters, I perceive."

"Christine? It was Lord Frome who

wrote to me. I have had no letters from Christine, why should I correspond with Christine?"

"I know that you correspond with her: she has told me so."

"In the past, yes. Why not? She is my cousin."

"But I – I don't complain," she said, almost timidly, a little bewildered perhaps by his insistence. "You mistake me. How should I complain? – I have known always, there has been no deception about it, that Christine is your true love."

Her hand with its glitter of diamonds lay close to his on the cool marble, though he did not touch her nor indeed was aware that she stood so close. He said, as though to himself – surely not to her? – "Ah, yes: Christine! I loved her, always I loved her from my childhood – it had become a habit. But she is too cold, she is too cold and pure and untouchable to hold all a heart's love. A man may worship at Chrsitine's feet, yet never know the passion to take her in his arms. . . ."

The colour flamed in her face, the patches of rouge were lost in it: ebbed away, and left them round and red on ashen cheeks. She stammered: "You are not . . . ?

Are not...? All this time – you have not been in love with Christine?"

Her hair was a deep gold glow in the candlelight, her great eyes looked up at him in their blaze of blue, her painted lips were parted, she swayed towards him, the white dress half off the ivory shoulders, hands outflung to him. "All this time – I have been free to love you after all...?"

He caught her: held her: thrust up his hand into the heavy gold of her hair as he had held her for that first kiss by the golden gates; and so, with her head supported against his palm, looked down into the two twin pools of blue – and was lost in them.

"I have always loved you – always, always...."

"And I, from the moment you walked into that room...."

"I knew nothing of the wager, you believe that now!"

"It killed me to think I should love you and you should – marry me through a trick...."

"I thought you mocked me, I thought you loved Christine."

"That was a boy's love," he said. "When I saw *you* – a man's love was born." He

202

looked down into the lovely, upturned face. "That night by the lake," he said. "What was I to do? I thought: If I ask her and she refuses – I have lost her; and if I ask and she accepts, then I have lost her indeed, for it means she is a party to the trick that was played on me. But – I had to ask you; or you would go back to Venice. . . ."

"To Venice!" she said; and started away from him gazing up at him in a sudden panic terror. "To Venice! I must go back to Venice."

He caught her to him again, holding her to him, smiling down at her. "Not now; not now – there is no need now to go."

"Oh, yes," she said. "Yes, I must go; I must go."

"What, leave me now? – now that we understand. . . ."

"You must let me go," she said, beginning to weep, struggling against the grip of his arms. "Just for – a little while only; but let me go."

"Is it your mother you wish to see? We can both go to Venice."

"Oh, no," she said, desperately. "No – I must go alone. Just for a little while – let me go alone, let me stay there a little while and then I will come back to you. . . ."

"Well, well," he said soothingly, "yes, of course if you long to go, you must go, of course you shall go. Only, now that I've found you, don't let me lose you again. How long must you go for?"

She evaded the question, turning away her head, crying now like a child. A little while; only a little while . . . She would come back to him. "Just for a little while. . . ."

He was puzzled, he grew serious, faint as gossamer a shadow of the old, cold doubt fell across his happiness. "For how long? What do you mean by 'a little while'?"

She shuddered, staring up at him, the back of her hand across her mouth. "I . . . Yes . . . I can – can come back to you; if only. . . ." She implored him: "If you will trust me, leave me alone – I will come back to you."

"Alone?" he said. "Leave you alone? And for how long?" She did not answer. "And why? What is wrong? Is there some trouble in your family? Is someone ill?"

She caught at it eagerly; yes, there was trouble, her mother – yes, her mother was ill.

"If you go because your mother is ill, then I can come with you." He said slowly: "If you go because your mother is ill, you can't know how long you must stay – and what is there to make a mystery about?" And he caught her wrist in a ring of strong fingers. "You're lying to me again. Why do you want to go?"

"I want to go home," she said flatly, almost sullenly. "For a little while."

"For how long? For a week? A month?" He said patiently: "It is August now. You will come back, when? Next month? In October, November?" She did not reply. "By Christmas, then?" he insisted; and he shook her wrist in his fierce grip and cried, "Answer! When?"

"In the spring," she said faintly. "Let me go now: I will come back in the Spring."

His hands fell away from her, he stood uncertain, incredulous, lost in astonishment. "In the Spring? You want to leave me now, to stay away six months? – more, seven, eight, nine months, till the Spring...?" But he shook off his bewilderment, he put his arms about her again, holding her to his heart. "Dearest love, think no more of it now, you're overwrought, we can talk about it again, we can talk later on...." And he lifted her head and kissed her again; and she lay in his arms with her poor masquerade of a doxy face

205

painted over the face of a young girl deep in love; and he pulled down the white dress from her warm shoulders as it had been pulled awry when she came down the stairs to him, and put his hand to her breast and murmured that she must refuse him nothing now, for now she was all his own: his to desire, his to lay claim to, his to possess – his wife.... The heavy white lids closed over the brilliant eyes; under his lips, her red lips parted, unresistant she lay, half swooning, against his heart, and he lifted her lightly and carried her through the tall doorway into the darkened bedroom with its glimmering of candles in the wall-sconces; and laid her like a white flower, all a-glitter with its dew-fall of diamonds, on the dark coverlet of the great four-poster bed. "Oh, Sapphire! – to see you lying there where all these long weeks of aching desire, you should have been: here on my bed, here in my arms at last...." And he fell across her, kissing her lips and throat, her arms, her shoulders, the lovely curve of her breasts thrust out of the torn satin dress; and raised himself to unfasten the diamonds round her neck and arms. "Take off these things, my love, and lie with me in your own true loveliness alone. What need have you of satin and jewels? – your skin is satin under my hands, as smooth as satin and as ivory white...." And he put his lips against hers and whispered that she was all ivory and gold and coral for all the world to see; but that her sapphires were for him alone; and these twin rubies for him alone.... And his hand tossed aside the diamond necklace, his mouth dropped kisses in the bare hollow of her throat, wandered, adventuring, down the satin and ivory of her naked breast....

Within the low bodice of the disordered dress – a locket: not hung by a chain but thrust away, hidden away there as though thrust out of the sight of men, close against her secret heart. Ringed round with brilliants suddenly glinting in the flame of a guttering candle – a pale handsome face with a lock of forward-falling hair looking back into a face grown suddenly sick with fear, staring down at it. A miniature, ringed with brilliants. A name: and a date. 'For ever – Anton. Ladyday, 1754.'

Nine

Sapphire wrote a letter; and, pale and trembling, Christine went to Lord Frome. "I have heard from Sophia. She is in great trouble. She wants me to go to her."

He took her hand kindly, he led her out on to the terrace looking down and away from Frome Castle over the lovely lawns and gardens, over the sunlit meadows, over the grey rooftops of Starrbelow lying in the plain beneath them. They leaned upon the balustrade of the terrace. He said: "Lady Weyburn is born to trouble, Christine, She is not of your world; you must leave her to her own."

"Oh, no," she said. "I couldn't. I couldn't desert her."

"She has disgraced her name, Christine, and Charles Weyburn's name: wantonly and flagrantly, as though of set purpose, she has put herself beyond the pale. She is no friend for you."

"She is the best friend I have in the world," said Christine, steadily.

"You did her a kindness once; she was grateful – but what has she ever done for *you?*"

She could not tell him that for her sake her friend had made herself Weyburn's cheap and easy prey, had longed to fly from Starrbelow, but stayed so that Christine might remain near Frome – she could not tell him how fully and faithfully that old, trivial debt was daily and hourly paid. "All she has done for me, is not to be told. I, at any rate, won't desert her now."

He leaned there, a quiet, dull, rather stubby man, looking at her in his own quiet way as she stood, so tall and slender, so white and china-blue, so grave, with the lovely upward-sweeping brows: her beauty had been ever touched with melancholy, she was not ardent and gay as her friend could be. He said: "Christine – of all women in the world, I think of you as one who could touch pitch and be undefiled, who could grow up out of the mud as pure a lily as the name they gave you; but even you must be blown upon by the reputation of this friend of yours...." He looked into her face, white and sorrowful but adamant. "What is this trouble she writes to you about?"

209

"It is – a secret trouble...." She looked down at the letter in her hand. She amended: "She has had a – a disagreement with Lord Weyburn. She wants me to accompany her back to Italy."

"To Italy?" he said, astounded. "This woman – wants you to go off with her to Italy?"

"She is – she is distracted. It is all something I can't explain to you, but she must go; my cousin, Charles, now insists upon her going at once, and – she has no friend in the world but me, she cannot go off alone, broken-hearted as she is...."

"She has no heart to break," he said, angrily.

"She has a heart; you do not know her, my lord, she has a heart . . . At any rate," she said, "I must go with her."

He was silent. "Your mother – what does she say to this?"

"I have not spoken to her yet; but she will weep and wring her hands and at last will yield because she must."

"She cannot allow you, Christine, to go off unattended to a foreign land with this – adventuress; it cannot be allowed." He thought it over in his deliberate way. He said at last: "If you are adamant – and I know your will, Christine – will you accept my escort to Italy?"

She looked at him absolutely confounded; the pink flush mounted up into her pale face. "*You* come! On such a journey! No, you could not."

"Is there something, then, disgraceful, after all?"

"No," she said quickly. "I cannot explain it to you, but it is not disgraceful, she is no way disgraced. As for your coming – would you lend your reputation to such a – a flight, I suppose it will be called?" He began to speak but she interrupted him. "It is the same for me, no doubt. But my friend is my friend, to you she is less than nothing, why should you harm yourself in her service . . . ?"

"It would be in your service, Christine; and I harm myself no more than you do."

"Ah, yes, but you do," she insisted. "What am I? – a young woman in society, with a respectable name, no doubt, but not a great one. . . ."

He interrupted in his turn. He said: "You might have a great name, Christine: if you chose."

It had come. She had known for many days now that it would come, it was not the

211

exquisite realisation of hopes and doubts that it would once have been: but it was the culmination of all her life's dream, that dream which, single in purpose, she had hugged to her breast from her childhood's days. And now it had come. He said: "I am a dull man, Christine: I am not handsome and clever as your cousin Charles is handsome and clever, who loved you too – who would have brought light and laughter into your life and a sort of gaiety I could never aspire to. While he was free... But he has ruined himself, caught himself up with this gypsy friend of yours – and so.... He broke off. He said: "I have not understood your feeling for Charles: I did not know. At your birthday ball... You must forgive me, Christine – I loved you, I have always loved you, but I held back on his account, because I thought he would be the best man for you, because I could not think but that you must love him. And then, to see you repudiate his love – and in such a fashion! I had to go away, to think it all over; since then I have waited, not daring to rush in too soon...." He muttered and stumbled. All England had known since her earliest girlhood that The Lily was in love with that dull dog Frome;

but now he, ordinarily so calm and strong, stammered like a love-sick boy to beseech her hand. . . .

But it was not till almost a year later that Christine dared leave her friend in Italy and creep back to accept as a gift of forgiveness and trust, the love he had offered so humbly – before she threw in her lot with that of the infamous Sapphire of Starrbelow.

On the morning of August the second, 1754, a gentleman waited upon Prince Anton of Brunswick. He came as a friend of Charles, Baron Weyburn of Starrbelow. In a matter concerning the honour of his family, Lord Weyburn called upon Prince Anton to meet him in a duel with such weapons as His Highness selected: the duel to be to the death.

Prince Anton stood, ashy pale. "So he hass discovered?"

Lord Pearsham stifled his curiosity. "You do not deny the imputation?"

"The imputation iss against the lady; but she was deceived, she is guiltless. The challenge is to me, and it is just. I will meet Lord Weyburn – with pistols – at such a place as he appoints." He said: "Is this

213

usual in England to add in a challenge, 'to the death'?"

"His lordship is prepared to leave England, to fight in Belgium or France."

"Very well. It iss just. He hass been greatly wronged. I will arrange for seconds," said Anton, wearily. But he caught at the man's sleeve. "My lord – you and I in the past haf been good enough friends. Iss it possible for me even for five minutes to see – to see Lady Weyburn before I fight?"

"To see Lady Weyburn! Good God, man, you must be mad! To see Lady Weyburn – before going out to fight with her husband...!" He turned on his heel. "My friend will brook no delay; how soon will you meet him?"

They met at dawn thirty-six hours later, on the bare sandhills of the Belgian coast, having left London secretly and in haste, before that morning was out. Lord Weyburn, twice wounded, still cried out, 'To the death!" and reloaded yet again, forcing back his seconds and the Prince's at pistol point. "Stand where you are – and fire!" This time he waited until the Prince – at close range – had fired; and missed. He said: "Now I have you!" and levelled his

214

pistol. "You have witnesses," he said to Lord Pearsham, quietly wiping the weapon as the rest rushed over to the fallen man, "that you all did what you could to prevent me; that I forced you off with threats to our lives; that I stood unprotected and let him take aim at me: that only then I killed him." And he walked over to the frantically working group and said coolly: "Is he dead?"

All about them, the coarse grey sand, thrust through with raggety tufts of coarse grey grass; in their ears, the mutter of the cold grey sea, splashing in monotonously along the endless cold grey line of the coast. In the sand where he had fallen, the body of a young man, who once had been handsome and tall, lying oddly angled, the head against a crook'd right arm: grey face grown rigid, grey eyes closing, grey lips muttering, monotonous as the waves on the shore. "What does he say?" said Weyburn, standing, gun in hand, blood oozing through his waistcoat and left sleeve.

"Listen for yourself," said Sir Adam Bodkin, getting up to make way for him, brushing sand from his knees; slipping something into his pocket as he stood aside.

Charles Weyburn knelt down by the

dying man. He caught the first syllables, the word, 'Lady...' and 'tell' and again what seemed to be, "Lady day." "He asked to see Lady Weyburn before he met you," muttered Lord Pearsham into his ear. "I refused of course."

"He did not see her?" said Lord Weyburn quickly.

"No, no: we were all out of town before a chance arose. But – he is dying, my lord – some message...?"

"You may take any message he can give you now," said Charles Weyburn, grimly. "He is gone." He stood up and threw down his pistol to lie by the dead body. "There is my weapon: let all the world know it is mine." He bowed to them. "I thank you all. I hope there is no trouble in this for you – remember that I shot him against your intervention, he and I by arrangement carried extra loadings, you knew nothing about it. For my part, a carriage is waiting – you will not see me again, I suppose, for a long time." He bowed to them all. He said to Lord Pearsham, not troubling to lower his voice: "You may tell Lady Weyburn that he died with her name on his lips," and turned and walked away from them, limping from the wound in his side, hugging his bleeding arm close to his breast. "To the hospital," he said in French to the driver of the fiacre, awaiting him, "and drive fast." He added: "You will recall that you found me by the roadside, wounded and bleeding, neither of us knowing how I came there; and, even if in the past half-hour you have heard it, that you do not know my name. Until I can leave the hospital, nobody must know who I am. I look to your promise." With his good arm, he clinked gold pieces in his pocket; the man assisted him into the carriage, and he looked out for the last time across the cold wastes of the water, towards the dim, half-seen, unseen, outline of the white cliffs of home.

Lady Weyburn had been back many years at Starrbelow, the child Nicholas was a sturdy boy – before Charles Weyburn saw those white cliffs again.

BOOK TWO

BOOK TWO

Ten

They stand one on either side of the rosewood spinet – two children, in the great ballroom at Starrbelow where, ten years ago, Lord Weyburn stood also, and watched the crimson curtain lift and Sophia Devigne come through. Two children – Nicholas, who up to this day at least has been known as Nicholas Weyburn; and Catherine, only child of the Earl and Countess of Frome. "Perhaps at this very moment the trial is ending! – or is ended already, Catherine . . . Is that not the sound of the wheels of a coach on the Camden road?"

"And then we shall know!"

"We know already," says the boy, stoutly. "My mother is innocent."

"That's not what the servants say, Nicholas. They say she was wanton and you born out of wedlock and not Lord Weyburn's son."

"They would not dare say it to me," he cries, fists clenched.

221

"Nor to me; but they whisper it among themselves. And such words! – 'wanton' and 'whore'...."

"You should break in upon them and bid them hold their vile tongues."

"Yet if it be true – why then you are nothing here, Nicholas; and I am my cousin's heir."

"What would you want with such an inheritance? – you whose father is Earl of Frome, ten times richer and greater than Baron Weyburn of Starrbelow."

"My father's estates will not come to me; since he has no son of his own, they must pass to his brother's line. Lord Weyburn, however, as you say," says Catherine loftily, apeing, poor little precocity, the housekeeper at Frome, "is but a mere baron and so his inheritance may go to his next of kin, male or female; and, my mother being dead, I am his next of kin. Besides, Nick, *you* want Starrbelow no more than I need it. You are no country squire and never will be. You had rather wander Italy with a fiddle tucked under your chin – you have told my mother as much a hundred times."

"Your mother understood me, Catherine. She alone could feel about music as I do, it was she who gave me my first violin, she said I should be a great master one of these days."

"Well, and now she is dead," says Catherine, bleakly, sharp-voiced, "and can say so no more."

"None loved her more than I, or will miss her more."

"And yet," says the child, "it was your mother who murdered her." But she relaxes immediately against his shoulder, throws her arms about his neck, hides her sweet face, grown childish and soft again, against his cheek. "Oh, Nicholas, my little cousin Nicholas, forgive me! – I am a vile wretch to repeat what they say, to speak so of your mother who would never have harmed a hair of my mother's head: your beautiful mother whom you love – and whom I love also, Nick, even though she would cheat me of my birthright. . . ."

"It is not your birthright," he says, pushing her away.

"And I say it is."

"To say it is to call my mother a wanton."

"Well, and so the world does call her a wanton; and whore and cheat and murderess to boot, my mother's murderess, my father believes it too. . . ."

And the sound of wheels is heard and the distant clang as the great, gilded wrought-iron gates are flung open and the coach comes through.

It was the Duchess of Witham, of course, who was originally responsible for the travesty of Sapphire Weyburn's 'trial by society' – the trial, to bring it down to its simplest issue, to establish whether, as Lord Weyburn claimed, his wife in fact remained his wife in nothing but name; or whether, as she swore, the marriage was finally consummated and the result of that consummation Nicholas, her son. The Wit was by this time in her middle age – a terrible old jade with her hard, bright, high-coloured face and her hard, high hooting voice; powerful in wealth and position, uninhibited in speech and conduct, armoured in vanity. She encountered him one day, in the spring of 1764, riding through the park. It was ten years since his marriage. Lady Weyburn had for the first weeks after her desertion remained quietly at Starrbelow; had then burst upon the world in an orgy of frivolity and much worse, and had then disappeared from the scene, going off to her mother in Italy – returning a year or two later with a

son who – tacitly at any rate, though she was
known to have made no overt claim for him
– was accepted as Weyburn's; his lordship
being elsewhere and unable to comment.
Since then she had remained in almost total
seclusion at Starrbelow, close neighbour
and once again close friend of the Countess
of Frome – whose husband, however,
refused her his countenance; visiting with
the Countess now and again in London but
otherwise never leaving home. Lord
Weyburn, for good and sufficient reasons
as all the world knew, had gone abroad and
stayed there; yet now was to be seen
cantering coolly through the park in the
thin, spring sunshine, as though he were
not still the most-gossiped-about man in
town. . . . "By all the saints! – 'tis Charles
Weyburn! Stop! Stop the carriage! Lord
Weyburn – Weyburn, come over here. . . ."

Only direct ill-manners could refuse
such a summons. He rode over reluctantly
and dismounted, standing with one hand
on the door of the painted carriage with its
enormous emblazonment of arms, his
expression saying clearly that it must be
done sometime and might as well be now.
"It's a thousand years since we saw you,
Weyburn. You look – older." She stared

at him appraisingly, avid for signs of awkwardness or strain. "It must be eight years since you left England – no, more, nine or ten. Let me see, that affair of poor Anton of Brunswick was in the Spring of '54 – no, that was the marriage, the end of May: the duel was in August, I remember...."

"Your Grace has an excellent head for dates," he said coldly.

"When the events are worth the recollection, no doubt I have. Why have you stayed so long?"

"I have been travelling," said Weyburn briefly.

"Oh, aye, travelling, we know all about that! Between the dressing-room of Madame Chose at the Paris Opera House and her dressing-room at home? – except for similar excursions at La Scala in Milan, and was there not also some little soprano in Lisbon, or was it Seville...?"

"I have been in both Spain and Portugal, certainly," he said, bowing, "but your ladyship exaggerates my devotion to music."

"Well, well, there was news of an interest in Terpsichore also." She rapped him archly over the knuckles with her closed fan and he removed his hand from the painted door and gathered up the reins on the arched neck of his splendid chestnut. "Come now, my lord, not so hasty! You did not suppose the world ignorant of the alleviations of your banishment?"

The ladies in the carriage exchanged naughty glances, the young men lounging about them nudged one another, concealing their grins behind their huge fur muffs. Lord Weyburn said sharply: "Banishment, Madame?"

"England has hardly been – comfortable – to you these past ten years."

"England is never comfortable to a man who has killed another in a duel."

"Oh, aye, that business; but a year or two would have served for that, even considering the fuss from Hanover. I spoke of a voluntary banishment. Why have you come back to England now?"

"I have been back several times, as it happens – without your ladyship's permission."

"Have you now? I'd no idea of it," said the Duchess, blandly. She thought it over. "To consult with your lawyers, I daresay: even a small estate like yours can't be left to look after itself. And to see your –

family?" She might ignore the shaft but it had not passed unobserved and now she paid it back in good measure. She said casually: "No doubt you are aware that your lady is at present in town?"

He stood very still for a moment, collecting himself: his handsome head steady, his pale, handsome features controlled to give no sign of the tiny cold shock the news had given him. But his tongue would not be guarded. He said sharply: "Lady Weyburn is at Starrbelow. My lawyers...."

"She came up yesterday with the Countess of Frome. You remember the Countess? – the Lily of Lillane they used to call her. Oh, but of course, she is your cousin, is she not? And was once your – particular friend?" He bowed, in silence. "Curious that she should nowadays be Lady Weyburn's particular friend."

"Anyone is fortunate," he said, coldly, "who has such a friend."

"And Lady Weyburn more than most."

"How do you mean?" he said, sharply.

"Why, that the Countess is – if a trifle dull – respectable; and Lady Weyburn therefore fortunate in her friendship."

His face was very pale, his knuckles

whitened, gathering the reins anew on his horse's neck. "Your Grace has not lost sight of the fact that she is speaking of my wife?"

Her Grace tossed her plumed head, winking round upon the small, shrinking group of her sycophants. "Why, even as to that, my lord – can you be sure?"

"I do not understand you, Madame?"

"It is perfectly clear. I say, simply – can you be sure that she is truly Lady Weyburn?"

"I can be sure at least that I married her – and having done so, if your Grace will pardon me, prefer not to discuss the matter."

"Hoity toity!" said the Duchess, laughing. She eyed him shrewdly. "It would never astonish me, my dear Weyburn, to learn you were a little in love with her yourself." He had thrust his foot into the stirrup, thrown his leg over the saddle and was starting away when she shrieked out after him: "Have a care, my lord, be not too soft or you'll find yourself saddled with a wife after all, and her bastard boy as your heir!"

All about them the sky was softly blue above the spare trees, the crocuses thrust coloured spears through the green satin of young grass; the Macaronis in their silks and velvets lost colour a little behind ringed white hands at her ladyship's daring, the attendant women in the ducal carriage exchanged scared glances; were, perhaps a little ashamed. And above the chuff-chuff of horses' hooves upon the soft ground, the rattle and jingle of harness, the cries of a coachman reining in his beasts to a peremptory order, a voice called, cool and clear: "Good day, Your Grace. Were you speaking of me? And of my son?"

His first thought was that she was more beautiful, by far, than he had ever remembered her – and God knows, he had remembered her with every waking hour and rebelled at the memory and, in the arms of this woman or that, had crushed the memory out of mind. Slender and upright, she leaned forward a little, her body, straight as an arrow, counterpoised against the lovely curve of the open carriage, emblazoned and gilded, in which she sat. Her hair was built, a la môde, into a high, moulded coiffure of her own, unpowdered gold, her skin was ivory against the clear, bold colour of her cloak and dress; as always the only touch of blue about her was in the hidden brilliance of her eyes. Against her warm glow, the dazzling whiteness and china blue of the Countess of Frome, sitting in the carriage at her side, was like ice against fire; but now as ever, ice upon fire, the small, secret, scornful, sorrowful smile flew its flag of defiance to himself and all the world: guarding against all comers, cruel or kind, the once vulnerable heart. . . .

The Duchess swung round in a flutter of ribbons and feathers, for a moment discomposed. "Why, 'tis you, Madame? Who would have thought . . . ?" But she collected herself. "Well, well – so you and your husband meet again!"

"Oh, is that who is it?" said Sapphire, apparently for the first time raising her eyes to the gentleman who sat so taut and motionless on the great chestnut horse. "Why so it is!" She gave him a cool little bow. "Good day, my lord; an unexpected pleasure. I had no idea you were in town." She added, before he could do more than bow formally to herself and to his cousin Christine in the carriage beside her, "You have returned perhaps for a public discussion with her Grace of Witham, of myself and Nicholas?"

He would have ridden off upon his bow,

but he reined in his horse to say, resentfully: "I have not mentioned your name Madame – but to defend it."

She raised her dark eyebrows. "You waste your time, sir. You have been too long out of England to know what is and is not indefensible. I am a law unto myself, the name of Sapphire Devigne need be no concern of yours."

"The name of Sophia Weyburn, however, is very much a concern of mine," he said, coldly. "I shall continue to defend it – within limits, Madame – while you remain my wife."

"And her son, your heir?" suggested the Duchess, spitefully.

He said nothing. Across the tossing feathers and fur in the intervening carriage, Sapphire said deliberately: What do you say to that, my lord – if you will 'continue to defend me'?"

" 'Within limits," quoted the Duchess. "The limits have been reached, you see, Madame – very early."

Sapphire laughed. "For God's sake, Sophia," said Christine, urgently whispering, "let us drive on and end this horrible scene. . . ."

But two or three riders had joined the little group, a coach had drawn up and a couple of bucks jumped down to see what mischief the Wit was meddling with now, a gig unable to pass had perforce stopped and its occupants looked down, grinning from a place in the gallery. The Frome coachman struggled in vain to release his team, looking back apologetically from his high seat. "Impossible to proceed, my lady: I have sent a man forward to try to clear the way...." Sapphire said, still laughing: "Aye, her Grace has you on the hip, my lord, your defences are vulnerable indeed! The first thrust and they fall. I had best rely, as ever, upon myself."

He did not answer; he also was hemmed in by the curious and could not immediately force a way out. "And what reliance, Madame, do you place upon yourself?" said the Duchess, flirting her great fan, ogling her sycophants, inviting admiration for her boldness. "Will *you* defend the throwing away your inheritance on the son

"Lady Weyburn will not reply to such a question," said Charles Weyburn, angrily, shouting it out now over the heads of the gathering, curious crowd of fashionables, tittering about the two carriages, some pleased, some scandalised, all agog for gossip; and he called out peremptorily to his cousin to order her carriage to drive on, to put an end to such a scene. She called back to him, helplessly, she was powerless, she was doing her best; and the Duchess, delighted, cried out in her strident voice that since neither would deny it, they must assume Lady Weyburn publicly acknowledged by herself and her husband to be – a whore.

Lord Weyburn sat for a moment, graven to stone. A silence had fallen, upon the ugly word; and he dismounted again from his horse and in the silence went to the carriage and stood by it, with one hand upon the painted door as he had before. "Madame, I take leave to tell you that I permit nobody in my presence to use such a word of Lady Weyburn."

"I? It is you who, by implication, use it of her, my lord." And she looked about her insolently, triumphantly. "For my part, I believe the lady to be honestly married and her child legitimate."

He bowed stiffly. He said grimly: "Whatever is your belief, Madame, I must refuse now, once and for all, to discuss my family affairs."

"Then you are the only man in England who does not," said the Duchess. "And for want of discussing them, are in danger of throwing away your inheritance on the son of Lord knows who.... And if you reply," she said quickly, "that this is no business of mine, then I say that it is: of mine and of all of us here. For we represent your world, my lord; and why should your world be saddled with this brat of Anton of Brunswick? – or of some other, for all I know; of Greenewode, Pardo Ryan, Lord Franks, or any other of the profligates about town because, forsooth, you are too proud to 'discuss your family affairs'! Though how in God's name," screamed the Duchess, looking once more triumphantly about her, "they can be called your family affairs when the boy is not your son and the woman in all probability not your wife...." And she rapped him with the great fan again and screeched out that the truth was that he was infatuated with the woman and wished the boy *were* his own – and that, indeed, for all they knew, so he well might be; but not legitimately so.

The coachman had succeeded in freeing a passage for his horses; Christine, more

235

white faced than ever, motioned him on. But Sapphire stayed him; and now she, herself, had lost colour, there was snow upon the ivory. The forward movement of the carriage had brought her more directly opposite the Duchess, Lord Weyburn stood only the width of the ducal equippage away from her; it was no longer necessary to raise her voice. She said: "One moment, Duchess. Of my son's claims to the Starrbelow inheritance I say nothing, I never have said anything; but you have now twice in my presence suggested that I am not entitled to call myself Lord Weyburn's wife." And she spoke across the high-coloured face with the bright malicious eyes and the beak of a nose, and said directly to Lord Weyburn, standing white-faced, grim and helpless on the other side of the carriage: "Do you deny my true marriage to you, my Lord?" She added, before he could answer: "Speak out now, if you please; since this enquiry has begun in public, it had better be concluded there," and brushed away Christine's pleading hand tugging at her sleeve.

Charles Weyburn waited quietly till she had finished. He said: "I have not questioned, now or ever, the legitimacy

236

of my marriage to you. I neither know nor care to know, what the Duchess refers to."

"I refer to a gentleman now dead," said the Duchess. "And by your lordship's hand."

"Do you mean Prince Anton of Brunswick?" said Sapphire, incredulous.

"Who is known to have conducted a 'mock marriage' at the Fleet with the lady whom Lord Weyburn so confidently refers to as his wife."

The last colour drained from her face, the faint traces of rouge now stood out like a clown's paint under the startled flash of her eyes, no longer guarded by discreetly lowered lids. But Charles Weyburn had, in his turn, relaxed, shrugging contemptuously. "There was some escapade – at a time when for a season, I understand, Lady Weyburn was famous for her escapades."

"Shall we say, rather, was notorious?" He bowed. "Your Grace, I believe, speaks with some special feeling in the matter," and he watched with satisfaction while the slack muscles tautened round the unkind mouth, while angry recollection flooded her eye: one of Sapphire's 'escapades' had most nearly concerned the dignity of her Grace of Witham. "Come, Madame – these events took place after my marriage, they in no way affect its legitimacy."

"Yet you later challenged Prince Anton to a duel – on grounds which he did not deny."

"These grounds, however, in no way concerned the escapades, nor, therefore, my marriage."

"Nor the legitimacy of your son?"

He looked across at Sapphire. Very pale, very taut, she speechlessly bowed her head in some motion, understood without words between them, of consent. He said: "Lady Weyburn has never – in so many words, at any rate – claimed my name, let alone my inheritance, for her son." He added deliberately: "Nor do I acknowledge the boy. For the rest, I repeat, and you, your Grace, have just declared your own belief, that she is an honestly married woman –"

"Honestly married, oh, aye," said her Grace of Witham. "But to another man."

There was a man standing, gaping, with the rest of that small crowd of the lords and ladies: a heavy, flabby man with small porcine eyes in a large porcine face. The

Duchess hailed him, over the nodding heads. "Hey, Sir Adam Bodkin, come forward, come over here!" As he shoved his way forward to the carriage, she poked out her fan at him, detaining Lord Weyburn with a hand on his sleeve, to hear further what he would say. "Sir Adam – were you not Prince Anton's second, when he fell with his lordship? Was it not you?"

"I was, your Grace, yes; and was obliged," said Sir Adam, resentfully, "to leave London myself, for a twelvemonth. The fuss over from Hanover...."

"Yes, yes, we know all about that, and about your sufferings; we have had ample reminder in the past ten years. But – of the event itself, Sir Adam – now what was it," said the Duchess, craftily, "that the Prince gave into your keeping, that day as he died?"

Sir Adam looked sullenly down at his fat hands. "He gave me a ring, as I think your Grace well knows."

"*I* know it, yes; but does Lord Weyburn know it? Come, Sir Adam – a ring? A plain gold ring from his finger – what sort of a ring?"

Sir Adam shrugged. "It looked like a wedding ring."

"It looked like a wedding ring. With an inscription inside, I believe – a date?"

"March the twenty-fifth," said Sir Adam. "March the twenty-fifth, 1754."

"March the twenty-fifth," repeated her ladyship, gleefully. "Ladyday, 1754. Prince Anton, dying, left the ring and a message, Sir Adam, was it not so? And the message?"

"Your Ladyship knows the message, if it was a message. He gave me the ring, as he died; he kept muttering, 'Ladyday! Ladyday!' as though it were a message with the ring."

"So." She looked round her, at the avid faces of her listeners, at the set white face bent over the clenched hand on her carriage door, at the ivory face with pink petals of rouge on an overlay of snow. She said, with malicious triumph: "So Prince Anton of Brunswick wears a wedding ring with the date, March the twenty-fifth, 1754. And in May of that year, 'Lady Weyburn' goes through a ceremony of marriage with his lordship. And in July of that year, 'Lady Weyburn' and Prince Anton are concerned in an 'escapade' during which some pages are removed from the registry of a chapel in the Fleet. And in August of that year,

Prince Anton, dying, leaves the wedding ring with its date inscribed and a message, a murmuring over and over of that date. . . . To whom, Sir Adam?" He did not reply and she raised her voice: "To whom, Sir Adam, did he leave the message and the ring?"

"To Lady Weyburn," said Sir Adam, still sulkily.

Aloft on their perches, the coachmen sat in their magnificent trappings, all ears; the footmen at the horses' heads craned their necks the better to hear and see the spittings and snarlings of their betters, saving up every scrap of gossip for retailment, richly embellished, in the servants' halls; only the proud horses arched their glossy necks, indifferent to human spite and folly, and the little dogs whined in their mistresses' muffs, and scuffled, unheeded, for release. Charles Weyburn said, looking into a bleached white face: "Is this true?"

"If it were," said Sapphire, speaking very stiffly, as though with pain, "it need not affect you, my Lord. On March the twenty-fifth, 1754 – on Ladyday – the Fleet marriages became illegal. So, anyway. . . ."

"*From* March the twenty-fifth, 1754,"

said the Duchess. "They were still legal on that day."

"Still legal?" She looked at her, absolutely ashen, with trembling lips. "You mean that on Ladyday...? On that Ladyday...? Her voice faltered away, she put up her hand to her forehead, swaying as she sat. "Sophia," implored Christine, white-lipped also, at her side, "for God's sake end this, for God's sake let us come away...."

But the coachman now as conveniently deaf to half-whispered orders croaked out from a dry throat; and a cold voice said, insistently: "I ask you again, Madame: is this true?"

No veiled lids now: she stared back at him, oblivious of the intervening carriage, with great, blue, terror-filled eyes, that for a moment you might have thought were a young girl's eyes, an inexperienced, young girl's eyes, in simple trusting anguish, imploring him. "You don't believe it? You don't believe it, you can't...?"

"For the third and last time," he said, "I ask you – is it true?"

His face was as cold as death and she moved her eyes from it, looking down, silent, for a long time at her hands, now lying quietly in her lap. But she raised her head at last and looked at him once again, quietly and steadfastly, and said: "No."

He looked up, startled. "You say that it is not true?"

"No," she said. "It is not true."

"None of it is true?"

"None that need concern *you.*"

"There was no marriage at the Fleet?"

"There was – an 'escapade'; but it was after my marriage to you."

"Then your marriage to me –?"

"Was legal. I am your wife."

"And Prince Anton of Brunswick –?"

"Was neither my husband nor my lover, my lord."

"I see." He was silent for a while, then he raised his head and looked her in the eyes. "I do not believe you," he said.

"You do not believe me?" She stared at him, utterly incredulous. "You do not believe me?"

"I do not believe you. You have lied to me, to my absolute knowledge, in one particular – why not in all?"

"Why not, indeed," cried the Duchess, eagerly – eagerly thrusting in on them. For a moment she had glimpsed that young-girl look and feared it might weaken him. She gave her high hoot of laughter. "Next she will be claiming that the boy is your heir. Why not?"

"Why not?" She had straightened herself up again in the carriage, had fallen again into her own lovely, studied, studiously un-studied pose, she raised her head, her eyes flashed once again their old, scornful blue. "As her Grace of Witham says – who sits like God in judgement upon us here – 'why not?' You ask me for the truth, my lord, here before all these people you ask me for the truth: and then you tell me you do not believe me, you tell me what I say is lies.... Very well, then, let us add another lie to the lies: I have never to this moment claimed one flicker of recognition from you for my son – but now here before all these people whom you have permitted to sit in judgement upon me and my – lies – to declare him, I declare him upon my most solemn oath, to be your heir." She shrugged. "As the Duchess says – why not?"

"Sophia!" entreated Christine, frantic. "Come away! How can you say these things? – for God's sake let us go...."

"Nonsense, be quiet, I know what I'm doing, Christine."

244

"But it's wrong, it isn't fair; Sophia, if you persist . . . ."

"Be quiet," said Sapphire; she caught the slender wrist in her own small, strong hand, forcing it down as though it were Christine's will that her own strong will forced into acquiescence; and called out, coolly: "I do not hear you repudiate the claim, my lord?"

"His Lordship is speechless at its audacity," said the Duchess.

"He has, however, a ready mouthpiece in your Grace."

"I need no mouthpiece," said Lord Weyburn, steadily, "to utterly repudiate the claim."

"Upon what grounds?" The blue eyes flashed on him now, afire with malicious fun. "Upon what grounds, my lord?"

"The grounds are obvious enough," said The Duchess. "Half the world can testify that he swore he would marry you yet never hold you in his arms; the other half, that he left you at the door of the church and has not seen you since."

Sapphire laughed outright. "Ah – that's all your ladyship knows!"

She swung round, startled. "Does this mean, my lord –?"

"It means nothing. If she is my wife, it is in name only: the boy is not my son." He repeated it aloud, steadily and slowly. "My private affairs are my concern and mine only. But I agree that my title and estate are a part of society and that if I claim my place in society, I must abide by its laws. I repeat, therefore, and I will do so whenever such a claim is made: if she is my wife, she is my wife in name only – her son is not my son."

("Sophia, you know it is true, come, leave it... Sophia, I shall tell my cousin, if you persist....")

"Be quiet, Christine: if you speak now, I will kill you! You don't understand, I'll explain. I'll explain later on....")

Sapphire stood up suddenly in the carriage, steadying herself with one hand on the curving, enamelled rim of the door. She stood looking down at him over the heads of the people, over the painted carriage between them with its flutter of ribbons and plumes; and he looked back at her with cold grey eyes. "Very well, my lord: then this is war between us. So let it be. I have asked nothing of you, all these years, but the name you thrust upon me when you wagered over me like a stable groom over his horse or his dog. I have taken nothing from you but the means to support such a name – since I bore it – as I should. But now you would trick me out of the name, as you tricked me into it – you and this whole yelling, belling pack you hunt with; and this time I'll not be tricked, this time you've a quarry to deal with grown wise in your ways, not the poor young hunted thing that once I was, alone at the mercy of your hearts of petrified stone.... This time I'll fight you back, my lord." She eyed him steadily. "Do you tell these people here that since our marriage day you have not seen me? – have not been alone with me?"

"Upon one occasion," he said, "I was alone with you."

"Two months after our marriage: on August the first, to be precise – when we were alone together for some hours?"

"I had an interview with you that evening, yes; at my London house."

"And during that interview – repented the vow you made?"

"Only such part of it," he said, coldly, "as had made you – in name – my wife."

"You did not upon that occasion take me in your arms?"

"I did not upon that occasion, Madame,

to make an end of this – consummate my marriage with you; and since there has been no other occasion, your son cannot be my son and is not my heir."

"Very well," said Sapphire. "Then we know where we stand. For I say that upon that occasion the marriage *was* consummated; and that I am your wife and Nicholas, my son, is your son – and is your heir." And she gave him a smile of devilish brilliance over the heads of the people and said, sweetly: "And you may go to law about it, my lord, and you'll find that the law of England is this: that a man may not seek to prove the illegitimacy of a child born to his own wife. So lie for lie – and one of us is lying – lie for lie, my lord, I win!" And she bowed to him, smiling her own derisive smile again, bowed to the Duchess and the ladies and the gentlemen, her white hand pink-tipped as a lilly with the pressure upon the supporting rim of the door; and sat down composedly and settled her dress to her satisfaction and felt for the safety of an earring and returned her hands to the cosy comfort of her small fur muff; and called to the coachman in accents that this time brooked no misunderstanding or delay: "Drive on!"

But Charles Weyburn already was riding furiously across the green grass, scattering the Sunday morning parties of strollers in a thunder of unconsidering polished hooves: not having waited to see the carriage go.

And two months later in the Sapphire Gallery of Witham House, the 'court' convened: that court that was no legal court, to try by a law that was no law of England or anything but the law of the narrow society in which they lived, the issue between Sophia, daughter of James Devigne, resident in Venice; and Charles, Baron Weyburn of Starrbelow.... The Trial-by-Society of Sophia, née Devigne, whom men called Sapphire and Sapphire-of-Starrbelow, and sometimes Starr-Sapphire: but could no longer safely call Lady Weyburn. To settle the burning question of the day: on that night of August 1st, 1754 – yes – or no?

Eleven

The trial of Sophia Weyburn was held in
the Blue gallery of Witham House as has
been said; and, as has been said, it had need
to be the largest room in town, for, God
knows, everyone in town was there.

His Grace the Duke of Orrell on the
bench – an old man, learned in the law, who
might have had more sense, you'd think,
than to lend himself to such a travesty of
law as this. For the prosecution, Sir Henry
Kidd, smarting still from the injuries of
those other days. In the jury-box, twelve
good men and true, recruited from the
London streets, scrubbed, clad,
entertained, promised reimbursement at
the end, if they would without bias listen
and pronounce a verdict – it would add a
fillip of excitement, it was felt, to have at
least some element of doubt as to what that
verdict would be. As witnesses – half the
social world, agog to give evidence of those
far-off, half-remembered, oft talked-over
days. For the defence . . . .

For the defence – only the accused herself: Starr Sapphire, Lady Weyburn of Starrbelow, age something under thirty, hair gold, eyes blue, skin smooth and creamy coloured as a pullet's egg, form slender, supple, disciplined to mannered grace: dressed proudly in formal magnificence, wearing the splendid jewels of her husband's house, no longer a frightened, friendless girl but a woman, cool, disdainful, faintly amused; undaunted and unafraid. She stood at one end of the long, pale, pinky-brown mahogany table shimmering with its high polish beneath the famous chandeliers. At the other end of the table, Lord Weyburn, not looking towards her; in mourning for his cousin Christine's death eight weeks ago. All round the great room, chairs banked in built-up rows almost to the ceiling; seated on his dais before the high, carved, marble mantlepiece, the Judge. . . .

He looks like an old sheep, thought Sapphire.

Footman-ushers hushed the court to silence. The Duke opened a great book lying flat on the table before him, peered at it vaguely, dived into a pocket for his snuff-box, took snuff, closed the box with a snap; and as though the snap had broken a string of silence held taut within him, began to speak. "My lord, ladies, gentlemen of the jury . . . .

"My lord, ladies and gentleman, we are assisting today at perhaps the most extraordinary trial ever to have taken place: a trial of course, without legal significance, held not before His Majesty's legal judges and according to the laws of this country, but before judges set up by the social world in which we, all here present, live and move; and in accordance with the laws of that society. Failing any possibility of solution in our courts of law, the case now comes before us, assembled here – by common arrangement and with the consent and agreement of both parties. . . ."

Lady Weyburn, coming slowly to her feet, adjusting with a careful hand the great sweep of her dress, silencing the old sheep's bleating with the simple, cool nonchalance, the practised dignity of her arising. "With – respect – my lord Duke: in my case with neither agreement nor consent."

"Your ladyship's presence here presupposes consent."

"I am present, my lord, under protest.

I wish to state plainly at the outset that I regard this enquiry as nothing but a frivolous diversion for the entertainment of the gossip-mongers: and that I come here only in obedience – as I have ever been obedient – to my husband's commands."

"As to these charges, Madame . . . ."

"As to these charges, to make short work of it they are, I take it, four in number. First, that my marriage to Lord Weyburn was not consummated and that therefore I lie in saying that my son, Nicholas, is his lordship's heir: to this I reply that, upon one occasion only, the marriage *was* consummated and – and for this I will fight to my dying breath – the boy is Lord Weyburn's heir. Secondly, that after my marriage, I conducted myself wantonly, and my son is the child of any of half a dozen gentlemen then about town: that he was so fathered, I totally deny. Thirdly, and alternatively that before my so-called marriage to Lord Weyburn, I had been secretly married to another – to Prince Anton of Brunswick; and therefore my marriage to Lord Weyburn was null. This also I totally deny. And fourthly, that to prevent the truth of these matters from becoming known, I have now murdered the only person who might have inner knowledge and could give testimony against me here: namely, the Countess of Frome, my best and only friend." She was silent for a moment; silent, standing with bent head, in the greater silence of the great room where for a moment even the flutter of fans was still. When she spoke again, it was in a new voice with – false or true – a new sadness, where before only defiance had been; a new bitterness where there had been only a cool, half-humourous disdain. "As to this last charge, ladies and gentlemen – if any so dares call himself while he yet condescends to lend his presence to this vulgar travesty, this mockery of justice – as to this last charge, I say, it is so monstrous that I shall not trouble to deny it. The law of the land has considered preferring it against me and, from lack of proof, evidence – even, I dare say, enough suspicion – abandoned it. It is not for you, therefore, to revive it, and to it I shall make no answer. I shall not reply to any examination on this score. In such matters as affect Lord Weyburn's honour, I shall – under protest and at his command – be at your service; but I warn you in advance that I do not acknowledge your court, I shall not be bound by any verdict of yours. As to the death of my friend, I shall not answer: for the rest, my marriage to Lord Weyburn was valid, it was subsequently consummated: and the boy is his legitimate heir." She sat down, unsmiling, not triumphant; cool and quiet – and gave her whole attention to the arrangement of her dress, the disposition of her hands, the angle at which she held her fan. His grace turned a page in his great book and while the court broke its rapt silence, seethed, resettled, fell silent again eager anticipation, pretended to read. . . .

The Duke of Orrell.

"My lords, ladies and gentlemen – gentlemen of the jury: her ladyship has put before you most succinctly the charges against her and declared her repudiation of these charges: a duty more commonly devolving upon counsel, but we are not now in a legal court and need not follow legal court procedure. . . ." (No, indeed! – vain to have expected any witness to volunteer evidence if he had understood it would mean exclusion from all these excitements until his turn came: protocol had been abandoned therefore, the rules of evidence had been thrown to all the winds; and witnesses for and against the accused, now eagerly packed the front benches, listening, as no legal court of law would have permitted, to the testimony of those who came before them.) "And from what Lady Weyburn has said, gentlemen, one thing will be clear to you – that the main issue here to be tried, (and all others are subsidiary to it) is the legitimacy of the boy, Nicholas; and his right to inheritance of the barony and estates of the Weyburns of Starrbelow.

"Very well. Now, by the laws of England, gentlemen, it is impossible for a man to seek to prove by his own evidence, that a child born to his wife, in wedlock, is not his own child. His only resource is to look for other people to prove the illegitimacy for him...." His old sheep-face looked into the sheep-faces of the twelve stolid jurymen, sitting ill-at-ease on their double row of chairs, looking dumbly back at him. "Do you understand so far?"

The jurymen did not understand at all. There was muttering among them. "Wot *we* don't see, moi lord," said their leader, at last, "is 'ow any other man can prove a woife's a woife, better nor a man hisself."

His face broke into a broad grin and he spluttered into his hand. His colleagues grinned also, or according to temperament, eyed her ladyship, hung their heads and went very red.

The Duke looked down his long nose. "Let me try to make it clear. Suppose a man says that a child born to his wife cannot, for physical reasons be his own – the law is this, that *he* may not offer evidence himself to this effect. But if he can find someone to prove, for example, that he was absent for, say, five years, in the middle of which period the child was born – why, then, you see, that other man may prove *for* him that the child was not his. Or let a priest come forward to say that before the man took the wife to church, she was married already – why then, again, the priest proves the man's case for him. It is to try to discover such outside witnesses to the illegitimacy of the boy Nicholas, that Lord Weyburn has agreed to this enquiry, to which her ladyship holds such strong objection: not, of course, proposing to rely in law upon our verdict, but trusting to some fact coming to light in the course of the enquiry, upon which he may be able to go to law...." He paused and took snuff, eyeing them warily;

the jury dully eyed him back. He said: "Lord Weyburn?"

Lord Weyburn upon his feet: very proud and cold, not looking at her ladyship, not looking at anyone, fixing his eyes upon the great book, his voice kept resolutely clipped and unemotional. "I declare simply that, in accordance with the vow I publicly made before my marriage, Lady Weyburn remained my wife – if she was indeed my wife, and not already married – in name only: and therefore the boy is not my son and is not my heir. . . ."

Lord Greenwode sat with Sir Francis Erick and Red Reddington, his ankle, emaciated to the thickness of a broomhandle by the slow progress of the disease that long had racked him, crossed painfully on a boney, silk-clad knee. "Well, well, it seems that between us we have fathered a splendid boy." He said over his gaunt shoulder: "And you, my Lord Warne, are you not a fourth door to which this poor babe has been laid?"

"A fifth, if you count the German princeling; and Lord Franks would have made up six – with, perhaps, as some have thought, more pretentions than most of us.

'Tis true, her ladyship sported a pair of red buckles...."

"I disbelieve it utterly," said Pardo Ryan. "I deny it."

"Aye, yes, and you also, Sir Pardo. Were you not there when the aunt was robbed of her wig and complexion? – and now we stand all accused of robbing the piece of something more!"

"We should form a new society," said Francis Erick, laughing, "to succeed the old Circle, alas so short-lived: The Fathers of Nicholas – he is welcome, God knows, to any inheritance of mine." He nudged his nextdoor neighbour in the ribs. "Eh, Red? You're rich: you've no brat of your own to endow."

Squire Reddington lounged with his chin on his breast, his short legs out-thrust before him. He opened one glazed eye, glanced sleepily at the straight back of Lady Weyburn, sitting composed and upright in the tall chair ahead of him, and closed it again. "Let him sleep," said Francis Erick. "He's drunk."

"I am stone cold sober," said Reddington, his eyes still closed, "and with my two bare hands I'll twist off the head of any man who says otherwise."

259

"You – are – drunk," said Sir Pardo, promptly, winking at the others, whispering loudly and clearly into his ear.

"So I am," said Red Reddington affably; and went back to sleep.

Lord Weyburn on his feet, cold and quiet, Sir Henry Kidd on his feet, nervously shifting. "My lord – in December of the year 1753, you made a wager that you would marry this lady, then Miss Sophia Devigne; and at the same time publicly declared you would make her your wife in name alone?"

"I did: and I now call upon Her Grace of Witham to represent at least two hundred people present, who heard my vow."

Her Grace of Witham, decked out like a cockatoo, triumphantly on her feet. "Perfectly true: I can testify, all can testify...."

Sapphire heard her out to the end. She rose. "I was at that time, Madame, aged not quite eighteen?"

The Duchess looked at her blankly. "Why, seventeen? – yes, I daresay you were."

"And you heard this wager offered and taken, and this vow made?"

"Certainly," said the Duchess, delighted. "Everyone heard it."

"And you let it go forward?" She bowed to her, softly smiling. "Thank you, your Grace; that is all." She sat down again.

Sir Henry also had heard the wager made and allowed it to go forward as indeed had they all. He continued a trifle hurriedly. "One week later, my lord, you proposed marriage?"

"Yes."

"And were accepted?"

Lord Weyburn permitted himself a small, cold smile, as contemptuous as any of Sapphire's own. "As to that – I had been accepted before ever the proposal was made: before even the wager was made – it having been made by the lady's accomplice, knowing full well it was she who would enter the room."

Lady Weyburn sat quietly on her high-backed chair, but her hands had tightened their grip on the ivory fan. "I had no accomplice: I knew nothing of the wager. How could I? Who could know in advance that you would utter such a declaration?"

"But as soon as the wager was made, of course you knew of it."

"I utterly deny it," said Sapphire, steadily.

"Very well." Charles Weyburn turned sharply and looked at her for the first time, fully, since they had both entered that courtroom. He said: "Then may I ask you this, Madame – why did you marry me?"

She opened her blue eyes full upon him and as directly looked back at him. "You asked me this question once before, my lord – on the night of August the first, ten years ago."

"This time," he said, with a face grown suddenly cold and white as stone, "let us have the true answer."

She smiled, half ruefully, she gave a little shrug. "Why, sir, I married you – because you asked me."

"May I remind you of the words in which I asked you?"

"You need not," said Sapphire. "I remember them."

"Perhaps you will not object to repeat those words to the court?"

"Oh, certainly," said Sapphire. "Since *you* do not, why should *I* regard them as any way private. You called me, as I recall a – a salted apricot." She paused to allow the audience the inevitable titter, taunting him with the deliberate belittling of that moment of tenderness. "I said that I should return to Venice. You said... You said: 'Let there not, at least, be any pretence between us two.' You said that I knew I could not return to Venice, for I knew I must remain at Starrbelow as your wife." She gave the little shrug again. "What you meant is clear enough now – that I had all along intended to become your wife, but since I was innocent of such intention...."

He cut across her sentence. "I further remarked, did I not? that I must be one of the very few men who actually had known at the moment he first saw her, that a woman was to be his wife."

"So you did, my lord."

"What other interpretation could there be to that – but that it was a reference to your entry into the ballroom when the wager had been made?"

"Why as to that – there *have* been men, my lord, who have looked upon a woman and, quite simply, loved her from the first: but I was yet to learn, poor silly child, that such naivetés as these are not for the fashionable world."

"You thought I had been struck in an

instant," he said, with a cruel mock bow, "by Cupid's dart?"

"A poisoned dart indeed it has turned out to be," said Sapphire, bitterly.

"It came from a poisoned source, Madame as you very well knew. For it came from Prince Anton of Brunswick, your vile accomplice and as I now believe your faithless lover...."

"Who, however, is dead, sir," said Sapphire, "and at your hand – so that I think you may spare him your epithets." She cut short the exchange, turning her head gracefully towards Sir Henry. "If you please, sir...?"

"Having engaged yourself to Lord Weyburn, Madame, you went almost immediately to Italy?"

"My father was ill."

"... And were absent almost all the time between the day of betrothal and that fixed for the wedding: so that there was no opportunity for Lord Weyburn to endeavour to release himself from the consequences of the bet?"

"Or for me to recognise," said Sapphire, "that it had been made; that all was not well." And she said almost piteously, shrunk back for a moment to that

264

tormented young creature of ten long, bitterly experienced years ago: "But when he was cold and – and undemonstrative, I thought it but the manners of a world I did not know."

"At any rate, on May 27th, 1754, you married him: or went through an invalid ceremony of marriage – we will come to that later. And immediately after the ceremony, Lord Weyburn left you, after handing you a note with the words. . . ."

"You need not remind me of the words, Sir Henry: I remember them well enough," said Sapphire: and the melancholy fell away from her, she said with a flash of her own old irony that the court appeared to credit her with but a poor memory for the major events of her life. "The note empowered me to collect the sum of a thousand guineas owing to Lord Weyburn from my 'accomplice.'"

"Precisely. May I ask you now, my lady – if you were so innocent – what did you think of that note?"

She looked back at him sadly: "Ah, innocence! – why, yes, Sir Henry. I think we may say that innocence was ended then."

He stared at her, electrified. He said

sharply: "Innocence was ended, Madame?"

"If by innocence we mean ignorance: ignorance of the cruelties of the world. For it was then that I enquired, it was then it was explained – the trick that had been played upon me: it was then, indeed, that I understood that a trick had been played upon Lord Weyburn also."

"And what did you then do?"

"I wrote to his lordship in the care of his lawyers: I told him that both I and he had been tricked." She sat with bent head, the hands holding the white fan, quiet in her lap and lived again the pain of those days when she had awaited, first eagerly confident, at last with diminishing hope dwindling to an agony of despair and disillusion, his return to her. She said quietly: "He did not reply."

Sir Francis nudged Squire Reddington in the ribs. "Here, Red, wake up! We're coming to our part in the mischief."

Reddington sat up, rubbing blearily sleepy eyes. "What? What? Where's the rest then? Where's Pardo?"

"Here at your side, you fool," said Sir Pardo, laughing.

266

"Where's the rest? Where's Franks . . . ?"

"Under the sod, poor brute: only you and I, Red, are left of the founder members of the Treasure Seekers' Circle. Anton of Brunswick's gone, and as for Honjohn – Honjohn's a married man, turned respectable now and will not sit with old friends. But they were gay days, eh, Red? Ah, sure," he said, with his own old lilting brogue, "they were the gay days in that Spring and Summer of '54. . . ."

"In the June of 1754, Madame, did you form friendships with certain – gentlemen?"

Sapphire sat erect, smiling again, hands folded, the tip of her fan just touching the gleaming edge of the mahogany table. "Why, yes, Sir Henry: yourself among them."

Sir Henry Kidd's bright eyes swivelled sideways, he jerked on uneasy toes, he briefly bowed. "It is true that I had the honour of your ladyship's acquaintance; but I speak now of certain others, of Lord Franks, of Baronshart, Sir Pardo Ryan, Mr. Reddington of Rede Manor in the county of Gloucestershire – were not these gentlemen among your friends?"

267

"Were then; and are now," said Sapphire. "Except for Lord Franks, who is dead."

"Was Lord Franks – such a man as Lord Franks – your friend?"

"Lord Franks is dead, Sir Henry."

"Do you know under what circumstances?"

"He took his life," said Sapphire.

"In despair at the pass to which his debaucheries had brought him."

"And therefore, we may leave him to the mercy of God, sir, and need not tear his poor memory to pieces here."

"I seek only to establish that he was no fit friend for a lady of virtue."

"Oh, as to that," Sapphire, shrugging, "you may find unfit friends enough among my connection, without desecrating the graveyards to look for them." And she laughed and glanced round behind her. "Come, Reddington, Sir Pardo, Greenewode, the rest of you – are you all too drunk to stand up and take a bow?"

There was a flutter of fans and a flourish of snuff-boxes, a ripple of excitement ran through the court: the notorious Lady Weyburn, it seemed, was getting into her stride. Behind her, half a dozen gentlemen stood up, laughing, and bowed this way and that (a little astonished, secretly, for the most part – for save Reddington and Pardo, the rest had not set eyes on her for years), and bowed to one another with mock congratulation and sat down again. And a motley crew, indeed, they were, and on the whole unlovely – the gay rake-hellies of an earlier day, grown already, too rapidly aging, into middle-aged roués, taking their dissolute pleasures now without joy, without the youth and the laughter that had lifted them once above mere brutishness. Sir Cecil Prout, he who had stolen her Grace of Witham's petticoat – foolish, effeminate, spiteful; Lord Greenewode, hollow-faced, fever-eyed, living from day to day at the brink of the grave; Francis Erick, the blue eyes bleared and the bright hair lustreless – kept clown, toady, clinging to the hems of his dying patron's winding-sheet. . . . And Reddington. "Mr. Reddington – you were neighbour to Lady Weyburn at Starrbelow?"

Red Reddington tumbled unsteadily to his feet. "I was, sir."

"And are to this day?"

"To this day? Why, 'tis true, sir, I have not moved house. My family have been

269

some four hundred years at the manor, we've grown used to the place."

"You were a friend of Lady Weyburn? – I speak now of the early summer of '54."

"I was then, and I still am."

"You were then and you still are." Sir Henry echoed it in the approved courtroom manner; his bright eyes swivelled. "You have agreed, tacitly at least, Mr. Reddington, to Lady Weyburn's description of you among others, as no fit person for a virtuous woman to admit to her friendship?"

Mr. Reddington gave an ironical, unsteady small bow. "Oh, certainly, sir." And he bowed again, with his hand on his heart, to Lady Weyburn. "And count it the more gracious that for ten years or more, this virtuous woman had admitted me to hers."

Sir Henry sneered. "You refer, sir, to Lady Weyburn?"

"Why, of course: I see no other virtuous woman here," said Red Reddington, and sat down with a bump.

Witnesses. Witnesses from the inn at Camden, buxom mothers who in those days had been giggling wenches, not entirely unknown to Squire Reddington and Sir Pardo: to give evidence of having seen her ladyship misconduct herself with the gentlemen, together and severally; of hearing of her locked by the hour together in a private room at the inn with one or other of them, of wine and laughter, of kissing and squeezing in dark corners, of coquetry on the lady's part and boldness in the men.... Of a quarrel one evening, all parties being in drink, when Lord Franks, him that was now dead, had assaulted her ladyship and her ladyship had thrown a glass of claret in his face and thrown the glass after it and his friends had fought with him, and her ladyship intervened and afterwards there was kissing and fondling and making up.... Of terms of love, of sly glances behind the backs of lovers, of disarranged dress....

Lady Weyburn waited till the last woman had done. Then she stood up. "I remember you – you are Laura from the inn: for whom the gentlemen, I think, had another name, which did not sound dissimilar. Now, Laura – I will ask you: what harm did I ever do *you?*"

"You dun me no harm, my lady," said Laura, puzzled

"Save that when I came among them, the gentlemen sat with me in the garden of the inn, and there were, for a while, no tumblings in the haycocks: no ribbons from London, no pieces of gold? And this you have not yet forgiven?" She paused. Laura cried out shrilly: "You throw back dirt for dirt, moi lady, and 'tis easy to do; but me, oi'm a decent woman and was a good wench."

"You are a decent woman? Married now, I dare say?"

"These eight year," said Laura, proudly.

"And have a quiverful of nine children, is it not so?"

Laura lost colour a little. "I have children, my lady."

"The eldest is twelve years old, Laura, is he not? And the second is ten? Who pays for their maintenance?" She shrugged; she looked round, laughing, towards the ragged two rows of her erstwhile associates. "Well, well – we will not give old friends away. Now, Laura – I threw a glass in a gentleman's face?"

"That you did," said Laura eagerly, glad

to be on safe ground again. "I see you with my own eyes."

"And why was this? What had the gentleman done?"

" 'Twas Lord Franks done it. He – he chucked your ladyship's chin."

"And for that, I – wanton and promiscuous – dashed my glass of wine in his face? A claret glass you say it was? And I threw the wine, and dashed the glass in his face . . . ?"

"I saw it with moi own eyes," said Laura stoutly, "and the blood drip down my lord's face and his face so pale. . . ."

"Very well," said Sapphire again; and she smiled at the girl, but quite kindly and said: "Sit down, Laura: you have done your best." She turned. "Sir Henry Kidd – I find I must look for protection to an unlikely source. You knew me, I think you have acknowledged, in those old days; and at that time, the exact time of this incident – had also some acquaintance, at least, with Lord Franks?"

"Reluctantly," admitted Sir Henry. "But, yes, I had."

"You observed, no doubt, the scars on his face, caused by these bleeding wounds which the claret glass had made?"

He was silent a moment. "It is true there were no cuts, when I saw him, new or old: the girl no doubt mistook the red wine for blood."

"And cherry brandy for claret?" suggested Sapphire, sweetly – and she smiled at him, her own old, wicked smile, not the smile of tolerant half pity she had given the girl. "The court no doubt will believe *you*, Sir Henry, when you tell them that you never at that time saw me with any but a tiny cherry brandy glass in my hand...."

Witnesses. Witnesses to the wildness, the recklessness, the wantonness that for a brief season had divided the town between shocked horror and shocked amusement; witnesses to disreputable friendships, to noise and laughter, to depleted wine-cellars in the house in Berkeley Square, to gambling parties lasting till the dawn.... Servants swearing they had seen her ladyship misconduct herself in this situation and that; servants swearing her ladyship misconducted herself not at all, save in over-much laughter, over-much gaiety, over-much freedom and fun.... Witnesses to her having entertained

274

gentlemen only at Berkeley Square, witnesses to her having entertained, on the contrary, actresses of vile reputation, all the rag, tag and bobtail of town.... Witnesses to having approached Lady Weyburn with amorous advances and having had knuckles rapped for it, to having made this proposition or that, and been laughingly, flirtingly, teasingly, but unequivocally repelled. No witnesses (naturally enough) to having been honoured with her ladyship's favours: whatever the gossips and the servants might say....

"Your ladyship in those days possessed a pair of ruby buckles?"

"I possess them still."

"Was it not a boast of Lord Franks that no woman's virtue was proof against a pair of jewelled buckles?"

More than one woman in court moved her feet, unconsciously hiding them away beneath the hem of her dress; Laura's own (garnet) buckles had long since gone to pay for comforts for a sick child. "I believe it was a saying of Lord Franks."

"Did not Lord Franks send you such a pair of buckles?"

"He did: with an apology – they were reparation for an insult." She paused to let

Sir Henry enjoy a moment of triumph. "I accepted the apology – but returned the gift."

"Having, however, asked him for such a gift."

"I had said to him, idly, that I craved a pair of buckles – they were the rage at the time and I had none. I later bought some for myself." But she was puzzled. "Lord Franks is long dead: who, then, has told you this?"

One who had listened, sick at heart, perched up on the driving-box of a coach, on that crazy, far-away night, to the boastings of a wounded man. 'Why this fuss about a kiss in public? – she's ready enough with them in private, as we all doubtless know. . . .' And, 'If her stick of a husband isn't here to give her gew-gaws, let others do it in his place. . . .' "Upon the occasion of your masquerade as highwaymen, Lady Weyburn – who drove the rear coach?"

"The coach? Why, what has that to do with the buckles? 'Twas only dear Honjohn – he drove the gentlemen home."

"You refer, I believe, to the Honourable John Fair?"

"The Honourable John Fair, yes – most

aptly named so. But it is a shame," said Sapphire, smiling, "to tell tales of his youth against him here." And she looked round the packed, bright room, leisurely, until she found him, his prim little wife sitting anxiously beside him. "He was very young," she said. "Let the rest look after themselves, who were so rash as to associate with Sapphire Weyburn in those days; but he was young and green and though he nowadays thinks it best, I believe, to deny my acquaintance, I beg leave to defend the memory of that young man I long ago knew: and say, in the words of Sir Andrew Marvel, that he 'nothing common did or mean' – in all those memorable scenes. I loved him for it then, and now, if I may; I thank him. Do not drag him into this." She sketched him a little, undulating curtsey, half-mocking as was everything she did. The prim wife turned away her head; but he stood up and bowed with a blush of shame; and had no evidence to offer, after all. He had loved her, with a boy's love, long ago.

Witnesses. Witnesses, witnesses, witnesses.... She drove home alone when the court was ended for the day, sitting upright and lovely in her carriage, not concealing herself from view, disdainful, unruffled, serene; but her maid could have witnessed that she spent the long evening lying motionless, exhausted, on her bed; touched no food, sipped only at a little wine. No visitors came. The men, perhaps, unwontedly delicate were afraid to compromise her by outward attentions at this time: only Reddington and Pardo, friends and neighbours still at Starrbelow where, since her return from Italy with the child, she had exclusively spent her time, sent her billets, folded into cocked hats. She glanced at them languidly. "Dearest lady – you were magnificent, down with the lot of them, how you put down that bawd from the inn and she with her glasses of claret, devil a sovereign more shall her brat see of mine. God bless you, Pardo," and, "Love of my life, you were splendid, you were magnificent, you are the love of my life...." Ill-written, half-illiterate, brought by the hand of some tavern runner. My only two friends in the world, she thought wearily, and even on this night they can't stay sober for me. And yet.... "Love of my life...' God help him, she thought, I believe it is true: and if it is true, who is to cast a stone at him because in wineing and wenching

278

he dulls down the pain? Not she; not Sapphire Weyburn who also had loved once and for a lifetime; who also was not loved in return.

The verdict of the court – if not of the jurymen after that first long day: Lady Weyburn found guilty of wanton conduct with any of a dozen men – and the child as likely the son of one of these as not.

Twelve

The second day: the day that was to prove the secret marriage to Prince Anton: Lady Corby called upon to testify against her niece....

Marcia Corby, at the age of fifty-two, lived with a dream – with an illusion and a dream: which, as the years crept by, as the ageing, haggard face more and more broke through the terrible mask of youth, and the philanderers and the flatterers fell away, grew strong within her: filled up at last every crevice of a mind grown sick with feeding on the illusion and the dream. For she saw herself now as a woman who had been loved, who in turn had given a great love; whose chevalier had been sans peur et sans raproche, whose own weary heart had been refined afresh in the fires of that clean young spirit. And this great love, Sophia Devigne had tried to steal from her; and, failing, had condemned to the murderer's hand. This was the illusion: and the dream – revenge. That Anton had been in fact Sapphire's lover – let alone that he had married her – she did not believe because she would not believe him faithless to herself. But even this, if it would harm the enemy, she was willing to swear. "I did what I could to prevent it, but I believe that Prince Anton of Brunswick was Lady Weyburn's lover, both before her marriage to Lord Weyburn and afterwards; and may well have married her as has been supposed."

"Your ladyship knew of this from the beginning?"

"Not at first, no. I saw that my niece was – attracted to him. . . ." But spite burst out of her, she hissed out suddenly and shatteringly into the avidly listening court that the girl was a natural wanton, who had seen that he was handsome, strong, manly, and had lusted after him. . . . "I did what I could to prevent it. . . ." She said at last, almost sobbing: "Many will testify to that."

Many indeed could testify to that – to that and to its apparent unsuccess. The first casual, kindly notice of this lovely protégée of his middle-aged mistress, the increase of intimacy after the disaster of her entry into society, the insistence upon the Christmas visit to Starrbelow ('I haf accepted, Marcia: I shall go as I said I would'). Taken unawares at the ball by the opportunity, suddenly presenting itself, to bring about what he had known would be his mistress's pleasure, he had carried out the challenge; but afterwards had gone out alone into the gardens and not returned to the ballroom that night; and later he had struggled to be allowed to go back upon the bet, had desisted only when she threatened him with his father's wrath. Had he married Sophia to prevent the challenge from being made good? And, perhaps, later tired of her? – or never loved her at all, married her only out of shame and now that it was done, grown afraid again, penniless as they both were, of Hanoverian repudiation? Obliged to be present at her wedding, he had looked white and sick; later, fool that she had been, she had taken him with her to Starrbelow again. "Your niece, in the June following her marriage, Lady Corby, invited you to Gloucestershire?"

"She invited me, yes, begging me to bring with me a party of friends. It was one 'friend' that she wanted, I see that now. She dared not invite him alone; but she knew he would be with any party of mine."

"You did not appreciate that at the time?"

"Not at first. When I saw that she was – though now a married woman – still seeking him out, I did what I could to prevent it."

"Lady Weyburn – took steps to remove your surveillance? This adventure of the highwaymen...?"

"I was ill," said Lady Corby briefly. "My nerves were shocked."

"You kept your room? And were later obliged to return to London?"

"To see my doctors. But she came also, she would not leave him alone, he came with me and so she followed...." But meanwhile at Starrbelow, she had disgraced herself with her pursuit of him, all the world knew it, ask the servants, ask the grooms in the stables, ask the Earl of Frome...."

Witnesses. Witness of a lady's maid to assignations in locked rooms, witness of stablemen to horses saddled for solitary rides.... Painful witness from the Earl of Frome, dressed in deep mourning for his wife's death, of those accidental encounters with the lovers in the Starrbelow woods....

"The Countess, my lord – then Miss

Lillane – had left Lady Weyburn's house?"

"She left because she would not tolerate Prince Anton's being there," said Lady Corby. "She would not be a party to such infamous conduct in her cousin, Lord Weyburn's, absence." She flung out a shaking hand at her niece. "Even her friend was disgusted with her behaviour and left her. Let her deny it."

Sapphire looked down at the painted fan she carried that day, and her own hands also were trembling. "I think Lady Corby is unlikely to have been at that time or any other, in Miss Lillane's counsels."

"It is true, nevertheless," said Lord Frome in his dry, reluctant and yet grimly determined way, "that she left, with her mother, because she disapproved Lady Weyburn's companions."

"Who did not at that time include Prince Anton; she had left before ever he entered the house," said Sapphire. "Or lady-ship either – who professes to know so much of Miss Lillane's intentions."

"Her intention was to disown you," said Lady Corby. "She never disowned me. She was my friend to the day she died."

Dates. "In the December, Madame, when you became betrothed to Lord Weyburn, you had known Prince Anton of Brunswick already two or three months – since, indeed, the time of your arrival in England? In the January, you departed for Italy; but you were in town again about the middle of March?"

"Yes," said Sophia.

"You were certainly in London on the twenty-fifth of March when, it is alleged, this secret marriage took place?"

"I was in London on that date, yes."

"Can you tell us, in fact, how you spent that day, Lady Weyburn?"

She shrugged. "At this distance – hardly. I was shopping, no doubt, for my approaching wedding: very possibly in the company of Lady Corby though I think she is less likely to remember it even than I!"

"On May the twenty-seventh, at any rate, you married Lord Weyburn, two months after that alleged marriage in secret. On August the first, did you, in the company with Prince Anton, embark upon what proved to be the last of your 'escapades'?"

The last of their escapades, the last adventure of the Treasure Seekers' Circle:

Lord Franks with his dressing-case, Lord Warne with his convent wine-cup, Sir Cecil with his petticoat-hoop, Honjohn, Greenewode, Tom Jeans, Francis Erick, Pardo, Reddington, the rest of them, each with his trophy – Prince Anton with the page from a Fleet Street wedding registry still to get. Tom Jeans called as witness. "Looking back upon that challenge, Mr. Jeans: does it now strike you that Lady Weyburn and Prince Anton may have determined it between them, long before it came?"

Poor Tom Jeans, shambling down to the mahogany table, a sick man nowadays, living on old memories, never at the best, acute of mind. "Determined beforehand? Why, who can say? I remember that several alternatives were put to the Prince and he refused. In the ordinary way," he ruminated, innocently, "her ladyship would have no challenge refused: once spoken, it was made."

"Who was it set the challenge of the page from the registry?"

"Her ladyship suggested first, as I remember, a page from Gossip Wit – from Her Grace of Witham's visiting book; the rest," he agreed, nodding his head with slowly dawning comprehension, "led from that. She said we must have a certain page from a certain book; and she would assist him." He nodded and dreamed: back again in the days of his youth, far enough already down the path to doom, but not so far as now. "I remember... I remember he said – it was when they suggested he filch a snuff-box from His Majesty – he said he could not, for he must not forget he was a prince: though he might forget he was a gentleman." He nodded and dreamed. "She said she would not contradict him in either; and she smiled. I don't know why she said that: nor why she smiled so. 'Twas as though he had not conducted himself as a gentleman towards *her*." He came-to with a start. "But I ramble, Sir Henry – I was far away...."

And Sapphire too was far away: was dressing herself again in the wedding-dress she had worn in the candle-lit chapel at Starrbelow in the last days of innocence: was hanging herself about with diamonds, painting her face to a travesty of its own beauty, perching a rubbish of wedding finery on her bright gold hair.... Was rushing, cloaked and veiled, down the curving stair. "Have wine and refreshment ready in the blue drawing-room. If any arrive before my return, show them up there and wait upon them until I come."

"Your ladyship will not have forgotten that his lordship returns tonight from Bath?"

"No, no, I have not forgotten: his lordship, I daresay, will not trouble my friends."

"Very well, my lady," the man said wretchedly, standing with bent head. She rushed on past him and into the waiting hackney coach.

Anton was already in the coach and Tom Jeans and – a woman: a woman with a raddled face beneath wedding finery to outdo her own in tawdry vulgarity as the sun outshines the moon; for the jewels were false, the dress cheap and shabby, the veil and feathers bedraggled and no longer clean. She stopped short at the door of the carriage, offended; but they were all hysterical with laughter and dragged her in. "We agreed to employ no women in these adventures," she whispered angrily to the Prince, jerking back into a place at his side as the coach rattled off. But he only shrugged. "Tom would bring her: he's far gone in drink."

"And you not much better; upon this of all occasions," she said indignantly, "when so much rests upon it...." She broke off. She said bitterly: "But you care nothing, you never have: what have *you* to lose?" She added sharply: "This is not the way."

("We have heard from Mr. Tom Jeans, my lady, that you spoke reproachfully to Prince Anton on entering the coach; that you appeared to remember the way to the chapel?"

"I was incensed that they should bring a woman with them: it had been agreed otherwise – I reproached him for that. As to my knowing where we were going: it had been arranged we should get a certain page from a certain book – the registry at the Savoy chapel where Mr. Wilkinson was then performing marriages: the coach was not taking us there, it was going to the Fleet.")

"We are going to the Fleet first," said Anton. "Tom, here, and his doxy haf a fancy to be wed." The three of them went off into hysterics again; but under cover of the darkness in the coach he pressed her hand. "Be patient, haf no fear – all shall be well."

Marriages were performed no longer within the precincts of the Fleet by the dissolute parsons committed there for their debts: the warden of the prison had long ago been forbidden to suffer them there. But within the Rules of the Fleet, there still existed, despite the penalties imposed by the Marriage Bill of March 25th. of that year, innumerable rooms in lodging-houses and taverns where at a moment's notice and without enquiry, a couple might be married by a so-called chaplain, who might be truly in orders and empowered to marry but who frequently was not. From the moment they arrived within sight of Ludgate Hill and the bridge across the Fleet Ditch, the coach was surrounded by a horde of hacks and 'plyers' only a trifle more furtive than in the days before the Bill. Hands in ragged sleeves clawed at the windows, faces seamed with dirt, bleared with drink, were thrust in. 'Parson, sir?' 'This way, sir, this way, ladies. . . .' 'Have no truck with these, my lords, these are no true parsons, come where the register is, my lords and ladies, come where it's legal. . . .' At sight of the wedding finery within, a howl went up that brought out a parson himself, in full canonicals, who was soon embroiled in hand-to-hand fighting with the barkers of a rival chapel. "For God's sake," said Sapphire, even her high heart failing at the filth, depravity and violence all about them, "let us get out of this: tell the man to drive on." But the man could not drive on, a drunken mob barred the way, howling in delight at the promise of liquor that would flow to celebrate the nuptials of such great folk as these. She grew desperate. "We shall be clawed to pieces, what can we do?"

Anton only laughed. "They vill not harm us – not while ve haf money to buy gin for them. Haf no fear."

To her right the other woman giggled and screamed with hinneys of high laughter. "But I *am* afraid, Anton: these two are in drink, they are no help to us. And I have jewels, suppose the mob guesses they are real and – attacks us." She huddled the cloak about her to cover the diamonds. "Thiss iss not like you, Sapphire," he said, "you are usually more brave." And he looked down at her with something of comtempt in the handsome face that was usually kindly enough and only rather weak. "You were brave enough when poor Marcia cowered before the demands of a highwayman for *her* jewels."

For once she had no reply; her pale cheeks flamed beneath their patched-on rouge, she looked down at her hands. But the sharp sting, nevertheless, had stimulated her. She rose from the seat, the cloak close around her; with her free hand, protected by its great fur muff, she thrust back the evil faces from the window, forced away clinging hands, herself leaned out of the window and above the heads of the crowd, suddenly falling silent at so unexpected an apparition – a lady of such beauty, such a wealth of bright hair, such magnificence of apparel where, nowadays, only the drunken sailors came with their bawds to be tricked into appearance of matrimony – cried out aloud, "Come, come, good people, let the coach pass! We are married already in May Fair and come home from carousing there, all our money is spent." As a low moan went up, becoming, with increasing realisation of their loss and disappointment, rather a growl than a moan, she added hastily: "Unless we can find a few coins in a purse, maybe, the which you shall willingly have to drink our health. But meanwhile – let us pass on! We are married an hour already and –" she laughed provocatively – "and long to be home." She had held out her hand behind her, dropping the great muff, and Prince Anton thrust a purse into it. "Fling out some coins from the other window also," she said, and held the purse high. "See you here, good friends – a purse of gold! Here a coin...!" – the crowd swung, watching its gleaming flight and the upthrust of a dozen hands, like spears, into the air – "and here another!" The crowd swung again, in the opposite direction, there was a swaying movement towards the falling guinea, she screamed out at the top of her voice, "And here the whole purse!" and to the man, "Drive on! Drive on! Drive on!" As the vehicle lumbered off, lurching over the filthy cobbles, she was tumbled once more back into her place. "You have done a wrong and stupid thing," she said, furiously, to Anton, "in coming here: you may well have spoilt all." To the still foolishly laughing Tom Jeans, to the wildly giggling woman in the opposite corner, she paid no attention at all. "Direct the driver to the chapel in the Savoy: Wilkinson's chapel," she said to Anton; and sat in her own corner with folded arms in an icy rage. "I supposed these outings were intended for outings of pleasure," said Anton, sulkily, looking between the two laughing faces and her face of cold fury. "This one was not," she said sharply, "as well you know." (This also was faithfully reported by Tom, dreaming stupidly in the court that sat in judgement on her ten years afterwards, not aware how he damaged her.)

Parson Wilkinson's chapel, where he presided with his partner in villainy, Grierson, was something more of a chapel than the usual tavern room where a table covered with a cloth served for an altar and constituted all the religious appointment of the chamber. He himself came forward and welcomed them in. He had kept a high standard, both he and his partner were in fact in orders and, though it was no longer legal for them to officiate, the marriages they had performed to the time when the Act took force had been legal and binding: their registers, probably for purposes of subsequent bribery and blackmail, were carefully kept, though nine-tenths of the signatures, or even mere initials, were false. Sapphire saw them at once as she entered the room, a row of big, leather-bound books, marked by their dates, quarterly. While they waited for his partner, the

Reverend Wilkinson put up a casual hand and hauled one down. Next to it, she saw the year's first quarter. She hustled the other three over towards it, all four tipsily gay. "Let's see who else comes here to be wed, let's look up friends. Was not Lady Anne Paulett married here but recently?" Lurching slightly under their weight, she began to tug down the great books.

Wilkinson intervened. "Lady Anne's daughter, Madame. But you'll not find her in the '54 register, 'twas last Summer."

"Well, well.... And here is the Ladyday quarter, Anton – search through and see if a Very Particular friend of your own is not here, my dear, as I've told you...." She shoved the great book over towards him.

Wilkinson, however, thrust both books aside. "Useless, probably. Ladies and gentlemen of the quality seldom put their true names – as we've found to our sorrow, Madame, since the blame falls to us; and especially those with Very Particular friends who may come later in search of them." He eyed them shrewdly. Friends of Lady Anne Paulett might well be emissaries also of the Duchess of Argyle whose outcry against the Fleet marriages had given them all an infinity of trouble.

"Come, ladies – your minds should be upon your own marriages, a solemn moment in your lives – and in the lives of those who must now lose you to these fortunate gentlemen." He case an anxious eye to the door where his partner yet dallied, and meanwhile encircled the waists of the ladies and gave them each a valedictory squeeze. Tom Jean's inamorata was, only too obviously, in no condition of health to be squeezed and she gave a shrill scream and relapsed into her inevitable giggles; Sapphire, shuddering, submitted to the endearment, releasing herself, however, with a dextrous twist and falling in feigned half-drunkenness into Anton's arms. Oh, God! she thought – if my mother could see me now; if my poor father could see me, whose hope for me ran so high that he would sacrifice us all – to this! In such a place as this, on such a work as this – and all for a moment of despair when all that was needed had been but a little patience, a little faith, to end in bliss. And she thought of the difficulties still to come, of the long, lonely path of sorrow that she, for love, had chosen to tread. We will go to Italy, she thought: Christine will come with me, we will go to Italy, there at least there will be smiling faces and blue skies, and my lovely Venice will open her arms to her weary exile and take me to her heart again. And perhaps, even yet, she thought, concealment might be possible: perhaps even yet, it might not be too late....

Parson Grierson came in, bowed, without further ado began rapidly reading out the marriage service, the two couples standing, one grim and silent now, one restless and sniggering, before the covered table. In the act of scratching an initial in the book, she put her hand to her breast. "Help! Help! I am faint...." Her companions moved round her, crowding out the two chaplains from view of the books and she edged the earlier volume towards Prince Anton. "Water – a glass of water ...!" As he stood, dismayed, looking down at the book, she hissed, "Take out the page."

"I can't," he said stupidly. "There's a clasp. The book's locked."

Wilkinson shoved his way back in among them; he had collected his fee and now wanted them only to begone – every moment they delayed was danger of discovery to him. "The lady would be best in fresh air."

"No, no," moaned Sapphire, doubled up again over the table. "A doctor – I pray you go, sir, and fetch me a doctor."

"There is no doctor here, Madame; save only," he said, grinning, "a doctor in orders. You had best get back to your coach and go yourselves in search of one." And he took her by the arm and hauled her bodily up from the table. Anton and Tom Jeans sprang forward in genuine horror. "Unhand her, sir! Lay your hands off her ladyship!" But he urged her forward, his partner taking the other arm, forcing her, violently resisting, towards the door. "It is time to begone, sirs, we risk transportation if you are found here, and the women in wedding guise. Get back to your coach and attend to your lady there." She struggled against them, casting imploring glances at Anton, hissing, "The book! Get the whole book!" but he was blind to all but the insult of their hands upon her and Tom Jeans only said, foolishly, "The book?" and might have given all away had she persisted. Almost weeping, she was forced out and into the coach, the two men still fighting off the rough grip of her assailants. "If ladies will come in such condition to be married," said

Grierson, guffawing, "they must do their fainting in private: we are interested only in marriage-beds, not sick-beds; in laying-with rather than laying-in." He gave the woman a shove and she scrambled after them, no longer giggling, concealing her great pregnant belly from his insults as well she might with the skimpy folds of dress and veil and cheap velvet mantle. For the third time that evening, the coach jolted into action, the two jeering faces at the window were left behind. Sapphire sank back into the corner in utter despair. "This night has been doomed to disaster from the outset; and now we have failed. We had better go home." She said to Tom Jeans: "Where do you wish this – lady – taken?"

"Let the lady speak for herself," said the woman pertly. She leaned out of the window and screeched up to the coachman: "To Berkeley Square!"

"I regret," said Sapphire, "I do not entertain ladies at Berkeley Square."

"You will entertain me," said the woman. "You forget Madame, I am now Mrs. Jeans."

"You are no more Mrs. Jeans than – than I am a princess of Brunswick. This ceremony was a farce; from last Ladyday, all such marriages have been illegal."

"Then why was your ladyship there?" she asked reasonably.

"I was there to obtain a – a trophy: did not Mr. Jeans tell you? 'Twas a jest (What in God's name will she spread about, if we tell her less than the truth?" she said angrily to Anton.) "All the world knows of the Treasure Seekers' Circle: 'twas a sort of – game: we went to secure a trophy."

"And where is the trophy now, then?" said the woman.

"We have failed," said Sapphire, bitterly. "We did not get it."

"You take it very hard," she said, curiously; she leaned round to peer through her veil at her ladyship, across Anton's broad shoulders. "Do you say then you will not entertain me, my lady?"

"I regret: I entertain gentlemen only, Madame. Let the coach drop me at my front door and conduct you on to wherever you wish to be delivered. . . ."

But when they stopped at the house it as the other's turn to be taken faint and call for help, for water, for a doctor . . . . And she, indeed, seemed in a condition that might just possibly make it a genuine emergency. "Better take her in," said

Sapphire at last, wearily. She watched the two men mount the steps with her. It is a hoax after all, she thought: she walks as well as I do – she meant to gain entrance. She left them and climbed up wretchedly to her room and let her maid take her cloak; and, sat for a little while, not troubling to remove the paint from her face or repair the tumbling of her dress, and rose at last and went down to the drawing-room. She had been absent only a short time but Tom Jeans met her at the door with a face of anxiety. "My – my wife! On the sofa here – given birth."

They all stood back watching her as she flew over to the sofa where, under a coverlet, the woman lay groaning. Oh, heaven! she thought, this drab delivered of a child here, in this way, none present but men – all grinning like apes, and – and He will arrive any moment. . . . She stood over the woman bewildered. "Do you say a child has been born?"

Tom Jeans at her side, also grinning. "A splendid child: felicitate me, Madame! A little brown in the complexion perhaps, a little leathery of hide for one so young . . . ." And with a swift movement he stripped back the coverlet. "If your ladyship cares to see . . . ?"

White veil, half hiding painted, simpering face; tumbled, tawdry dress: a pair of large feet squeezed into white satin shoes sticking up in the air: and clasped to the stomach by a pair of large white hands – a square book of brown leather.

She caught it up, ripped through the pages: January – February – March – April – May. . . . She looked no further. March, 1754.

And a burst of laughter, and that wretch Cecil Prout, oddly masculine in feminine attire who ordinarily looked so feminine in man's dress – sitting doubled up on the sofa in an hysteria of giggling, the white veil all awry.

"I will thank you for ever," she said to him, and though her mouth laughed, her eyes were not laughing. She had ordered a fire lit, to the astonishment of the servants for it was August and the night stifling; and now she went over with the book in her hands to the fireplace and stood there. "With your permission, gentlemen: this book holds secrets which are no business of ours. Prince Anton will be content, no doubt, to hold as his prize the story of its acquiring." Without further ado she took it, riffled through its pages, looked earnestly for a moment at one page – and threw the whole book in the fire. "This is the happiest hour of my life," she said.

The happiest hour of her life: standing there in her draggled finery, a glass of red wine thrust into her hand, with her painted face and her dress half pulled off her body by the filthy hands of two rascally renegades: with her rabble of tipsy profligates about her and God knew what secret burning to merciful ash in the grate at her feet: and a servant standing whey-faced in the doorway – "If you please, your ladyship – my lord is here."

"At eleven o'clock on the night of August first, Madame, did Lord Weyburn seek an interview with you?"

"First dismissing all the servants to bed," said Sapphire. "Yes."

"Did his lordship accuse you of wanton behaviour with gentlemen now in court?"

"He did, yes."

"And ask you the reason for what seemed like a determination on your part to disgrace his name?"

"To what end are these questions, Sir Henry?"

"Did you, Lady Weyburn, request his lordship's permission to return to your home in Italy?"

"I did."

"And he taxed you with thus behaving so that he might wish to be rid of you, might pack you back home to Venice 'where your heart had always been.'"

"In marrying an Englishman, Sir Henry, I exiled myself from Venice: would I have done so –?"

"Would you have done so had he not been rich, Madame, and able, blackmailed by you with dissolute behaviour, to pension you off in wealth to 'where your heart was' . . . ?"

She had borne many insults in that court – deserved or not: but at this she flushed up for the first time, she brought the ivory fan down upon the table before her with a crack that rang through the gaping, eager silence of the crowd. "My lord! – will you permit this to be said, will you hear me called a – a whore, that would sell herself for a competence abroad? What need had I for your money? I had a home, I had a loving father and mother, I – I couched there like a bird in its nest, safe from all harm, till this woman, this bird of ill omen, this eagle, beaked and taloned, swooped down and carried me forth to know suffering for the first time and cruelty and callous indifference, to lose my young innocence and all my joy for ever.... And will you let any man dare to say that I came in greed and infamy to sell myself for gold? Will anyone dare to say it of that girl who came, so ignorant and afraid, into your world?" She was silent, eyes bright, head held high, waiting. Nobody spoke. "It is you who are disgraced," she said, looking round at them; and her face took on the old careless, scornful smile again. "It is you – not I."

"I asked you, Madame, if that was your purpose in defiling my name by your conduct. You denied it; but afterwards you said you would protest no longer; that 'perhaps that was the reason after all.'"

The fire had gone. She said carelessly: "Oh – did I say that? Very well then. Have it as you will."

"But it was not true, was it? – after all."

She shrugged. "You say first it was true, now you say not."

"You acknowledged then that it was the reason – so as to disguise another, the true reason. We ... I ..." He stood trembling for a moment, not able to control his voice. "We came to – an agreement; I – invited you to remain in England to become, in truth, my wife." Over the suddenly whipped-up storm of sensation in the court, his voice rose high. "You consented: – upon one condition, Madame did you not? – that you return to Italy for a certain time."

The storm had died away to silence as swiftly as it arose: all ears listened for the answer, all eyes stared, fascinated at the two pale, proud faces, deep blue eyes flashing defiance, cold grey eyes relentless, meeting them. "This was the first of August. Your marriage to Prince Anton of Brunswick is said to have taken place at the end of March. You had had four months in which to conceive a child; and you asked me for six months – alone – in Italy. Your child in fact was born there in the following Spring."

She said steadily: "My child and yours."

"My marriage with you remains unconsummated: you had no child by me."

"Our marriage was consummated on that night of August 1st. The boy is your heir."

"I deny it," he said: as steadily as she.

"You lie, my lord." She rested her finger-tips on the table before her, their nails whitened by the pressure upon them to control their trembling. "Do you deny that upon that occasion, you took me in your arms?"

He gave her a small, cold bow. "I do not deny it. I have told the court that we came to an agreement: a reconciliation, if you will. But – the question of your visit to Italy arose. Even then – I was unsuspecting, I might yet that night have made you my wife. You will tell the court, my lady, what locket I found in your bosom; we may leave them to judge whether, having found it, I turned with love to you."

"With love! Ah, no! A man does not love a bawd, sir, that he tumbles into bed in some brothel of the town; and nor did you love me. But...." She laughed out on a high, crude, tearing note that made them wince who heard it. "But – tumble me you did, my lord, bawd that I was to you and wearing Prince Anton's locket in my breast where, in tearing aside my dress in your lust, you found it." And she laughed again as at a memoried picture, vile and unlovely. "The servants a-bed and by your orders, and I in your chamber in the dress I wore at our bridal ... I remember your words, sir: they were the last, I think, coherently spoken, I ever heard from you: 'Since every other man in London appears to have known you,' you said, 'why so will I.' "

And the fruit of that bridal bed, she said, looking round upon them, deliberately shameless, shaming them by the very scorn of her own violent pandering to their hunger for her shamelessness, was Nicholas. "Whom I say again, and will say despite what this trumped-up court of yours may find to the contrary, is Lord Weyburn's heir."

Verdict of the jury, sniggering behind large, red hands, that with all this consummying and not consummying, you couldn't make head nor tail of it; but the quality did seem to be up to some rare old tricks all right, and if they'd bin in 'is lordship's shoes, they'd've consummied the marriage quick enough, I'll warrant you. . . .

Verdict of the court – if not of the jury – at the end of the second day of Lady Weyburn's trial: that she married Prince Anton of Brunswick, secretly, on March 25th., that being the last day of legal marriages at Savoy chapel: two months, that is to say, before her mock marriage to Lord Weyburn at Starrbelow. That on August 1st., she and Anton conspired to remove all traces of the marriage from the register. That that night, knowing herself with child, she endeavoured to seduce Lord Weyburn to an act which might father the child on him; and that she failed. Verdict of the court: that the brat might be legitimately Anton's by a marriage which now, thanks to their action in destroying the register, could never be proved: but was not Lord Weyburn's heir.

Thirteen

The third day. For the prosecution – sick with grief, grim, resolute, deadly with the blind purpose of an honest man bent upon a just revenge: the Earl of Frome. For the defence: only the accused. And the charge – murder.

She stood in her place at the head of the great, glowing table: her dress today was of a stiff, creamy silk, she wore no glittering jewels but a circlet of seed-pearls exquisitely wrought in a pattern of lilies close about her lovely throat: her fan was of mother-of-pearl. "My lord Duke, my lords, ladies and gentlemen – I do not answer to this charge."

"The charge, my lady, is that, to preserve your secret, which she, only, could disclose, you administered laudanum to the Countess of Frome and so brought about her death. . . ."

"I understand the charge very well, my lord Duke: and I have said and I now repeat that I shall not answer – I shall not condescend to answer – to so monstrous an accusation." She sat down quietly, and slowly, serenely, like some white swan preening its feathers before its progress down the ruffled waters of the muddy stream, arranged the creamy folds of her skirt, composed her white hands in her lap, opened out with a flick the white wing of the iridescent-gleaming fan. The Earl of Frome stumbled to his feet.

"My lord Duke, my lords, ladies and gentlemen, gentlemen of the jury ... I wish to make it clear from the first that my wife, the Countess of Frome, was not in the habit of taking laudanum. Most of us take laudanum now and again for sleeplessness or pain; I do myself and in a closet adjacent to her room was a small phial, a sufficient dose to which she might have resorted if she had found herself in need of it. But that she would resort to it of her own accord, is unlikely in the extreme; she was violently prejudiced against it, I have never known her to use it; and, as it transpires, the phial in the closet remains untouched. I make this point to prove, my lord, ladies and gentlemen, that if my wife were offered a dose of laudanum, were persuaded while in a state of over-emotion to do what in

311

other circumstances she would never do, and accept it – she would be ignorant of the proper dose. Lady Weyburn, on the other hand, though she also seldom resorted to it as I understand, did now and again use laudanum, did understand laudanum; kept always a large phial of laudanum in a locked box.

"This phial of laudanum, since the morning of my wife's death, has disappeared; and in the embers of the fire in Lady Weyburn's room, were found some remains that might be splintered and molten glass.

"My lords, ladies – you will hear the testimony of the coachman who drove the carriage when my wife, the Countess, and her friend, Lady Weyburn, encountered the Duchess of Witham in the park – now eight weeks ago – with Lord Weyburn. He will tell you that throughout the argument that followed, the Countess was scandalized at Lady Weyburn's conduct, that she repeatedly begged her to desist, that when Lady Weyburn publicly claimed recognition for her son as Lord Weyburn's heir, the Countess exclaimed that it was wrong, unjust and dishonest to do so and that if Lady Weyburn persisted she herself would tell her cousin, Lord Weyburn, the truth.

"My lords, ladies, gentlemen of the jury – Lady Weyburn replied to this: 'If you speak, I will kill you."

Witnesses: to the conversation in the carriage, to long arguments afterwards, the two ladies being closeted in Lady Weyburn's room – she was at this time staying at the Frome mansion in London with her friend, the Earl being away from home. Witness of a footman to voices raised in argument, in protestation, in pleading, half-heard through a closed door; of a butler to a meal taken up and returned hardly touched, to white faces on either side of the table, lips silent in the presence of servants, ringed hands trembling.... Witness of the Countess's own maid, "It was near midnight when my lady retired. No, there was no laudanum in her room. Yes, my lady would know of the laudanum in his lordship's closet close by. There was one phial of laudanum only, in the closet; in the morning it was still there." Witness of Lady Weyburn's maid. "It was near midnight when I prepared my mistress for bed. My lady was silent, but she was never one to gossip with her maid. Yes, there was laudanum, a large phial of laudanum, in her ladyship's medicine chest. My lady would take laudanum sometimes, but not from that phial: she had some small quantities measured out into tiny phials, each sufficient for a dose. As long as I have known her, my lady has had the large phial and it has not been touched."

"It was kept in her medicine chest? And, on this particular night, the chest was placed – where?"

"The chest was placed in a closet, my lord, with her ladyship's jewel-case. The chest was locked, but the key in the lock. I put both boxes in the cupboard and locked the door, and put the key of the cupboard door in a hiding place: this was always our habit when we were from home, we changed the place each night. Upon this occasion, I said to her, 'I will put the key here, my lady,' and slipped it into the toe of a shoe. My lady the Countess had then retired to bed, we were alone in the room, no one but her ladyship could have known where the key was hid for I did not know myself until I put it there."

"Very well: you have been very clear. Now – as to laudanum, what did Lady Weyburn say to you?"

314

"My lady looked ill, my lord, and very tired. I said, 'Shall you sleep, my lady?' – this was before I put the medicine chest away, sir; and she said, 'Leave me out one small phial of the laudanum, in case I do not.' In the morning, my lord, this phial lay broken by her bedside, there were dregs of laudanum in the glass by her side and her ladyship had to be woken from a heavy sleep."

But – had woken at last – to the news that Christine could not be awakened, would never wake again; lay dead on her bed no glass beside her, no broken phial – but with the smell of laudanum heavy on her lips.

Witnesses. Witnesses to Lady Weyburn, being awakened, having exhibited grief and horror at her friend's death, witness to her having stammered out, still half-hazy from the drugged sleep, some explanation of the Countess's having perhaps come through to her room, found her already asleep, helped herself from the chest and, ignorant of the correct dose, taken the larger phial. ... Witness of the maid again, however: in the morning the closet had been found locked and the key in its hiding place.

The heavy lids lay like twin shields across

the blue eyes, guarding her thoughts from the prying eyes of men. Composed in their studied arrangement in her lap, the fan held open between relaxed fingers, her hands lay motionless. Through all the terrible indictment, she spoke not a word. "What answer have you to make, Madame, to his lordship's charge?"

"None. I make no answer to so monstrous a proposition."

"In default of an answer, we are free to infer your guilt."

"You may make what you like of it, my lord: I refuse to answer."

Lord Weyburn got suddenly to his feet. "My lord Duke – Lady Weyburn is in the right of this matter. The law has – tacitly at least – absolved her of complicity in the death of the Countess of Frome. I say it should form no part of the present enquiry. I say she should be regarded as absolutely innocent."

His Grace looked down, astonished, his finger between two pages of the great book, as though about to open it out at a relevant passage and pass wise and instant judgment. "If her ladyship is innocent, my lord, why does she not simply say so?"

"Her ladyship does say so: she had rejected the accusation."

"To reject is one thing; to offer an explanation, (which only she can give) of the Countess's death, would clear her of suspicion."

"As to that," he said impatiently, "there may be a dozen explanations."

"You will find if you examine it, my lord, that there are none. Lady Weyburn would have us believe that she slept through the night and knew nothing. If, then, the Countess came through – it's true there was a communicating room – and helped herself, how could she have found the key?"

"Perhaps Lady Weyburn has forgotten – perhaps she left the key in the lock."

"But she had no occasion to go to the cupboard; her own dose of laudanum had been left out by the maid and none other was used. In any event, the closet was found locked and the key still hidden. Even had the Countess found the key in the lock, how could she have known where to replace it?"

"As to that – the maid may have talked, may have mentioned the hiding place casually; perhaps to the Countess's lady's-maid. . . ."

Witness of the maid, recalled, that she had spoken to no one. Several members of the servants hall could testify that she had spoken to no one but gone straight to bed (and one of the footmen that she stayed there all night – which corroboration, however, she did not put forward).

"The Countess perhaps came back; and the hiding place was referred to."

"Then why does not her ladyship say so? And supposing it true, why not ask then for the laudanum? And supposing she came again later, and finding Lady Weyburn asleep, as she says – overlooking the smaller phials, took the too-large one: why lock the closet again, why hide the key...?"

"The closet contained Lady Weyburn's jewels."

"Very well. The Countess of Frome, having talked exhaustively with Lady Weyburn since early afternoon, retires at last at midnight; returns again and enters into a conversation which for no imaginable reason turns to the hiding place of the key; retires again, feels the need for laudanum, ignores the dose close to her hand, comes to her friend's room, recollects the hiding place of the key so providentially mentioned a little while earlier, unlocks the cupboard, ignores the proper dose put up in small phials and takes one enormously larger; relocks the cupboard, hides the key again and then ... Where is the glass, my lord, from which the Countess drank? What has become of the phial?"

"You know what became of the phial," said Lord Weyburn, angrily. "Its remains were in the embers of Lady Weyburn's fire. The Countess may well have tossed it there, thinking nothing of it."

"And the glass?"

"She used Lady Weyburn's glass," he suggested, shrugging. "There was a glass at the bedside, already with dregs of laudanum in it. May not the Countess have broken the phial into that glass, drunk down the contents, not knowing she had the wrong, the too-large phial, and tossed the empty phial into the embers of the fire?" He shrugged again: it all sounded so simple – if you said it quickly.

His Grace of Orrell thought so too. "All this is dependent, my lord, of course, upon Lady Weyburn having told the Countess where the key was?" It was his turn to shrug; he looked round the court, very meaningly. "But if she did," he said, "why doesn't she say so?"

He was silent, defeated. She raised her eyes and looked over at him with a small, ironical smile. "So soon, my lord? Are you already vanquished?" She was resigned to it. "Ah, well – it was good of you to constitute yourself my champion in this matter at least; you did it so once before, if you recall, though 'within limits,' and that time also, failed at the first throw. So trouble yourself no further, I beg of you: you will only damage your cause and I need no champions. I did not kill my friend, I had no quarrel with her, she knew no secret of mine, I had no motive." She gave him a small bow, bending forward slightly in the great chair.

The Earl of Frome struggled up to his feet again. "As to motive... As to motive..." He was silent a moment, shaking his head like a wounded bear, shaking off the fog of grief that closed in on him like a grey blanket, muffling his mind against sense and clarity. "As to motive – in August of the year 1754, Madame, did you not – did you not write her a letter? – did you not write to her that you were in great trouble, ill, distressed, and obliged to leave England immediately, did you not implore her to go with you...? I – she –

against my counsel she went with you, we – we quarrelled...." His voice broke, he stood staring down at his twitching hands, tears in his eyes, muttering to himself, oblivious of them all... small, choked-off sentences... The only disagreement... Parted... All that time lost to them... And all through *her* – through *her*....

She sprang to her feet. "My lord – why do you distress yourself, what good can it do to you; or to Christine? I pray you, for your own sake, let it rest."

He seemed to come back to the present with a start; he stared at her heavily. "How can I let it rest – until I *know*? How did she die? You killed her – because of what she knew...."

"I did not kill her," she said sadly.

"Then prove it to me: answer me!" He pursued the advantage quickly, before she hardened again in her resistance. "She agreed at last: she went with you to Italy?"

"Yes, she went with me."

"And so was witness to all that happened there?"

"All the world is witness to that, my lord; I have not denied it. My son was born there."

"Upon what date, Madame, was your son born?"

"On February 15th., my lord, as I think you know." She waited for the hiss of indrawn breaths to die away, the dry rustle of fingers tapping out the tally of the months from August to February: from August 1st to February 15th. Into the subsequent chill silence she said, steadily: "He was prematurely born."

He showed no triumph; he repeated heavily: "Two months prematurely born."

"Rather more than two months: yes, my lord."

"Having been conceived upon the single occasion of the consummation of your marriage with Lord Weyburn?"

"Yes," she said.

"Am I right in saying that the child was born in Florence?"

"In Florence, yes."

"Why," said Lord Frome.

She looked a little startled, "Why in Florence?"

"Why not in Venice, Madame, where your home was?"

She feined indifference; but she looked at him warily. "I was in the care of my mother. My mother is restless since my

322

father died, she ceaselessly changes her home. Moreover..." She shrugged. "I did not want my affairs known to all Venice."

"Why not? You had come back there as a married woman: why should you not be having a child?"

"Well, as to that...." She thought about it a little. She said quickly: "As to that, my lord, the ways of our world of fashion are not quite clearly understood in Venice. In Italy, if a woman is married, she remains with her husband; to be apart while the first child is coming would seem to the simple people of Venice – curious. Moreover, Florence was my mother's birthplace, she knew of a doctor there...."

"So you left Venice where everybody knew you; and went for the birth of this – premature – infant, to Florence?"

"Where, as you wish me to agree, no doubt – nobody knew me."

"Where nobody knew you. Or rather," he said, and once again the heavy, baffled, look came about his face, the pain of grief for a moment half-forgotten, came flooding back, "or rather – where one person knew you. One person who was with you, one person who saw all, knew all, one person who alone could have told us the secret

323

truth: and cannot tell us because – because she has been silenced, because she's dead. . . ."

"The truth?" she stammered. "The secret? I do not understand you, my lord: what truth could she know, what secret could she have told?"

"She could have told," said the Earl of rome, "whether the child was or was not – prematurely born."

For if not – then the case was over: for he could not possibly be Lord Weyburn's son.

The last day. The last day of sitting in torment in that lovely room, the great room with the crystal chandeliers, with the painted ceiling and slender marble columns, which for the past long week had been a prison; a prison where one sat in studied grace, wearing a proud face, smiling a scornful smile, spreading a painted fan to lie, fluttering only a little with the gentle movement of a jeweled hand, across a breast that hid a sick and despairing heart. The last day, perhaps, of wearing a proud title – for rebel how she might against the verdict of the court, that verdict must govern every hour of her life to come; and to whom would she be 'my lady' when my lord declared her none of his? The last, the final day....

"My lord Duke, my lords, ladies and gentlemen, gentlemen of the jury... We come now to the last, the final day....

"We come at last to the final day – the final day of this Trial-by-Society, as I may call it, of Lady Weyburn of Starrbelow – as I may, for a little while yet, call *her*. Before the day closes, I shall bring before you one more witness: but this witness, whose evidence I venture to say will prove to be of paramount, of clinching importance to my presentation of the case, comes from abroad and has been detained upon the way – will be here today, but is not here yet. While we await him, let me amuse you, my lords, ladies and gentlemen – with a story....'

"In the summer of 1753, there came here among us, a certain young lady from Italy who – innocent or guilty – succeeded by an apparently accidental displacement of her dress, in attracting the notice of the town: and specifically of two gentlemen, one of royal, one of noble birth. Under pressure from her guardians, she accepted the hand of the rich nobleman. But she had already given her heart, perhaps had already confided her honour, to the other: despite the engagement, she married him secretly on Ladyday, March 25th., 1754. Some time about six weeks later, a child is conceived (and was born, in February of the following year). In the meantime, she is faced with her undertaking to marry Lord Weyburn at the end of May.

"Members of the jury – we shall, perhaps, never know just what went wrong: the Prince was at this time, a poor man, dependent upon august relatives abroad, going much in fear of them. Did they quarrel? Did they fall out of love altogether? Did they simply grow afraid of the future, now that the deed was done? At any rate, they came to a mutual plan: she was to proceed with the marriage to Lord Weyburn, the child – if they even yet knew about the child – could be fathered upon him: they would somehow destroy all records of the previous marriage – and that would be that.

"That would have been that indeed; but now something occurred to wreck all their plans. Lord Weyburn left his bride at the church door; and a child was positively on the way.

"For a fortnight she hoped, prayed, struggled with the situation – and, sitting brooding at her window at Starrbelow, evolved alternate plans. She would send for the Prince, effect a reconciliation, deny her marriage to Lord Weyburn and throw in her lot with his: but should this fail, it was imperative that Lord Weyburn never discover the earlier marriage – the child must be fathered upon anyone but the Prince. With this in her mind, she lost no time even before she could discuss the matter with her true husband, in embarking upon a career of flagrant misconduct – with a circle of profligates one of whom might later be suspected of fathering the child – for no time was to be lost. And it was as well she did: for from those long, secret, anxious discussions with Prince Anton, while his mistress was meanwhile 'got out of the way,' no reconciliation was effected. She must continue to be Lady Weyburn and let her 'husband' accuse her of infidelity if he would – he would find it hard to prove in law that a child born in wedlock to her was not his own.

"Members of the jury – between us we have puzzled out the facts: and to all of us

– to me as well as, I hope, to you – new light has come. For, looking back upon the first day of this trial, what evidence have we of any real, of any positive, misconduct on Lady Weyburn's part with any of these gentlemen? The evidence of village wenches – tainted, as she herself showed us in a neat piece of 'cross-examination' with envy and and spite; the evidence of servants resentful of the new mistress who appeared to have tricked their master into marriage – and much of that conflicting; the evidence of men boasting to one another, each doubtless believing the other favoured by her and anxious not to appear himself rebuffed. And – the evidence of herself, the evidence of deliberately publicised wild behaviour, of such trivia as the apparent acceptance of a pair of jeweled buckles (which she now denies, and which it has never been proved she did not buy for herself...). That at the beginning of this trial, I myself believed her guilty, of wanton-ness, I do not deny. But I now believe, and hope to induce you also to believe, that this was all part of that carefully thought-out plan – which, moreover, was a plan with a dual purpose. A plan first, to provide half a dozen names or more whom Lord Weyburn might suspect of fathering her child, thus drawing away attention from her marriage of Prince Anton; and a plan to facilitate the abstraction of that book of records from the chapel in May Fair. For, growing up naturally enough no doubt from the episode of the 'highwaymen' in Gloucestershire, this I now believe was the whole secret purpose of the 'Treasure Seekers' Circle': to disguise the theft of the register, in a dozen such escapades.

"Members of the jury – I appear in this court of ours as a friend and champion of Lord Weyburn, not as the personal enemy of Lady Weyburn. It is no part of my case to smear her with calumny in which we need not believe. All Lord Weyburn requires is proof that the boy, for whom she claims his inheritance, is not his son and heir. Well, as to that – a child was born in Italy who, to be his son, must have been prematurely born. There is no dispute as to that. Lady Weyburn makes no claim that the marriage was consummated upon any date earlier than August 1st. A child of that consummation must, in the natural order of events, have been born in about the following April. Lady Weyburn – failing, perhaps, to anticipate in those early days the difficulties she was later to encounter – has from the beginning made no secret of the fact that her son was born in the middle of February. There can be no question therefore that to be Lord Weyburn's son – and heir – that child must have been at least six weeks or more premature.

"Members of the jury – as to these facts one person alone in all England was able to speak: one person alone, besides Lady Weyburn, was present at the time of the birth and could have told us whether or not the child was a normal, full-term child. That witness, under what circumstances I do not presume to say, is dead. But, members of the jury, I have said, and said advisedly, one person *in all England.* For the child was not born in England; and I bring before you now...."

Sir Henry paused dramatically and, in the suddenly seething excitement a small, dark, jerky little old man darted forward from the doorway where he had but very recently appeared and, smiling expansively right and left, advanced to the table, bowed graciously to Lady Weyburn and stood looking expectantly into Sir Henry's face.

Sir Henry said, quietly: "My lord Duke, my lords, ladies and gentlemen, members of the jury – I present Signor Pietro Perraci, for many years the leading doctor in Florence and –" he paused dramatically once more – "devoting himself principally to cases of women in childbirth."

Doctor Perraci bowed right and left again, devoting himself principally, as Sir Henry might have said, to Lady Weyburn. Sir Henry let the ripple of comment die down to what seemed a long silence; and into the silence said sharply: "Signor Perraci – why do you do that?"

The little doctor looked startled: not for this had he come, arriving belated and weary, all the way from Italy in response to their importunings. He said in his halting English: "Eh? I do not understanding?"

"Why do you bow particularly, Signor – to this lady?"

"To this lady?" He threw out protesting hands. "Is this not the lady?"

"It is the lady, yes. But, Signor – how did you know that?"

The old man bowed with his hand on his heart. "Once I have seen such a lady, can I forget her?"

"Ah, that is the point, Signor Doctore,

isn't it? This is not the first time, then, that you've seen her?"

He was old and weary, the point dawned upon him but slowly. "Si, si, I have seen her; many years ago, but I have seen her."

"In Florence?"

He shrugged. "Where else but in Florence? I do not move very much out of Florence." And after this journey, his expression added, am not likely to do so again in any sort of hurry.

"Is this then the lady you attended in Florence, in the year 1755? – who gave birth to a boy there."

He shrugged and smiled. "Many ladies gave birth to boys in that year in Florence; many ladies have done so since – how can I remember. But in that year – there was only one English lady."

"And her name, sir?"

He shrugged and smiled. "A Signora – Smith, sir."

The court tittered, fluttering a flower-bed of fans, bright and delicate as petals. "You have a record, then, of a Signora Smith, your only English patient at that time in Florence – who gave birth to a boy on February 15th., 1755? Can you

332

tell us, Doctor . . . ? This child? Premature? Or normal?"

And the breeze that had fluttered the painted fans was still, the rustle of silks was hushed, the glitter of jewels muted to an unwinking glow upon hands held motionless, breasts that ceased to rise and fall with the suspension of their very breathing. Doctor Perraci looked into the beautiful face and saw the pain there and the dread in anticipation. But – what could one do? The truth was the truth and lovely ladies mustn't be naughty. "The birth?" he said. "Premature? Oh, no – perfectly normal."

She had risen. She stood very still, very pale, and faced them; and Sir Henry Kidd also stood quietly, for once his dancing feet ceased their movement, his bright eye fixed steadily on her cold, pale face. "So, Madame – this is the end; and I, who came here to accuse you, find myself, if I may say so to you, with a mind and heart much changed as must be, I think, the minds and hearts of all who have watched out for so long stand before the tribunal of this court . . . For, Madame, I submit to the court that you be judged Not Guilty of much that must have forfeited for you the respect of society. I submit to the court that you be judged Not Guilty of wantonness, or marital infidelity, of aught but a few trivial sins against the social code of good manners and propriety – and those sins committed deliberately for a special purpose. I absolve you of all but these – and of one far greater: that you have allowed yourself to live under Lord Weyburn's name when you have never in fact been his wife: and that you falsely claim your son as his heir. And even this...." He looked round at the avid, stoney faces about him, he looked into the beautiful face gazing back now pitifully into his. "And even this – a mother protecting her child, fighting for her child, sacrificing her all, her good name, her peace of mind, her place in society, facing insults and scorn, placing her very life at last in jeopardy – for the sake of a child who, at the time this all started was even yet unborn...." And he looked back at her, looked back into the blue eyes clouding over with his every word into a sort of blank despair; and said almost gently: "Has it never occurred to you, Madame, that the boy may lose the Starrbelow inheritance and yet gain a greater inheritance by far? For the marriage with Prince Anton of Brunswick was legitimate; and the son of that marriage is Prince Anton of Brunswick's heir."

She stood stiff, motionless, as though paralysed into her own carefully ordered pose of grace, a creature of marble. Her white lips stammered out: "His heir?"

"Had you never thought of it?"

"No," she said. "I never... We never..." And she put her hand to her forehead, striking the hard knuckles with violence against the frontal bone as though to drive through to her reeling intelligence a whole new conception too vast for her comprehension. "His heir! Oh, God! yes, it is true... All this time, he's been Anton's heir...." And she gave a little moan and fell forward across the great table and lay there with her bright hair gleaming against the gentle glow of the mahogany; her face as pale as death.

Fourteen

Now the rattle of wheels is heard, the thunder of hooves in the winding lanes, the clang of the wrought iron gates thrown open, the clatter of hoof and harness and wheel and screaming spring as the coach comes lumbering up the long approach to Starrbelow; once again the bright flowers are flecked with loam flicked up by the silver shoes. Two children fly to the open window, fly out to the terrace, come tumbling down the steps to the great, portico'd front door – a girl, white-skinned, blue eyed, golden of hair as her mother was; and a boy dark and slender, with a lock of forward-falling hair. "Is it known? Is the verdict known. . . . ?"

Sophia steps out: terribly pale, terribly beautiful, with a dark velvet cloak thrown over the rich dress she wore yesterday like a proud queen for the final ordeal in court; for she has driven all night to come to Starrbelow before anyone else shall get here. She says nothing to the boy but she puts out her hand with its glitter of rings, to take his. She says sharply to Catherine: "What are you doing here?"

Seven years old: but old for her years in an age when children are but miniature grown-ups, her young mind warped with the gossip of servants made more than ever careless in the fever-pitch of excitement in the past months since her mother died. She looks back at Sophia, half insolent, half afraid. "Have I not a right here, Madame?"

The boy looks up into the beautiful face, sees the curved lips straighten into a thin, cold line, need ask no longer, 'Is the verdict known?' But she says only, "Since your mother died, Catherine, your father has given orders: you are not to come to this house."

"But it is *my* house," says Catherine. She looks up again, slyly. "Is it not?"

"It is Lord Weyburn's house," says Sapphire, shortly; and she calls to the nurse who has hastened up and now stands, awed and irresolute, at the foot of the great, pillared portico of the house. "Take her back to Frome and keep her there."

"I shall not leave Starrbelow," says Catherine. "I am my cousin Weyburn's heir, I can see it in your face, and I shall not leave Starrbelow." And she sets her small white teeth in her lower lip and grows suddenly deathly pale and falls down in a faint. Sophia starts forward and the nurse, terrified, flings herself on her knees beside the child and lifts the lolling head. But the boy shrugs coolly. "It is a trick Mother, she can do it at will, she has done it a hundred times when I have opposed her. Leave her alone, seem indifferent, she'll soon come to. (He has practised it often in the privacy of his bedroom, finding it is advantageous an accomplishment, but succeeded only in achieving a few minor bruises: such guiles are for women!) He says to the nurse: "You know it's all nonsense. Ignore her."

But the woman is alarmed and anxious. "I must carry her into the house, my lady, let me lay her down for a while on a bed and apply restoratives. . . ."

"Do what you like," says Sapphire, wearily. She takes the boy by the shoulder. "Come, Nicholas, come with me; we have no time to waste." They go together into the house, she seeming hardly to observe the frigidly bowing servants – for it is true, the verdict is written on her face – through the the great hall and, by some common consent, into the ballroom. She sits down upon a brocade covered couch and puts out her hand to him again; and, still holding him, puts out her free hand to brush back the straight lock of hair falling over his eyes and smiles a little, as though reminiscently, but drops her hand at once and sits sad and musing. The silence lasts so long that he ventures at last: "The verdict has gone against us, Mother – hasn't it?" She looks downward again, sadly, not denying it. "Is there, then, nothing more we can do?"

And she smiles again directly and pulls him down to kneel beside her, all the time keeping his hand in hers. "Why, as to that, Nicholas, yes, there is something still we can do. We are not two poor lost and helpless creatures, you and I. We have one another, which is much; and there are – three things, three courses open for us to choose from." She pauses a moment; but she goes on resolutely. "I have come to you now, wasting no time for there is none to lose, to ask you to choose which of them it shall be."

"To ask *me* to choose, Mother?"

"Yes, you. It's for you to decide. And I – I shall abide by what you say. I shall not urge you nor argue with you, I shall not influence you. You shall choose." And she

339

looks at him with pity and tenderness, and with terror too, to think that on the whim of a child of nine, so much must depend. And yet – he is very wise: true and wise beyond his years as the other child is sharp and precocious beyond hers; and in his little wisdom and his honest heart, her own strength must rely for it is not enough to support her in making this resolution alone. She releases his hand at last and from the pocket of her muff which has been laid aside, she takes out a folded silk and from the silk takes three lockets, ringed with jewels; and spreads out the silk upon a small, inlaid table and upon the silk lays the three lockets – three small, oval crystals, set with jewels, each containing a miniature. "Between these three, Nicholas – you must choose."

Three lockets, lying on the little table against the rose-pink brocade. Three faces, looking up at him. Her face: his mother's face as the Guardi portrait shows it, a miniature taken from that picture, the blue-green cloak and the golden ship, pearl-studded, riding the smooth gold waves of her hair. And Lord Weyburn's face, cool, proud, defiant – so much like the face that looks back at him each day from the dressing-mirror in his own room. And a third face: handsome, smiling – with a lock of forward-falling hair.

His mother: Lord Weyburn of Starrbelow: and Prince Anton of Brunswick. And between these three he must make – poor, bewildered, uncomprehending little boy – his choice: and hers.

The day wears on. She goes to her room, refreshes herself, but does not change her dress. She orders food and wine and they are brought to her by servants overtly doubtful of her continued right to command; whose demonstrations, however, she scorns even to recognise. The boy drinks some wine with her and they eat a little food; and all the time she talks to him, gently and quietly, trying to straighten out truth and untruth for him – and yet not tell all the truth; trying to teach without guiding, to inform without influencing him this way or that. "And now, Nicholas, which is it to be? It grows late; and if we are to throw in our hands, we must leave Starrbelow without delay for it means we have no right to be here."

"No right? To be at Starrbelow?"

"If we give in you see, we renounce such rights."

To leave Starrbelow! He has other longings, other dreams, born of the long, ecstatic days in the studios of Venice, Milan, Florence, Rome on their annual visits to Firenze, ever restlessly changing her abode, everywhere finding friends; but always in the background, Starrbelow has been familiarity, security: to his mother it has come to mean home. "Even if I am not the heir here, even if I renounce my rights, if Catherine is to succeed, while my – while Lord Weyburn lives, could we not remain here as we have always done?"

"We can remain and fight. No legal court has rejected our claim."

"Or we can go elsewhere and fight – for that other claim?"

"Go elsewhere and fight – for a right to wealth, no doubt, to position, power, place, for a right to the estates Prince Anton of Brunswick would have inherited had he not died – leaving, however, a legitimate son. A right to fight for a new life – in another land. "But we should be foreigners there, Mother, unknown, not wanted; supplanters, for some other must long ago have succeeded, knowing nothing of this

342

claim. . . ." A ten year old claim, springing up without warning from out of a mist of secrecy and shame. "Who would want me, Mother – even were I proved his son?" He glances up at her uncertainly from beneath dark, slanting brows, anxious, bewildered, afraid to directly question. "Even though – even though I *were* his son?"

And still she will not, or she cannot, answer him directly. She gives a little shrug. "I am but putting it to you, Nicholas, it is for you to decide if you wish to make the claim." She thinks it over, musing. "And it would be a fight. The registry records are destroyed, the men who performed the marriage are long since deported and probably dead; the witnesses were strangers brought in from the street. We have nothing but – this." She picks up the miniature, holding it in the palm of her hand, looking down into the painted face, looking up from it into the grave young face above. 'Forever – Anton'; and a lock of unruly hair! "It isn't very much, my little one, to claim a royal title and a royal fortune on."

Was this then his father, after all? – this handsome stranger whose home would hold out so cold a welcome to him – to him

343

who, also, would be a stranger. He lays the two miniatures side by side, the pale dark face and the fair, handsome face; and takes up the third. "And if I choose neither Starrbelow nor Brunswick, Mother – but only you?"

It is what she has hoped – and dreaded: the decision to go, to sever all connections, to end once and for ever the wild, sick folly of hope deferred and yet never quite dead in her. She looks up at him, smiling. She has been very cool towards him always, very reserved, she is not a mother to kiss and fondle and call pet names: her magic for him has been in her very remotion, in her pride and her beauty, in the absolute integrity that even a child can sense of her love for him, of his own strength and safety in that love – in the smile that, of all the world, she reserves for him alone. She smiles that smile at him now: that smile with no trace of the mystery, the disdain, the cool mockery of the smile she has shown to the rest of the world. She says: "Do you love me, Nicholas?"

He lowers his eyes because, for the first time in his life, he sees tears in hers. He mutters: "Yes."

"More than Starrbelow? More than

Brunswick?" She bows her golden head, a tear falls on the small brown hand she holds tight in her own. "Oh, Nicholas – I am weary, weary, I think that my heart is breaking.... Shall we go away together, then, you and I? – shall we go away from all this, shall we end it for ever, shall we go to Italy? We could live simply – somehow; we could work, you could study your music seriously as you have longed to do, and I could work, we could manage somehow. You are very young, but wise far beyond your years, life has made you so; and I am not old – twenty eight isn't very old. And Italy is lovely, free and lovely; we might not have rich clothes and jewels, which would mean nothing; we must leave this dear house and this lovely land, which would mean a great deal; but in Venice every stone is a jewel, Nicholas, the whole city is clothed in a beauty we needn't be rich to see. And the skies are sunny there and – hearts are kind. But it would be a great step, a desperate step for us. If we fight, we fight for great stakes; if we give in – we have nothing. My mother will be happy beyond all dreams to have us with her, but she's poor too, there could be no help for us there. We should have nothing."

"Would not – it's not for myself, Mother, it's for you – would not Lord Weyburn...?"

"We would take nothing from Lord Weyburn; and nothing from Brunswick. We will fight for our rights, Nicholas; or resign from them altogether, taking nothing. We will not blackmail them into giving us an income for keeping our mouths shut." And she opens her blue eyes suddenly full upon him. "It is all or nothing. It is Starrbelow – or Hanover – or Italy. Lord Weyburn – or Prince Anton of Brunswick – or me."

He stands staring down at the three lockets. He stammers, "But it's a matter of rights, Mother. Starrbelow or Hanover – it can't be both and you don't tell me...."

The heavy lids fall again over the dazzling blue. "As to that – you must be content to trust me. One day I will explain; meanwhile, answer because we must go or stay; I will not be caught here, dithering. What is it you wish to do?"

What is it he wishes to do? "What have I ever wished but to be in Italy, to be a great musician one day as my aunt Christine always told you I should be. What have I ever wished – but to be in Italy, not idling

346

here, a young lordling, waiting for his father's shoes, but studying and working, living my life among musicians, among the poets and painters and sculptors, among the thinkers...."

"There are 'thinkers' in England too, you know," says Sapphire, mildly. "And poets and painters and even musicians too."

"Not at Starrbelow. If I could go up to London...."

"I don't think you'd care very much for London," she says, no longer smiling. "I myself, I know, have found little comfort there. At any rate it will be closed to us now; if you want a world outside Starrbelow, you must go to Italy." And she asks him sharply, as though, suddenly she can no longer endure the anxiety of waiting for his answer: "Is this then your choice?"

He swings away from her for a moment, paces across the room a little, comes back to her. "You see – I don't understand that it can be a matter of choice. It's a matter of rights. A – a man may put aside lands or possessions or fortune that have come to him this way or that; but as his inheritance is a part of himself, so he is a part of his inheritance – isn't he, Mother? If it lies within me – in here," he insists, striking his breast with a small, closed fist, "to be a prince of Hanover or lord of Starrbelow, then I can't make myself less by saying, 'I give up my rights.' I am what I am: I am my inheritance." He looks up at her anxiously. "My heart is in Italy; but – if I chose to stand by my rights because I – I thought it wrong to deny them: you wouldn't desert me?"

She turns away her face from him to hide her despair, the weariness and despair at the thought that the long struggle against her own heart is not to be ended for her after all, by any childish grasping at the easy way out. "No, no – whatever happens, I shan't desert you."

"But you too would have chosen Italy?"

"As an escape," she says. "Not for happiness – only for peace."

"For me it would be happiness. For me it would be the other way about, you see: it would be happiness – but not peace. I couldn't feel at peace, I couldn't give my heart to my music, knowing that I had been cheated of my birthright. And if I bow to the ruling of this court and renounce it, I shall still, in fact, have been cheated of it; and if you can understand me, Mother, I shall feel it's been cheated of *me*. I wish it weren't mine: that's the truth, I wish it weren't mine; but since it is... I can't. I can't so dishonour my own birthright by appearing to admit that it has never been mine." He raises his eyes to her again, dark, candid eyes under the upward-sweeping brows. "Nor so dishonour *you.*"

She meets his eyes. She says steadily: "And as to that, there is no dishonour. My marriage was legitimate: let who will doubt it, you and I may be satisfied of the truth."

"Of course I don't doubt it, Mother. I have never doubted you. Only...." He stares down at the two handsome faces, the dark face and the fair face. "Only, Mother – which?"

Once again, she does not answer directly. She says: "So we are to fight?"

"For my rights. It's no question of a choice. But which *are* my rights? Brunswick or Starrbelow – it can't be both."

She rises. She stands beside him for a moment looking down also at the two miniatures, then she puts an arm about him and turns him to face the great gilt mirror overhanging the high mantelshelf. She says. "Look in the glass, Nicholas – and decide for yourself."

A pale dark face looking up from an oval miniature; and a face with a forward-falling lock of hair. And from the mirror, the same pale face looks back – from beneath a lock of forward-falling hair. Weyburn or Brunswick? Starrbelow or Hanover. "Choose, Nicholas; choose!"

And there are voices in the hall.

She stands very still, looking over the boy's shoulder at the face reflected in the glass; and there are voices in the hall, the voice of a servant, and a voice that for many years had not been heard there – the voice of Lord Frome. While she lived he had trusted his wife in all things; from the time of their only quarrel, he laid no veto upon her friendship with Sapphire, but he himself refused Lady Weyburn his countenance, never saw or acknowledged her son, would not entertain her at Frome, never came to Starrbelow. Now, however, his voice, cold with anger, is heard in the hall. "I am but now returned from London. I am told that my daughter is here?"

And the voice of the servant stammers an admission and the voice of the nurse protests from the stairs. "She would come, my lord, we dared not brook her, and she with her mother so lately dead: she has been here every day. And when I would have taken her home. . . ."

"Fetch her at once," he says.

"My lord, she is ill, she is a-bed, she was taken faint. . . ."

And the voice of the child, shrilling down also, from above. "I am not ill at all, but I would not leave: for is it not true, my lord, that the verdict is known and this is my house?"

"What nonsense is this?" he says, heavily and angrily. "It is your cousin Weyburn's house."

"But when he dies? Is it not the verdict –?"

"There is no 'verdict' affecting you, Catherine; come down at once and come away with me. . . ."

"Let them go," says Sapphire, whispering, to the boy. "Let them go, not knowing we are here." Through the mirror she watches the great door through which, so many agonies ago, she came to meet her destiny. "Let them go and then, quickly, we must make our decision: if we are to go, let us go and not wait to be ignominiously sent. If we are to stay. . . ." And she puts up her hand, trembling, watching his face in

351

the glass, and smooths back his hair and thinks with pity for the child that it was wrong to leave so great a decision to him; and with pity for herself that her own will was to weak to make the choice that would cut her off for ever from tormented hope; and with terror for them both that on a boy's whim all their future, peace or happiness, must depend. Catherine's voice cries, coming closer towards her father down the stair. "But my Aunt Sophia is come and she does not deny –"

There is a moment's blank silence. Lord Frome says sharply: "Lady Weyburn is here? But she can't be – we started at dawn...." and the servant's voice mumbles out that her ladyship has driven all night; and a third voice cries out: "She is *here?*" And the door opens; and Lord Weyburn comes in.

Just so had they stood long ago and looked at one another across the great length of the ballroom: not speaking. Behind him, Lord Frome also entered; in the hall, the child Catherine set up her shrill clamour and he closed the door behind him sharply, and the sound was muffled into obscurity, and faded. She turned from the mirror and so confronted them, her arm about the child's shoulders, as they advanced, staring down the length of the room. Lord Frome said at last: "Dear God! What boy is this?"

He stood very close to her, his dark head at her shoulder, his hand holding tight to hers. "I am – Nicholas, my lord."

Silence. But very low, she said to him at last: "The moment has come: you must choose now. Yes, you are Nicholas. And – is that all?"

"Yes," he said. "I have chosen. I am Nicholas and nothing more." He looked into Lord Weyburn's set white face. "Those others wouldn't want me: and *he* – he doesn't want me, either, Mother. I'd rather be plain Nicholas."

"But you are not plain Nicholas," said Lord Weyburn. "You are Nicholas of Brunswick. It is written in every line of your face: you are Prince Anton's son." He had known it always, but now he was sick with the shock of the proof of it. He said to Sapphire, almost sullenly: "No wonder you would not bring the boy to the court!"

"You are mad," said Lord Frome. "Anton's son! Look in the mirror, man, hold the boy at your side and look into the

353

glass. Can you not see – he's the living image of yourself?"

"He is Anton of Brunswick: the shape of the head, the shape of the face, the whole carriage, the air; and when he wore no wig – as he often did not – his hair fell ever forward as this boy's does. . . ."

"You are mad, Charles. He is Weyburn all over – look at his eyes, his nose, the Weyburn nose; look at his mouth, the upward sweep of the brows. . . ." A look of terror came into his face. He stammered: "The brows. . . ." Weyburn said impatiently: "The boy is the image of Anton; he cannot be both."

"He cannot be either," said Sapphire, quickly. She pulled the child roughly back to her, away from them, and put her hand up to his dark head, holding it close against her shoulder, the face turned inward to her breast as though she would have it no longer canvassed between them. "Let us go now, my lords, we have made our choice. We go back to Venice. We will trouble you no more." She moved past them to the door, holding the boy still close. "Let us be gone."

"No," said Lord Frome. "Wait."

But she pushed past him, urging the boy

354

forward ahead of her. "My lord – let us go, let us be gone. Say nothing, I beg of you, I beseech you – say nothing, keep silent, and in one moment we shall be gone and never, I swear it, never shall you hear from either of us again. Only keep silent now," she implored him, only say nothing and we shall have passed out of your lives for ever...." But he caught at her wrist and dragged her back. "Oh, God!" she cried out, "don't say it, don't speak. When I have given so much, have lost so much...."

But he dragged her to the little table, the boy following lost in bewilderment, Lord Weyburn rushing forward to catch her as she fell forward, half-fainting, into his arms; and took something from his breast and laid it down with the three miniatures upon the rose-coloured silk....

Dazzlingly fair where her cousin Weyburn was dark: but with the Weyburn nose and the Weyburn mouth and the Weyburn carriage of the beautiful head – resembling her cousin in all but her colouring and the lovely, upward, winged brown sweep of the brows....

Christine.

'If passionate gratitude can make a friend – you have one in me, Madame, to the end of my life. . . ."

Fifteen

And time put back the hands of the Great Clock over the hours and the days and the months and the years: and from this very room, a weeping girl fled out alone into the starlit gardens; and Prince Anton of Brunswick, having sold his soul to the devil, went out also into the night – where his Master awaited him.

Anton of Brunswick – and the Lily of Lillane.

They had seen a good deal of one another while, at the behest of his mistress, Prince Anton played watchdog to Sophia in the days of her first coming into society – to Sophia and her new and inseparable friend, Christine Lillane. Now, both of them sick and ashamed of what they had lately done, they met in the gardens, while, within, all interest was concentrated on Lord Weyburn and Sapphire Devigne; and he for a moment forgot his shame and misery in consoling hers and she hoped to pique the errant Lord Frome by accepting attentions from this new source – which, however, she thought, innocently wise, he could never suspect her of seriously considering. ('This is a comedy only too often played,' Sapphire had said to her bitterly later, in her room; and, 'Yes,' she had said – her mind far away, not thinking of her friend at all.)

But – Lord Frome was errant indeed, was gone, was lost to her; and her cousin Charles also was lost; and her friend was caught up in Lord Weyburn's pursuit and their betrothal. And meanwhile Prince Anton's ache remained with him, and in all his world, there was only this one who knew nothing of his shoddy wager, who still accepted him as the man he would wish himself to be. And Sophia and Lady Corby went off to Venice and they had only one another, under the chaperonage of the blind, trusting, doddering old mother. And he was kind and easy-going and gay, and his attentions were balm to her wounded pride; and she was gentle and lovely – and, after the practised fires of his middle-aged mistress's passions, her cool, white purity refreshed, enchanted, and at last inflamed him. By the time the travellers returned, he could think of nothing but that he must possess her. Only under the seal of matrimony could attainment be possible; nor could he hope for one moment for permission from home – he was promised in marriage to another and moreover by family arrangement and under the royal consent. But she was irresistible; and as it proved, hardly resisting. Innocent and ignorant, she was easily persuaded that she had by now too far compromised herself with him to be able to refuse him: that secrecy was imperative on account of the inevitable family opposition – which would all be resolved, however, in a happy reunion, when a fait accompli was made known. On March 25th, while she yet doubted, played for time, begged to be allowed to confide at least in her dear Sophia – he sprang the news on her that the day had come; and hustled her off to the chapel in May Fair.

But what in pursuit had been exquisitely, provocative evasion, in possession proved only chill, loveless and shaming; and for this he had jeopardised every hope of the solid Hanoverian happiness in which his real future lay. Within a month he was bitterly regretting the whole business, another month and she had fled from their secret embraces for ever; by May 27th, his mind was made up. He followed her down to the Weyburn wedding and there, hangdog but triumphant, informed her that it was all over. Such marriages as theirs had been illegal 'from and after March 25th, Ladyday' according to the Act; that included the day itself, and under such circumstances they had not been married at all.

She was happy beyond words, no doubt, to find herself free. Lord Frome had returned at last for his friend's wedding, and was treating her with all his old loving kindness: her life-long devotion, never for a moment grown less, seemed fated to be rewarded after all. But that she was being deceived never for a moment entered a mind which itself was free from guile; nor any thought of deceiving. She had entered into her supposed marriage in perfect confidence, had given herself in what she truly believed to be the bonds of wedlock: she had done no wrong, had been only foolish and mistaken, and now found herself to her exquisite relief, not bound by her mistake. That she should one day confide in Lord Frome, she may well have contemplated, and with some misgiving,

360

too well knowing his rigid sense of propriety; but even this might not be necessary, the past was the past, was over and done with, both had their reasons for secrecy, nothing she did not choose to tell need ever be known. In her sky-blue dress, matching the radiance of suddenly carefree blue eyes, she danced at Sophia's wedding with a light heart; and the future she had ever dreamed of, held out welcoming arms....

Two weeks more and she knew that the dream was over. She was going to have a child.

The mother, as a confidante worse than useless, readily allowed herself to be carried down to Starrbelow again – for was not the Earl of Frome in residence 'next door'? Sophia dragged herself from her stupor of pain to hear the story.

"Well, but Christine, you must inform Prince Anton – of course he will marry you now."

The room in which they sat was panelled in daffodil-coloured brocade, the furniture painted French satinwood with exquisite spindley legs, the ornaments of ormolu and the deep blue of Sevres porcelain – richly glowing against the yellow silk; from the

361

window, the drive curved away and down to the wrought-iron, gilded gates. And beyond the gates, the woody hills rose up to where Frome Castle stood in its splendour of cool grey stone. Through those gates, had passed out all that Sophia Weyburn loved in life; behind those grey walls, lay Christine's happiness, lost to her for ever, now. She said at last: "After what has passed, even if he were willing, Sophia – how could I marry him?"

"You have married him once already," said Sapphire dryly.

"When I thought Lord Frome had abandoned me. Oh, I know," she said, quickly, not raising her head, staring down bleakly at the clasped hands, "that that dream is over But – the other. I never loved him, I married him for wrong reasons, in a moment of madness: all this I know. But now – now, I think, Sophia, that we hate one another."

"There is nothing to hate in poor Anton."

"Not when he has pretended to marry me –?"

"You can't think, Christine, that he knew at the time it was illegal?"

"I don't know," she said drearily. "He says he did not."

"I don't believe it of him. He is weak and has been ill-taught by Lady Corby; but he is not calculating and mean."

"In any event, Sophia, what does it all matter? He is repugnant to me now, I could not live as his wife; and for his part, he was undisguisedly happy to be rid of me. How can I now, by blackmailing him with this threat to my honour – impel him to marry me?"

"There is no blackmail – it is his responsibility as much as yours; more, since he persuaded you into this 'marriage.' He must be told, Christine, at any rate. You must see him."

"How can I see him? We have foresworn all communication, he's day and night again in Lady Corby's pocket."

"Write and tell him "

"I did write asking him to meet me; he ignored my letter."

"Did you tell him the reason?"

"Of course not, Sophia – how could I commit such tidings to paper? If your Aunt Corby got hold of it...."

"She may have got hold of the letter – and suppressed it. Or he may suspect the reason; and it would by typical of him to evade the issue, to let things slide, to put off decision. But you must discuss it with him, Christine; it's only right, and only fair to him to do so. I'll ask him here."

"He won't come. She has always been jealous of you – little knowing it was I he was attached to, Sophia! – and she wouldn't let him."

"I'll ask her too, then; where she goes, he will go."

And she wrote off privily to Anton: it was necessary that he should come to Starrbelow, an excuse had been made to invite Lady Corby, she was to bring 'a party'; he must insist upon being included in it. She sent the letter by a private messenger, riding post haste, and twenty four hours later received his answer. "He is coming," she said to Christine, entering the room with the letter in her hand.

It was the room Christine had always used at Starrbelow: the small room with the naked cupids playing on the painted ceiling, all tangled up with their pink-and-blue ribbon bows; with the tall windows over the wooded park, looking out, as so many of the Starrbelow windows looked out, towards Frome. She had

364

dismissed her maid and was in her long white muslin night-robe, ready for bed, the fair hair falling in its soft curls on her white shoulders. She said dully: "Very well."

"But – he refuses to come while you are here. He says he will discuss what is to be discussed with me."

"Christine raised her head. "Then surely we need not trouble him to come at all? He cannot marry me, if he will not see me."

"Of course he must see you. But I am obliged to send an undertaking that you have left the house. Very well, then, you must stay near at hand and I'll arrange a meeting when he gets here."

"How *can* I 'stay near at hand,' Sapphire? Are my mother and I to leave Starrbelow the moment Prince Anton of Brunswick chooses to come there, and move to some inn? What reason could we give?"

"You must say.... You must give out that you disapprove his coming, Christine, in your cousin's absence. My aunt's jealousy was no secret, it was widely believed that *I* in the past was Prince Anton's object: even I didn't know," she said, half rueful, half laughing, "that all the time it was you!"

"Oh, Sophia, as if I could lay you open to such gossip; should seem to criticise you?"

"I am used to gossip," said Sapphire wearily, "and past caring; such things seem merely pinpricks to me now. But if you prefer, you can say it's my aunt you object to. Lord Weyburn never approved her, you can declare that you will not condone her presence here with her riff-raff of friends."

"But in that case I would return to town; I should not go to an inn."

"Who asks you to go to an inn?" said Sapphire, losing patience. "Go over to Frome: let your mother put your complaint to the Earl, seek refuge there from the goings-on at Starrbelow." She shrugged. "He will be only too ready to take up your cudgels; for, love him as you may, you cannot deny, my dear, that your Lord Frome is something of a prude." People came to you with their burdens, she thought, and from that moment made you their enemy, fighting your efforts to help them as though you yourself were in some way to blame. "We will talk about this again tomorrow, Christine," she said, and went away.

But sitting in her own room once again,

staring out unseeingly and down towards the gilded gates as, she knew, Christine would be sitting staring out toward Frome, her heart smote her for unkindness to her friend. Why should her love be less passionate than mine, she thought, because it is not mine – why should her pain be less keen? We have both lost our loves: but I, at least, need not now demand marriage with a man I hate and who does not conceal his dislike for me: need not be dragged off, unwilling and unwanted, to a strange land where I shall be rejected and resented for the rest of my days. . . . It was a pity in the end, she reflected, that this had not happened to herself rather than to Christine: Christine had a world of hope still before her but for this; but she – she knew now that for herself hope was past, that he had not loved her after all, he would never come back. . . . I could have gone to Italy, she thought, to my mother, I could have had my child there and who would have known? or, all the world knowing, who would have cared? One more black mark against poor Sapphire Devigne who had been gossiped and scandalised over for a brief season and would soon be forgotten as anything but the object of a notorious wager. But it had not happened to her – could never have happened to her; it had happened to Christine, to Christine the stainless one, the Lily, the irreproachable, whose fall would therefore be infinitely more great: Christine the gentle, the loving, the steadfast, the guileless of heart. And in all the world nobody could offer her help and comfort but herself; and she had been impatient and unkind. She got up and went through again to Christine's room.

Christine was sitting in the window no longer, but she stood there still; and still stared out – for the last time – towards Frome: the triple vial of laudanum in her hand.

She rose from a night of sleepless watching, the plan all formed in her mind. She told once again a single lie – one lie to persuade Christine into agreement, which later must be retracted – but not until it was too late for them to change their minds. Lord Weyburn, she said, had in fact come back to Starrbelow after the wedding, for a single night, secretly, seeking some solution to their unhappy marriage; and, arriving at none, had quarrelled with her irrevocably and gone again. He could not deny it, however, if she declared herself with child by him; she would insist upon going to her mother in Italy for the birth, would insist upon her friend going with her; they would wait there till Christine's child was born and she would then claim it as her own. No need for any marriage with Anton, no need for the alternative gossip, obloquy and shame. Christine had but to be patient a few uneasy months, and then come back to England and her happiness there.

Christine, of course, protested, argued, pleaded, disclaimed: stumbled at last upon the objection affecting inheritance. "You could not claim the child, Sophia, as Lord Weyburn's; for that would make it his heir."

"And so it *would* be his heir," said Sapphire. "You are his present heir; and your child would be, after you."

It would never arise, for Lord Weyburn, of course, had not set eyes on her since the wedding two weeks ago, would know the child not his; but for the moment it silenced the last argument "We will see what Prince Anton says, Christine, and let it rest upon that. Only promise me – no more laudanum!"

But the bottle of laudanum, anyway, was

369

safe in her own keeping; she carried it with her from thenceforward, a reminder lest ever her resolution fail in the path of self-sacrifice mapped out for herself: that same phial which ten years later was to fall again into Christine's hands.

So the plan went forward; and within the plan, her own, her secret plan. Christine retired to Frome, permitted it at least to be believed that she disapproved her friend's behaviour in Lord Weyburn's absence. Sapphire began the systematic collection of names that might be associated with hers when the time came to question the fatherhood of the child – names so numerous that, as Sir Henry Kidd long after was shrewdly to deduce, none could be singled out for responsibility; began the course of conduct that would give credence to the mystery of a child born in secrecy abroad, of whom any of half a dozen men might be the father. That the birth itself might be kept a secret remained, of course, her first hope; but she dared not count upon success and alternative plans must be layed in advance.

Red Reddington, Pardo Ryan, Lord Franks – they were easy prey; and meanwhile Prince Anton came down, and the watchful mistress was disposed of and the consultations began, long talks during the solitary rides in the woods above Starrbelow, secret meetings there with Christine, ridden over from Frome: secret meetings now and again interrupted, obliging Christine to admit to the Earl that he had 'accidentally' met with her friend and the Prince.... Long discussions, cold as death but for the most part without acrimony; ending always in the same decision – he and Christine must part. If she made the thing public and so forced his hand, of course marry her he must. "But you vould not be happy in Hanover, Christine, vith me...."

"She would not be happy in Paradise, with you," said Sophia; and she looked him up and down, slowly, while he went first white and then red beneath her look; and smiled the smile. "You need not have struggled so hard, Prince: I would not, now that I know you a little, have let her marry you if you had come crawling to her on your knees. A prince you may be, but by God," she said, in the new language she was learning so readily at the hands of Pardo and Red, "by God and Mary, you are no gentleman!"

371

Less, even than they knew or dreamed of. And his concern now was to have all record wiped out of that marriage, which he alone of the three knew to have been a true marriage after all. "Well, that too we can accomplish," said Sapphire. "I have thought of it already and laid a plot." She said to the silent, white, shuddering Christine: "Go back to Frome, dearest, we will meet no more. But when the time comes that I summon you, be ready to come away with me; and see that you quarrel with his lordship about it (where I am concerned, that will be easy enough!), or we'll have him dog-trotting out to Italy after you and finding you the size of a house, with this fine gentleman's child." She did not say again that Lord Frome was a prude; but the thought that had he been otherwise, all this might be resolved without her self-sacrifice, roused her whenever his name was mentioned to irritable scorn.

And so the Treasure Seekers' Circle was born and ran its brief course, and at last came – had the other members but known it – to the last 'escapade'; and in the distress and anxiety of that unlovely evening, she forgot to hand over to Anton the love-token

Christine had given her to return to him.

It lay still hidden in her bodice when her true love took her at last into his arms – and found it there: this miniature, this pale face framed by the fair, forward-falling hair, that now looked up at her from the rose-coloured silk, laid out upon the little rosewood table in the ballroom at Starrbelow. 'Forever – Anton.'

But now he held her in his arms again: and would never let her go. Lord Frome sat heavily on the brocaded couch, his head in his hands: raising it only once to stammer out, "But – the doctor. . . ."

"Of course he recognised me. He had seen me often enough at Christine's bedside. I was anxious; but he was old and weary, he had forgotten, he recollected only that he had seen me before."

The boy stood staring at her with troubled eyes. "Do you tell me, then, that I am not your son? That you're not my mother at all?"

"Oh, Nicholas, I am more than your mother, you are more than my son. What have we not been to one another, all these long years?" She left her lover for a moment and went to the child. "I could

373

have left you in Italy, my mother would have cared for you; she loved Christine too. But...." She said to Lord Weyburn: "I had to come back to Starrbelow; hope would not die in me, I wanted to be at least in England where you must some time come. But I could not leave you, Nicholas, I loved you too much; you had been all mine since Christine had come home and left you with me." But she saw again a darkening of the eyes, a lowering of the winged brown brows, she said swiftly: "And she loved you too, always, your true mother, your 'other mother'; she broke her heart at leaving you in Italy, she begged me to come home, to bring you with me to Starrbelow so that at least, living close by at Frome, she could see you often, be always near you. And so she was, dearest, and loved you and cared for you: gave you her own divine gift of music and taught you to love it and use it...."

"I see," he said, gravely. He thought it over. "And that man – that Prince who was no gentleman: that was my father?"

"He is dead," she said gently, "and in his death, perhaps, showed himself a gentleman after all. For he accepted the challenge – the challenge to the death. He thought, of course, that it was on account of her – of your mother, Nicholas. Lord Weyburn, in his challenge, referred to 'a matter concerning the honour of my family' – a lady's name would not be mentioned, naturally. It was I, we know, whom Lord Weyburn intended – having found the locket in my keeping and believing me with child by Prince Anton. But Anton was guiltless towards me, how should he think it was I? – he knew nothing of the finding of the locket, knew nothing of my having seen Lord Weyburn. No, he thought, of course, that it was Lord Weyburn's own family he referred to: that he had discovered the wrong done to his cousin Christine. And he accepted that, Nicholas: he said it was just, though he must have known that it well might mean his death."

Lord Frome spoke for the first time; his heart was too full to trouble about the boy. He said grimly: "He made no effort, however, to put matters right for her – for Christine – before he died: to tell her that she had been truly married and her child would be legitimate." No doubt, he said, heavily ironic, he preferred not to trouble his precious principality with a posthumous heir.

"No, no," protested Sapphire, her eyes on the boy's face, "it was not that. I think, indeed, he never considered the matter of inheritance, he was young, he was at that time without money or estates, how should he be looking forward to the future of an unborn child? – none of us thought of it. Christine and I, of course, believed the marriage illegal, but even when we knew otherwise, the thought did not come into our heads. And I think he did, in fact, try to protect Christine. He could not ask to see her before he fought – believing as he did that she was the reason for the duel; but he tried to see me, and that surely must have been so that he might tell me the facts? It was refused, of course, and then they all left for Belgium hastily and there was no chance."

"He might have written."

"To write would be to commit her secret to paper."

"And to embarrass himself," said Lord Frome, doggedly, "in the event of his surviving the duel."

"Well – perhaps; in the event of his surviving, it might have embarrassed them both, for to his mind everything was now satisfactorily settled: it had been arranged that I was to claim the child. But – she was in his thoughts, for he wore on his finger the wedding-ring she had returned to him, with the date inscribed; and this, as he died, he sent me with messages, and murmured over and over again, 'Ladyday... Ladyday...' hoping, no doubt, that I would see the significance of the date at last. Even then, you see, Nicholas, he was scrupulous not to mention her name: only a message to me and that muttering over and over again of his anxious conscience, 'Ladyday... Ladyday...'" She said to him carefully, hesitantly, "If you would like it, Nicholas, I still have the ring."

"No, no," he said quickly, "I don't want the ring."

"It was your mother's wedding ring, dearest: given by your father on their true marriage day." And she thought: Such a little boy, to be burdened with so much knowledge; and yet for his years so right-thinking and so wise! He said, breaking into her thoughts: "I won't call him my father. He disowned me, he left my mother to bear me in secrecy and shame: and I now disown *him.*"

"He was to have great possessions, Nicholas, when he came to his inheritance;

377

which now would be rightly yours. You would be a prince."

They stood watching him, such a very small, slender little boy among all the tall grown-ups, so preternaturally resolute and grave. He said: "I will not be a prince. I do not call his inheritance an inheritance, I will not call him my father – I repudiate him as he repudiated my mother and me."

"You have his blood in your veins, royal blood, Nicholas; you cannot make yourself less than you are. May you not have a duty, dearest, may you not one day believe it your duty to the inheritance of your father –?"

But he interrupted her. "Haven't you heard me say it? – he is not my father. I have no inheritance, I refuse to call him my father." He said: "There will be no 'one day': no power can make me ever think of it or speak of it again. I will be a gentleman if I may; I will not be a prince."

"A man may be both a gentleman and a prince."

"*He* could not," he said, "and I would rather be neither, Mother, than call myself his son." He corrected himself quickly, however, painfully flushing. "But you are not my mother after all, are you? What shall I call you now?"

She had always been very cool towards him, remote and reserved; but now she kneeled down beside him and put her arms about him. "Oh, my little son," she said, "my brave, my true and honest one, my perfect gentleman – if you will not call me mother still, I think it will break my heart."

Lord Frome forced himself up for a moment from his abstraction. He said kindly: "It is what your own mother in heaven would have wished."

"Whom you say she murdered," said the boy sharply, spitting it out at him suddenly, holding her close to him with his reedy arms, as though to champion her against the world; and she rose, her heart at ease for him at last, and faced them with his hard little hand clasped tight in hers. Lord Frome said heavily: "I do not say so, I never said so; she would not answer to the charge, she would not explain. . . ."

To answer would have been to bow his own proud, prudish, obstinate head in the dust, to tarnish the stainless family escutcheon Christine had died to defend. How could she have answered, when to answer would be to reveal Christine's secret? How clear her own name, at the expense of Christine's, now that Christine was dead...?

For Sapphire, on that last day of Christine's life, had come at long last to the end of her patience. Driving home from the park after the encounter with the Duchess of Witham, when a dozen words had made clear to her the real truth of their position.... 'On March the twenty-fifth,' she had said, 'on Ladyday, 1754, the Fleet marriages had become illegal...' and, *'From* March the twenty-fifth'; the Duchess had screeched out, 'they were still legal on Ladyday....' "Do you not see, Christine, what all this means? If Anton were wrong, or was deceiving you – but it is too clear he deliberately deceived you; and we have been mad all these years, to take it all for granted, not to make sure – if indeed the Marriage Act took force, not from the day he married you but from the day after: why then you were legitimately married after all, you were truly his wife."

She was bemused, she could not think clearly; but, single-hearted as ever, one thought flew up to the surface of her mind. "But Sapphire – then my marriage to Edward...?"

"Oh, pish, child, you think of nothing but Edward! You are safe enough there, poor Anton had been dead eighteen months before you married again; we had been on a little trip to Italy in the meantime, if you remember? and you had come back, and dillied and dallied, and your precious Edward had at last forgiven you your association with the notorious Sapphire of Starrbelow. But Nicholas – I vow, Christine, sometimes I think he is more my son after all, than yours: you care nothing for him nor for Catherine either, it is all for your prig of an Edward. . . ."

"He is not a prig," said Christine, angrily. "It is a word you use too often, Sophia. You have never understood him; he is stern it is true and rigid in his principles, but he's open-hearted and generous as the day."

"Very well, then, now is the time for him to prove it. For, in this case, Christine, Nicholas was legitimately born; and therefore, after you, is Lord Weyburn's heir."

"Nicholas! Heir to Starrbelow! But Catherine –"

"Pouf! Catherine – what does it matter to her? She's a girl, she will marry; and though Frome's title and estates must pass to a male heir, she will be dowered enough for a dozen women. But Nicholas – Nicholas would have had nothing but what you and I could privately give him; and you and I have nothing of our own. And now he is heir – my Nicholas, your Nicholas, is, after yourself, legitimately Weyburn's heir!"

"That's why –? Just now, with the Duchess – I thought you had lost your senses, suddenly crying out, claiming the inheritance for him, after all these years of silence...."

Sapphire laughed. "With you clutching at my arm, protesting! – 'Sophia, this is not just.' 'Sophia, I shall tell my cousin...!' I thought at any moment you would blurt out the truth."

"But now –?"

"But now, after all, it is the truth that must be told: though not screeched out over the heads of the mob to Gossip Wit in her carriage in the middle of the park!" And her heart rose at the thought of what it all might yet mean to herself: for when the truth was known....

"You have the ring, your wedding ring, Christine, which Sir Adam sent to me, after

Anton was killed; with the date inside it. You have but to show it as proof of the day of your marriage. . . ."

"For God's sake! Tell the truth – about the child, about Anton . . . ?"

"You know now that your marriage was legitimate, Christine; there is nothing to be ashamed of."

"But all these years . . . Sapphire, I told Edward nothing, my life with him has been a lie. . . ."

"It shouldn't have been so: if he had been any other kind of man, it needn't have been so. You believed yourself married, you did nothing wrong: he should have been asked to understand that, to accept you."

"To accept me? The Earl of Frome – to take a woman disgraced and dishonoured, with an illegitimate child by some dissolute princeling whom none of them approved of: the Lily of Lillane, fallen to this, to be Countess of Frome . . . !"

"Very well; but now we know you were not dishonoured, your marriage was legal."

"But Sapphire, I have lived a lie with him. I – I was obliged to pretend, I – deceived him, I came to him as – as a virgin. . . . Am I to tell him now that in truth I had lived as another man's wife? Am I to

383

tell him that I, his wife, had had a child already, by another man . . . ?"

"To whom you were honourably married," insisted Sophia.

"But Sophia, I lied, I – I dissembled: all these years I have lived a pretence and a lie. Edward will feel – he will loathe and despise me, he will feel that I tricked him . . . ."

"I told you," said Sapphire in her own dry way, with that touch of scorn she used ever when she spoke of Lord Frome, "that the time had come for dear Edward to prove his vaunted magnanimity."

And the storm blew up again and small gusts of it carried to the coachman on his box, to be repeated later at Sapphire's trial for murder; and was carried into the house and lasted the long evening, to the delight of eavesdroppers, only half-hearing, all uncomprehending, but ready to run with tales of it to my lord, when their mistress was dead. "Could you not, Sophia, simply claim Nicholas as your son and Lord Weyburn's? If he justly inherits, what does it matter through whom the inheritance comes?"

"Lord Weyburn knows very well he is not his son."

"How can he know? If on that night of August 1st –"

"On that night of August 1st, my dear Christine, your cousin, having earlier done me the honour to make me his wife in name, in anything but honour made me his wife in fact. He believed at the time and he will never believe otherwise – moreover, he was perfectly correct – that Prince Anton's child was already on the way: he believed that was why I had asked him to let me go to Italy – and, as I say, he was right. He will never believe that Nicholas is his son. You heard him deny it in the park today, you heard him deny he had ever made me his wife."

"But in that he lied."

"He lied because he knew that that evening had nothing to do with the birth of the child. To admit it would be only to complicate matters, the lie did not affect the truth about Nicholas; so he told the lie."

"And you also lied: you said you give lie for lie. You claimed Nicholas for your son – and his. Now you say we should tell the whole truth: why didn't you tell it then?"

"What, screech it forth without preparation in the middle of the park? It was your secret, Christine, not mine; and

385

I hadn't had time to think, I saw only that Nicholas was in fact heir to Starrbelow and that I must fight for him. But now I *have* had time: and the answer is clear. You have done no wrong, your honour is unimpaired; you married, you bore a child – you kept it a secret, and that is all. Now you have but to tell the secret, bear a few reproaches from your so-generous husband . . . ."

"But the gossip! The scandal! It is not for me, Sophia, but for Edward. I am Countess of Frome; is his name to be dragged with mine through the mire?"

"My name and your cousin Weyburn's have been dragged through the mire, Christine, and for your sake."

"I know, and I will love you forever for it, and thank you forever. But – I am not you, Sapphire. I have lived – as I have lived; a reputation was thrust upon me as a young girl which I grew to live up to, to live by, the Lily of Lillane; I have lived by it ever since and so has he, so has my husband. If I were to lose it now, to drag his name down with mine, I think I should die."

"*I* did not die," said Sophia.

"You died in spirit, Sapphire; in those first days after the Duchess of Witham's rout, you died in spirit: you were never again a young, carefree, careless girl. And then, when Charles left you, more scandal, more gossip – I think you died again. After that – oh, dearest, don't think I don't know what you did for me, all that you did for me, all that you lost in the last shreds of your reputation, all that it cost you. But . . . ."

"But? But what? But it was only the shreds, after all," suggested Sapphire bitterly. "That's what you mean, Christine, isn't it, by your 'but'? What I had to lose, I lost for you, and willingly, and you're grateful – but after all it was not much, for there was not much to lose; and in fact, though you dare not say it, you rather suspect that I enjoyed the losing – the wineing and the winning, and the flirting and philandering, the company of all my gay riff-raff, the whole wild masquerade. . . ."

"I have never underestimated what you did for me: nor what it cost you, not what it had meant to me. I owe you everything I hold dear in the world."

"All you hold dear in the world, Christine, is Edward, Earl of Frome; and if I thought you stood to lose him now, I would still take the alternative path, I would seek the protection of the law of

England and defy Lord Weyburn to deny that the child was his son. But you don't stand to lose your husband, or if you do, then he's not worth the keeping. You must tell him, or I will, that Nicholas is your son, born in wedlock: so that Nicholas may be acknowledged, without argument, what he is – heir through you to your cousin's title and to Starrbelow."

"Nicholas has no interest in Starrbelow – Nicholas has inherited my own gift of music, as you know, Sophia. He could be a real violinist one day, he would far rather –"

"Nicholas is heir to Starrbelow: it is his right to inherit, and it will be his duty."

The room was sombre, the curtains drawn, a dull fire glowed in the grate on this chill spring evening. Outside the great Frome mansion in Hanover Square the hooves of horses clip-clopped, there was the sound of carriage wheels rattling over the London cobbles – elegant and gay, the great lords and ladies sped hither and thither agog with the tidings of Gossip Wit's exchange with That Woman in the park this afternoon; and actually Weyburn present, and staring at the Harlot, my dears, with all his eyes...! Can it be

388

possible he is in love with the creature? It is sure, she's lost nothing of her beauty: tucked away down in Gloucestershire, what should impair it? – for the gossip is, she lives very quietly since her return from Italy, Squire Reddington, of course, the lover, and they say Pardo Ryan tumbles her occasionally, and poor Franks, no doubt, till he cut his throat – on account of the pox, they say, in which case...? But within, they sat across the fireplace from one another, two lovely women, elegantly disposed upon their stiff chairs, as long-training, grown to habit, enjoined them: in the splendid dresses into which, habit still prevailing, they had permitted their maids to apparel them for the evening, after the drive in the park. They sat in Lady Weyburn's bedroom, the vast four-poster, hung with rich embroidery, shadowy in the backgrounds: Sapphire vivid, alert, imperious, Christine pale and weeping. "I cannot. I cannot." She repeated as always: "It is not for myself – it's for Edward."

Sapphire struck the little table before her till its ornaments jangled and it seemed as though its legs, slender as the legs of a deer, would crumple beneath it. "Oh, God damn Edward to everlasting perdition! I have been sacrificed long enough to Edward. Why should I suffer, why should Nicholas suffer . . . ?"

"You need not suffer: I would not ask you, if you and Nicholas need suffer. But all you have to do is what you have done already once today – claim Charles Weyburn as his father. . . ."

"He is not his father."

"He cannot prove that, Sophia. You said so yourself in the park today, you warned him that the law of England. . . ."

"Good God, Christine, am I to foist upon Lord Weyburn an heir he knows to be not his own? – teach him to believe me a fraud and a cheat for gain, as well as all the rest . . . ?"

"You care nothing, after all, for what he believes of you."

"Do you think not?" said Sapphire.

"And even if you did . . . I would not ask this of you if there were any chance of his changing towards you. But how could that be? It is not as if he ever loved you."

"Might he not love me now?" said Sapphire, "– knowing the truth."

"But dearest, what should change him? For what you had done for me and suffered for me – he would respect you, it would

390

explain much that no doubt has made him angry. But that is not love. And why should you wish him to love you? You have never loved *him*, Sophia. But I....” She rested her arms on the table, bowing her lovely golden head in her hands. “Sapphire, you don’t know what it is to love, to have your whole heart and soul in another’s keeping. I have loved Lord Frome from my childhood. It’s true when you say that compared with my love for him, my children, are nothing. I love them. I love Catherine and I love Nicholas, my belovéd, my secret child; but beside him, they are nothing. I can’t help it, that is the way my heart lies – and if he should turn his heart away from mine....” She broke off. She said: “You have never loved, Sapphire, you can’t understand me.”

Sapphire rose to her feet. Opposing elements, they confronted one another, fire and snow, earth and cool water, orchid and lily. She said: “I have loved Lord Weyburn from the first moment I saw him – and from that first moment until for your sake I destroyed his love, Christine, he loved me.” Christine cried out, but she silenced her. ‘Till that night in August – even though he believed me a party to the wager, he had

391

loved me. But that night..." She swayed, sick with the memory of it, pressing her palm against her burning forehead. "That night was to be the end of it all. The page from the register was destroyed and there need be no more 'escapades,' I need consort no more with Anton, that poor, false, fickle wanton lover of yours. The last chance for me to return to him the locket he had given you; and I, in the horror of that visit to the Fleet, in the agony of presenting myself before my husband in that guise of debauchery – forgot to give it back. He found it there, hidden in my bosom, as well you know, Christine. Had I spoken then ... But I didn't. I kept your secret still. He loved me: but for your sake, I held my peace – and so, once and for all, I say it again, Christine, for your sake I destroyed his love." Loyal, true, generous, but pitiless at last, she looked down at the golden head. "When he knows the truth, perhaps – perhaps after all, he may love me again. For you I might even yet sacrifice this tiny flame of hope – as I did before. But, to save Lord Frome's precious sense of propriety – no. This is the end."

Christine stared up at her, utterly

thunderstruck. "You and Lord Weyburn –?"

"You are not the only woman who can give her heart, Christine; or feel it break."

"But dearest, but Sapphire – you did this for me, you have suffered all this and said nothing for all these years . . . ? How could I know? Should I ever have allowed . . . ?"

But she would not melt, she would not risk her self-control, she dared not be kind. "Be silent. I will not speak of it; never refer to it again. I have told you only because you must make up your mind, you must do what has to be done." She crossed the room and rang the bell for her maid. "Go to bed, Christine. We are both exhausted, tomorrow we can talk again. But my mind is made up: you must tell the truth to the world."

And the silent disrobing, a kindly word from the maid: "Shall you sleep, my lady" "Leave me out a phial of the laudanum," she said, "in case I don't." And the locking of the cupboard, the hiding of the key. "Goodnight, my lady."

"Goodnight," she said. When the maid was gone, she went through a small, communicating boudoir to Christine's locked door. She called: "Christine?"

"Sophia? One moment. What is it?"

"Has your maid left you?"

"Yes, I dismissed her: I am not yet finished undressing."

"When you are ready, bring me Prince Anton's ring." She went back to her room. Five minutes later, prepared for bed, Christine came through with the ring. She took it from her. "I had better keep this. It may yet serve as proof of your marriage, and proof may be needed, for the record was burned; and I don't want you destroying evidence, my dear." Christine cried out in repudiation, but she was sick, weary, exhausted, she could bear no further argument, she would not hear. "Give me the ring: I will lock it away with my jewels."

And she went directly to the hiding place and took out the key and unlocked the closet and put away the ring in one of two boxes there which Christine knew well, and hid the key again. "Go back to bed now: tomorrow we will talk again." How deeply grateful was she to be in the days to come, that she had gone to Christine then and given her that last kiss.

For in the night.... Who could know what dread of the future impelled it, what remorse for the past? Gliding through, the gentle, sorrowing ghost in the long white gown, crowned with the aureole of pale gold hair – gliding through the intervening boudoir, past the silent, sleeping figure in the great bed, taking the key from the hiding place, abstracting the phial; standing looking down with what turmoil of emotions, at the bedside; taking up the glass, tossing the empty phial, unconsidered, into the fire. . . .

Her first instinct, awakening to the news from a drugged, exhausted sleep, was to mask, to conceal all suspicion of suicide: the first impulse, born of long years of evasion and deceit for protection of Christine, to deny that Christine could have known where the key was hid. That step once taken, it was impossible to retract; to acknowledge that Christine could have taken the phial herself, was tantamount to admitting her suicide. That she, Sapphire, could ever be seriously threatened by a suspicion of murdering her friend, at first never entered her head: and when at last it came home to her – well, one more stone to be thrown, one more accusation which could never be proved. If the danger grew real, she must at last tell the truth: to die for such a secret would be wrong – she was weary of a life that, once again, held out no hope for her; but now more than ever Nicholas needed her. And for the rest . . . .

Bitterly weeping at the white bedside, holding the cold, still hand that wore only Lord Frome's wedding-ring, she knew. 'If gratitude can make a friend, you have one in me to the end of my life. . . .' Gratitude, love, the devoted protective friendship of so many years. Because she could not live to see her fair name sullied, Christine had died; how should Sapphire now, for the sake of her own heart's longing, sully the fair name of the defenceless dead?

Outside the great ballroom, the light grew dim, the brocades and satins were a jewelled glow in the last rays of the setting sun, the crystal chandeliers that had blazed there on that night ten years ago, were glimmering ghosts in the shadows of the high ceiling. Lord Frome stumbled to his feet, came over to her with dragging steps, blundering like an old man; took her hand in his. She could feel the slow, heavy tears hot against her skin as he raised her hand to his lips. "I can only beg the forgiveness of your most generous heart."

"Nothing matters to me, if your own heart forgives Christine."

Forgive Christine! – whose sin had been that she had come to him not the pure lily she pretended. Forgive Christine – whose life with him had been from beginning to end a lie. Forgive Christine...? At his side the boy stood, quivering, waiting. He burst out at last: "You say nothing, my lord. She was my mother – she did no wrong. What is there to forgive?"

"Only that she – she was not true. She lied."

"She lied for your sake, to save you pain. For that she sacrificed everything: she sacrificed me, she sacrificed him –" the small hand gestured to Lord Weyburn, "she sacrificed my – my other mother, here, who, I think was my true mother after all. She lived for you, she died for you. What is there to forgive?"

"There is nothing, little son," said Sapphire. "You are right: the word was mine. Lord Frome knows well, there is nothing to forgive."

"There is much to forgive," said Lord Frome, "but, God help me! – all of it in me." He released her hand. "I must go home to Catherine." He gave the ghost of a smile. "I must break it to her that she is dispossessed."

"By her brother," said Sapphire.

"By her...? Oh, Mother, am I Catherine's brother?"

"Her half-brother, Nicholas, since her mother was yours also. But...." She looked between the two men. "As to all this – what are we to do?"

Charles Weyburn stood with his back to the high marble mantlepiece, where long ago he had stood and watched her come into that room – and loved her from that hour. Now she stood by his side, soon night would fall and he would hold her once again in his arms and make her his own at last; not in violence and angry contempt as on that other night, but in tenderness and love. "Let it rest as it is. I have her at last, nothing more matters to me. Nicholas is my heir, let me simply acknowledge him my son, I will say that I lied about that night in August...."

"This leaves Sophia's reputation still undefended."

"Nothing matters," said Sapphire, echoing, smiling back into her lover's eyes. "I have him at last, nothing more matters. Let the wicked Lady Weyburn live on in the minds of the gossips: what would her Grace of Witham do without her?" She gave her hand to him again. "While she lives on, our Christine rests quiet in her grave."

He withdrew his hand. "No, Sapphire, it will not do." He had never called her by her nickname before. "It is proved that the child was conceived long before August."

"Who cares what's proved?" said Charles Weyburn. "I claim him as mine."

"They will think you are duped. Her name will suffer more than ever."

"We will go back then to the story she told Christine: that I came to her, secretly, after the wedding." He smiled at the boy. "Let us begin now, Nicholas; let us forget that other father – you are my son, and most proudly I am your father. You are heir to Starrbelow."

He was heir to Starrbelow: he was a prisoner here in this belovéd home which thus imposed its burden upon him for ever – when all he longed for was to be gone from it, to be free. . . . And this much-loved mother, to whom he had been all in all, was not his mother, and this man, who so kindly and proudly claimed him as his son, was not his father: and he was all in all no longer.

399

And yet – for his rights, they were prepared to sacrifice their own fair names to the end of their days; or sacrifice, alternately, the fair name of his true mother, who had died to defend it; to tarnish the great name of the Earl of Frome, and of his sister Catherine.... And all for an inheritance he must accept if it were his; but which he would give his whole, music-starved young soul to avoid.... They watched him as he stood, small and slender in his narrow coat of dark brocade with the lace ruffles at his bony, childish wrists, and the child's face, sick with a child's intemperate, heart-whole longings.... To claim Starrbelow – and eat his heart out all his days for that other destiny, for the kingdom of his mind; or to choose that kingdom and renounce his rights.

And, young as he was, child that he was, yet, reared in the high tradition of the best of the great landowners of England, living upon their own land, among their own people, dedicated in the service of their own inheritance – he knew there could be only one answer. The one was a matter of choice; the other of duty. He was heir of Starrbelow.

Until....

He turned at last. He said, suddenly smiling: "In all this, my lords and my lady Mother, I think you've forgotten – we've all forgotten – one person. One person yet to be born." And he came to Sapphire and slipped his thin hand into hers and laid his weary head against her arm and kissed the brocaded sleeve of it, lightly and lovingly, in the very ecstasy of his happiness.

"I am your heir, my lord," he said to Charles Weyburn, "until you and she have a son of your own."

Sixteen

The painted pole made a plop and a splash, the water racing down its length to merge again with the unruffled pewter of the canal. A boy's voice called gaily in stumbling Italian, "Hey, poppe! – let me try now."

"A fine mouthful I shall get from your grandmother," said the gondolier, laughing, "if you fall in and half drown yourself. She says you are too much, my little lord, with the gondolieri."

"And this is the one," said Catherine, loftily, looking out from beneath the canopy into the sunshine, "who was too dedicate his life to musicians and 'thinkers.'"

"You should not try to say 'musicians' while your baby teeth are missing and you have not yet got your new ones," said Nicholas, grinning. "And a man may think, let me tell you, while he poles a gondola along – and make music too." And he threw back his head and sang in his high, boyish voice, the first line of a love song. The gondolier caught up the melody, a girl looked down from a window and smiled at them and waved and began to sing too. "You see," he said. "It is my tune; and already everyone in Venice is singing it."

"The more's the pity – I think it a very silly little tune."

"That's unfortunate," he said, "since it was written especially for you."

She could not resist his good-temper, she burst out into genuinely childish laughter. "Oh, Nicholas – you fibber! It was written for your mother – for my aunt Sophia."

"You can call her my mother," he said. "She is more than my mother – more than any mother...." He spoke without bitterness, only lightly and lovingly.

Firenze met them at the steps of the pallazzo – that old home which so long ago a girl whom all Venice called La Zaffiro had gone forth to meet her destiny. "My dearest boy – are you safe? You have not been trying to pole the gondola? It is so dangerous."

He leapt out on to the steps and hugged her briefly. "Oh, Nonna – how you fuss!

Come Catherine...." He put out a thin brown hand and hauled her not very ceremoniously up from under the canopy. "This girl! – you'd think she was out and about in society already, with her airs and graces."

"The Earl of Frome's daughter does not scamper about like a barefoot Venetian guttersnipe," said Catherine.

He might have retorted that the guttersnipe referred to was a Prince of Hanover; but he only laughed at her – he did not even remember. She said to Firenze: "Where is my father?"

"He is within, child. He is writing a letter...."

Gossip Wit received the letter and soon all London rang with the news of it. He wrote without the consent of his friends, Lord and Lady Weyburn, said the Earl of Frome; but justice must be done, and after long thought he had decided that there could be no better way of – of dispensing it, than to confide in her Grace: to inform her Grace of the truths which now, for the first time, had been made known to him. For who could doubt, wrote the Earl, with one of his own rare gleams of ironic humour, the pleasure with which her Grace would disseminate the knowledge that would clear Lady Weyburn of every suspicion against her – would expose to the world her loyal and generous self-sacrifice for the sake of her injured friend.... And as for her, as for his own most deceived and greatly wronged Lily – as her memory remained pure and sanctified in his heart, so, he knew, would the world at her Grace's kind hands, respect it. Her child, after her, was acknowledged Lord Weyburn's heir, until such time as his lordship might have a son of his own to succeed him; the Hanoverian inheritance was to be formally renounced. Meanwhile he himself had brought both children abroad and here in Venice was establishing the boy where his heart longed to be, under music masters, in the care of Lady Weyburn's mother. Lord and Lady Weyburn remained at Starrbelow....

Lord and Lady Weyburn remained at Starrbelow, Lord Frome and the children were far away beneath Italian skies; and the storm broke and raged and blew over all their heads, uncaring; and blew itself out and a new scandal arose to take its place. For Prince Anton of Brunswick might be proved a villain but he was dead and therefore dull and was forgotten, and the Lily of Lillane kept her purity still, but was dead and therefore was dull and was forgotten; and the wicked Lady Weyburn was wicked no longer – and therefore was dull and was forgotten. True, the story reached Hanover and there was an exchange of letters, alarmed on one side, reassuring on the other: Prince Nicholas of Brunswick, while asserting his full right to the title, herewith through the medium of his guardians formally renounced it and all other claims, in favor of his late father's brother and of his brother's heirs after him – offspring, it now appeared, of complaisant Gertrud. . . .

"Poor Anton used to say," said Sapphire, laughing, "that she was like a young carthorse."

They stood in the Long Gallery – that gallery where on a December night, Christine had walked with the Earl of Frome; and now once again it was December. "The carthorse remained it seems," said Charles Weyburn, "in the stud that had been planned for it: and now there are lots of Hanoverian foals kicking up their heels as friskily as little carthorses may. And good luck to them! – what would our young racehorse have done in such a stable as that?"

"My Nicholas! Oh, Charles – I worry about him. He writes home so gallantly; yet do you not think he sometimes must miss me, far away in Italy?"

"Who, Nicholas?" he said, laughing at her. "You women are insatiable – must there be two men to whom you are indispensable? Nicholas is as happy as the day is long, even if he did step backwards into a canal and get a ducking, besides ruining his precious fiddle. Leave Nicholas alone. It is I that miss you."

"Miss me? How can you miss me? I am with you."

"I know – that's what makes it so dreadful. And he laughed again; but he took her into his arms and held her close, not laughing. "Oh, the long years – the long, lost years! How should I not be in the habit of missing you?"

"We are together now, dearest, for ever and ever. We begin again."

"We begin again, yes: now that at last I have found you." And he forced her head back as, long ago, he had held her in that first wild kiss in the December woods at

Frome. "Give me your soul, Sapphire! – open your lips under mine and give me your soul; press your lovely body close against my body, let me feel you one with me, never to leave me, never again to be less than all my own. . . ." In the steel ring of his arms, he felt her tremble, relax, succumb: suddenly stiffen again. Her white hands fluttered against the brocade of his coat. Shaken with longing, he held her a moment more – and then released her. "What is it, my heart? Don't you want to be here in my arms?"

"Oh, Charles!" She stood, trembling, her two hands gripping his coat sleeves, her cheek pressed against his heart. "It's only that . . . only that. . . ." She looked up into his face, blushing a little, and contrived a rather shakey laugh. "It's only that I know too well where all this leads."

"It leads to the heaven of heavens," he said. "A four-poster bed."

"Not at seven o'clock in the evening, my lord, if you please!"

"Is it but seven?" he said, also laughing; and he looked out into the late sunshine lying silvery over the long green lawns, the honey-coloured stone, the woods and meadows and streams, all the lovely curve of the land about Starrbelow. "How strange it is, Sapphire, that until I knew you, I never discovered that the day lasts far too long!"

Hand in hand, they wandered through the great galleries, under the moulded and gilded ceilings, through the splendid rooms with their treasures of porcelain, ormolu, crystal, rich tapestried hangings, marbles, paintings, marquetry, rosewood, inlaid mother-of-pearl; and so came at last to the long ballroom where now the Guardi picture hung above the tall white mantel – the painting of the 'Woman of Venice' in her green and crimson and gold, wearing in her deep gold hair the little golden ship with its rubies and pear-drop pearls: wearing on her lips the old, inscrutible, sorrowful, scornful smile. And he left her and went and stood between her and the picture, facing down the great room. "Stand there in the doorway," he said, "where first I saw you. I want to see you smile."

And she stood there, framed by the crimson curtain, where she had stood that night so long ago; and the blue eyes met his across the long, lost years and looked down

into his inmost heart; and she smiled at
him.

A new smile, all his own.